CW00971872

The Emperor

The Emperor

Fall of the Swords Book IV

Scott Michael Decker

Published 2016 by Creativia
Book design by Creativia (www.creativia.org)
U.S. Copyright # 1-1575322441
Cover art by http://www.thecovercollection.com/

Titles by the Author

If you like this novel, please post a review on the website where you purchased it, and consider other novels from among these titles by Scott Michael Decker:

Science Fiction:
Bawdy Double
Cube Rube
Doorport
Drink the Water
Edifice Abandoned
Glad You're Born
Half-Breed
Inoculated
Legends of Lemuria
Organo-Topia
The Gael Gates
War Child

Fantasy:
Fall of the Swords (Series)
Gemstone Wyverns
Sword Scroll Stone

Look for these titles at your favorite book retailer.

To Bobby Foster,
Who gave me the idea over a cup of coffee in the town of Ft.
Bragg on the north coast of California, and who to this day has
no idea what an epic it became. Thank you, Bobby – SMD

Prologue

I T WAS was a sword. It did not look important. Three feet long and slightly curved, the blade looked tarnished. The metal's dark color suggested it was simply brass. The edge was sharp and without a nick. The haft was pewter-colored, contoured for the human hand, and unremarkable – except for the single ruby set in the pommel.

Despite its modest appearance, the sword was skillfully constructed. The blade itself had been made from microscopic sheets of a chromium-antimony alloy layered one atop the other. The painstaking process made the blade very flexible and the edge very sharp. Even the best swordsmiths found the alloy difficult to work, however, making reproduction improbable.

In addition to its precise construction, the sword was ancient. Forged more than nine thousand years before, the sword had withstood all manner of use and misuse. The number of warriors who'd wielded the sword was a figure lost in the past. The number of warriors who'd died on its edge was many times that. The number of warriors mortally wounded while wielding this sword, however, was fewer than a hundred.

Called the Heir Sword, it assured the succession by preparing an Heir's mind for the Imperial Sword. No different in appearance, other than its slightly larger ruby, the Imperial Sword extended the range of an Emperor's psychic powers to the farthest corners of the Empire. Thus, the Imperial Sword was the figurative and literal source of the Emperor's authority. The Imperial Sword electrocuted anyone inadequately prepared by the Heir Sword, killing the unfortunate (or treacherous) soul. Thus, the Heir Sword was the only way to obtain that authority.

Each of the four Empires had its own pair of Swords, each pair adorned with a different gem. The four Imperial Swords all served the same function: To grant the current Emperor total dominion over his or her Empire. The four Heir Swords all shared their own function: To assure a smooth succession.

Although they shared the same function, the most valuable of the four Heir Swords was the one adorned with a ruby, the Heir Sword for the Northern Empire. Because of this Sword, the Eastern Empire had slaughtered all the people of the Northern Empire. Because of this Sword, a civil war had riven the Eastern Empire. Because of this Sword, bandits besieged the Eastern Empire from across its northern border. Because of this Sword, the four Empires' nine-thousand-year-old political systems were faltering, even though, ironically, the eight Swords had been forged to preserve them.

The Northern Heir Sword did not look important, but because of a single fact, it was the most important object in the world:

The Sword was missing.

Chapter 1

O F THE thousand ways the bandits might have retaliated against Flaming Arrow for his assassination of the five bandit leaders in 9318, the least expected was peace.—*The Gathering of Power*, by the Wizard Spying Eagle.

* * *

"Peace!" Aged Oak grumbled. "Five years ago I wouldn't have thought it possible!" Prefect of Cove, twelfth Patriarch of the Oak Family, and Commanding General of the Eastern Armed Forces, he glanced briefly over his shoulder at his mate, as if for reassurance.

The Matriarch Shading Oak smiled pensively. Standing beside her was the Commanding General's personal servant, Crow.

Glumly, Aged Oak looked out the rain-streaked window. "Five years ago the Eastern Armed Forces swept through the Windy Mountains in the Heir's wake like nets through a school of albacore. Eventually, we hauled in a total of thirty-five thousand bandit heads. What a catch! A full third of all bandits in the empty northern lands. We had 'em by the gills! Everybody thought Flaming Arrow was the mariner who'd ram the bandit navy from Imperial waters once and for all!"

Shading Oak smiled, knowing that the bandits had no navy. Her mate had lapsed into the dialect of Cove, the city of his youth a fishing port on the east coast. Like her mate, she was a native of Cove. Unrelated to him, she had the same surname as he. Like her mate, she was small in stature. Unlike him, she was without a wrinkle, despite her sixty-five years.

"They were wrong. *I* was wrong, eh? Another man beached their fleet." Aged Oak shook his head. "I'm *still* not sure I believe what happened. Who'd have thought that a bandit would be the shipwright of peace? That a *ban*dit would pilot their foundering fleet into safe harbor?" He sighed audibly. "Remember how it happened?"

Standing behind him, knowing he couldn't see her, she nodded, keeping her mind carefully shielded. When upset, he liked to be alone. Any reminder of her presence would likely annoy him. Right now, she knew he felt very upset, his years weighing on him like the overloaded hold of a ship.

"A few months after the last Imperial warrior left the empty northern lands, on a blustery autumn day, the northeasterlies were cracking open the topsails like a dolphin slapping the water. Seeking Sword—Lofty Lion's son, Purring Tiger's mate and Scowling Tiger's successor—declared himself Emperor of the Northern Empire. In the same breath of wind, he promulgated a law that penalized the initiation of hostilities against a foreign power with expulsion. The Bandit ordered all bandits to stop their banditry like a ship captain ordering all the winds to stop their blowing, eh? The audacity!

"No mystery that most of the bandits laughed at him contemptuously. The effrontery of a single man to tell *them* what they could and couldn't do had to be beyond belief. For over thirty years they'd roamed their seas at whim, going where the wind and the tide and their own sails would take them. Most of the bands insolently sneered at the Bandit's new law by carrying out a series of raids on both the Eastern and Western Empires." Snorting, Aged Oak shook his head. "The pearl in that oyster stew of diplomacy is that Seeking Sword forewarned us it'd happen, sent a messenger to Emparia Castle under the Inviolate Insignia—unbelievable in itself, eh?" Aged Oak chuckled.

Shading Oak smiled, knowing her mate had forgotten her.

"*Then* what'd he do? Unattended and unguarded, the Bandit visited the leaders of the bands who'd violated his law. He told them that to rebuild the Northern Empire all the people who lived in the empty northern lands would have to act like citizens. During the first year after promulgation, the penalty for violating the law three times was the band's expulsion from the empty northern lands. Some leaders genuinely saw the advantages of stopping the raids, and acceded to Seeking Sword's request. Some leaders protested their inability to control their warriors, and shrugged at him. Some leaders pretended to acquiesce, and the moment he'd gone launched a raid. Some leaders laughed in his face, and ordered a raid in front of him. What a mutinous crew, eh?

"Remember the Wolverine Raiders? The Heir and I didn't leave much of them behind. They were the first band to violate Seeking Sword's law three times. The day after their third raid, the Tiger Raiders fell on the camp, bound and dampered every single member. Then they shipped them like common criminals across the border into my waiting hands. The Imperial executioner was busy that day." Aged Oak grinned at the memory.

"After that, nearly all the other bands obeyed the Emperor Sword's law, most of them appreciating the ironic justice of his beaching the pirates onto the very beaches of the foreign power they'd attacked. The penalty changed after the first year, only individual bandits suffering the consequence for raiding.

"The Bandit brought peace to the northern border of the Eastern Empire." Aged Oak sighed, shaking his head.

"The Emperor Sword wants more than peace, though. He wants to rebuild the Northern Empire. Shortly after stopping the raids, Seeking Sword drew up a treaty of non-aggression with the Western Empire. He negotiated for the repatriation of every homesick Western sailor stranded under his rule. During the next three years, twenty thousand bandits sailed home.

"Within the first year of the Emperor Sword's sovereignty, Snarling Jaguar joined the Infinite. Despite Stalking Jaguar's popularity and benevolence, not all citizens were content with the new Emperor. The mutinous Southern citizens sailed north, expecting to find a new home port. Instead, they received a cold welcome. Capturing them all, Seeking Sword asked the Emperor Stalking Jaguar what he should do with them. Facing charges of treason and sentences of death if the Bandit repatriated them, the emigrant Southerners were a political nightmare for Stalking Jaguar. Not wanting their blood nor the expatriates themselves on his hands, the newly-invested Emperor Jaguar left their fates to the Emperor Sword. Seeking Sword put them to work, commuting their sentences in exchange for a year of their labor, then offering them citizenship for a second year of work.

"Work they did. Expatriates *and* natives. Every single bandit, new and old. In five short years, they rebuilt everything that Flaming Arrow and the Eastern Armed Forces destroyed. What took Scowling Tiger and the Bandit Council fifteen years to construct, block by painstaking block, the Emperor Sword surpassed in a third of the time. Without wars to wage, the bandits turned their industry on the land. Rich with tender care, the ground bore fruit.

"Even though I still don't believe it, I welcome the peace.

"Oh, I'd like the peace between Empires to extend to the internal affairs of the Eastern Empire, but discontent grows among us like barnacles on a hull! Our own mutinous crew's becoming disaffected with the Heir, Flaming Arrow."

Aged Oak sighed, looking out the window of his office in Cove, a city a hundred twenty miles from the northern border.

"As am I." Beyond beaded panes, rain slashed down on an already inundated city.

"I've known the Heir most my life. I don't doubt the boy myself. The brutal and callous Flaming Arrow who has emerged in the past five years dismays nearly everyone else. Oh, he denies the Bandit's every act. Most citizens simply refuse to believe that the Emperor Sword's capable of such a long succession of heinous deeds, and instead blame them all on the Heir.

"We know what the Bandit wants, eh? The Northern Empire may have stopped the raids, but they haven't stopped wanting the Imperial Sword from Flying Arrow. They've shown they'll obtain it regardless of cost, regardless of method. Cunning of the Emperor Sword to abort the senseless physical assault on the Eastern Empire and begin a personal assault on the Heir's reputation, eh? A master political strategist couldn't have planned it better.

"Remember the first incident? It seemed so insignificant. Three months after Flaming Arrow earned the title of man, he has an unpleasant encounter with a peasant—just a shoving match. Four weeks later in Nest, though, the Heir gets angry at a boy who jostles him, and grinds the boy's face into the mud. Three months later, a drunken Heir sings bawdy shanties staggering along an avenue in Emparia City at midday. Four weeks after that, the Heir accosts the mate of a merchant in Burrow. When she refuses, he drags her into a nearby alley and rapes her like he's some despicable corsair.

"That was the first year. After that, the incidents became more frequent and more reprehensible. At first, the Heir was patient, Infinitely patient, assuring the victims that they'd suffered at the Bandit's scourge and offering compensation not from Imperial coffers but from his own inestimable wealth.

"Why do you suppose Guarding Bear bequeathed the Caven Hills to Flaming Arrow five years ago, instead of his own son Rolling Bear? Smoking Arrow granted the peasant hereditary rights to the prefecture. Like a schooner tacking against the wind, Guarding Bear turns around and gives it to Smoking Arrow's grandson! Incomprehensible, eh?

"Anyway, as the opprobrious acts escalated, the victims became more disinclined to believe the Heir. Refusing his personal recompense, they sought legal redress instead. The Patriarchs and Matriarchs resolving these politically explosive situations initially ruled for the Heir, or at least pressed the litigant to accept the Heir's offer of compensation. When the incidents continued, however, the plaintiffs began to ignore the advice of their elders, insisting that the Prefects decide the Heir's punishment.

"Remember that? Right here in Cove, three thousand people watching, the Heir worked his way from one end of the marketplace to the other. He destroyed every object in his path like typhoon winds through thatch huts. Damage estimates stood at thirty-five hundred taels, a measly sum for the Heir. The litigants wanted more than damages and what they deemed 'silence taels.' They wanted the Heir's expulsion from Cove. I had to grant their request and expel him immediately to quiet the furor. After I traveled to Emparia City to consult with the Lord Emperor, Flying Arrow wisely reversed the decision, despite the protests and denunciations that followed." Aged Oak sighed, wincing at the memory.

"Well, what could I do? What could the Heir do? Gradually, he gave up trying to convince everyone of his innocence. When accused now, he quietly denies perpetrating the Bandit's misdeeds and quietly endures the subsequent legal proceedings. Most citizens look at him these days with loathing. They don't see how he tries like the Infinite to be stoic and strong. He lives his life above reproach, his every act more exemplary than an admiral's. They don't see that, either.

"Outwardly, he's still Flaming Arrow. To me and others who know him intimately, the Heir *has* changed. That boy broods too much, spending time by himself too much. Even his mate

Rippling Water privately longs for the Flaming Arrow of old, eh? The Flaming Arrow who'd always find time to talk with her, never ignoring his two lovely children, Trickling Water and Burning Arrow. What a pair they are, eh? Despite his exemplary execution of his offices of Heir and Prefect, Flaming Arrow virtually neglects his family and friends. Back when the waters were calm, if he and I happened to walk the same stretch of corridor, the old Heir bantered easily with me, like a crewmate who'd survived the same shipwreck. Now the Heir pleads urgent business and hurries onward, as if I've turned pirate."

Someone discreetly scratched on the door. Shading Oak poked her head out into the corridor, nodded at the servant, and looked toward her mate apprehensively. She put her hand on Crow's shoulder, her request unspoken. The General's personal servant nodded in understanding. Shading Oak then unobtrusively left the room.

* * *

"Well, I know what he's thinking," Aged Oak said, wincing. "Flaming Arrow reasons that if he socializes with fewer people, fewer will share his shame and perhaps his fate. Unfortunately, he presumes the effect and therefore the fate. I detest such reasoning! As if we don't know which direction the wind's blowing, eh?"

Not wanting to remember what he'd done three days ago, Aged Oak put his face close to the window. Here in the offices of his home in Cove, he felt secure. Above was the storm, below was the city, and beyond city was ocean. A sob escaped his lips. Aged Oak fell to his knees, trying to deny the memory, his gnarled and calloused hands clutching the window sill.

* * *

Aged Oak approached the gate to enter Emparia Castle. Coming the other direction was the Heir, pretending he didn't see the malevolence in the glances of passersby.

"Lord Heir," Aged Oak called, further from the gate. He lengthened his stride to intercept him.

Flaming Arrow stopped. "Yes, Lord General?"

The General placed a hand on the burly, sun-browned shoulder. "I want to talk to you, Lord."

The shoulder slid back, unobtrusively, intentionally. "Not now."

"*Now*, Lord!"

The fire in the Heir's gray-blue eyes could have melted iron.

"I won't let you put me off like some barnacle-scraping drudge!" Aged Oak said. "I'm your friend, by the Infinite. I don't care if you *have* forgot the fact!"

The tension in Flaming Arrow's shoulders eased; the fire left the eyes.

"I want to know what you're going do about this seaweed-slinging Bandit, Lord Heir. Why don't you retaliate?"

"Retaliate for what, Lord General?"

Aged Oak grabbed the lapels of Flaming Arrow's robe and shook the larger man roughly. "You're just going to let him drag your reputation through the sand and give your head to the executioner?!"

"No," the Heir said, not trying to disengage himself.

"Well, blast you to the Infinite, what *are* you going to do?" Aged Oak despised his speech when he became upset, the dialect of Cove marking him as a muckraking clam-digger from the east coast of the Empire.

"I'll do exactly what I need to do. If that includes telling you my plan, then I'll be the first one to inform you."

"You insolent sea-slug!" With a strength he didn't believe he had, Aged Oak hurled Flaming Arrow at a nearby wall.

The Heir struck so hard his lungs emptied.

Spitting epithets, Aged Oak planted himself a foot from Flaming Arrow and unleashed a barrage of blows into his midsection. Several sets of hands dragged him away, the General screaming curses in a voice already hoarse and struggling to free himself to administer more blows.

Rage had so consumed him that only later in the day, as he set a grueling pace toward Cove, did he learn that the Heir hadn't lifted a pinky to defend himself.

When he arrived in Cove, Aged Oak heard the extent of the Heir's injuries on the psychic flow: Five broken ribs, a ruptured spleen, a punctured lung, multiple lacerations across the back, and bruises from navel to nipples. Ashamed of his behavior, the damage terrible, Aged Oak immediately fell to his knees, bared his abdomen and unsheathed a knife. His soul screamed for release.

From the west a psychic lance penetrated his brain. Only twice before in his life had he received a personal communication from the Emperor using the Imperial Sword. The blue and white seven-arrow quiver filled his sight, the voice of Flying Arrow ringing in his ears. "Lord Commanding General Aged Oak, the Lord Heir Flaming Arrow requests that I spare you, pending an investigation. I order you to withhold your knife from your belly. You'll wait in Cove under house arrest for further instructions, Lord Oak." With that the six-inch wide beam of psychic energy withdrew, the message finished.

His knees in the mud, his stomach bared to the cold ocean breeze, the knife in his hand forbidden to strike, the shame of what he'd done permeating his soul, Aged Oak glimpsed for the first time how Flaming Arrow felt. The glimpse only tripled his shame.

* * *

They told him later that his scream had awakened the whole city.

He didn't remember.

Rain streaking the window, tears streaking his face, Aged Oak wished he could completely forget the past three days. The family Wizard had adjusted the General's emotional balance several times. Without those adjustments, Aged Oak's guts would've been in his lap.

Flying Arrow's two days of silence mystified everyone. Most people expected Flying Arrow to retaliate despite Flaming Arrow's request. At noon that day, the psychic flow had reported that the Heir had left Emparia Castle for the Caven Hills, sufficiently recovered from his injuries to travel. An almost palpable cloud had lifted from the Empire.

Not from Aged Oak, though. The grey, cloudy skies darkening with dusk, the General said, "Crow, summon an Imperial messenger please."

"Yes, Lord." Crow, the General's personal servant, relayed the order to a servant in the corridor, but did not leave the room.

Aged Oak couldn't live with this shame any longer, and wanted to request permission to fall on his knife.

Moments later Shading Oak stepped in to the office, her face beaming. Stepping up beside him, she slipped an arm around his waist. "I've brought you a visitor, my love. Smile for him, would you?"

"Don't want a visitor," he grumbled, her presence comforting.

"This one you will," she replied, turning him to face the door.

Soaking wet and wincing, Flaming Arrow grinned at the General. On the pommel of the Sword at his side was a diamond, confirming that this was indeed the Heir—and not the Emperor Sword.

Falling to his knees, Aged Oak put his head to the floor, sobbing.

Stepping forward a pace, the Heir gestured Shading Oak and the servant to leave. They closed the door behind them.

The two men were alone. "You were right to question me like that, Lord Oak. Someone had to pound some sense into me, eh?"

Aged Oak looked up, tears pouring down his face. "Oh, my boy, I shouldn't have struck you like that! I shouldn't have!" He rose, reaching out his arms to embrace Flaming Arrow.

* * *

With blinding speed Seeking Sword drew and slashed. The head leaped from the neck and a fountain of blood sprayed the window. From beyond the door came a scream and a thump. The Bandit grabbed the head by the hair and spat in the face. "How dare you touch the Imperial person of the Lord Heir Flaming Arrow!" He hurled the head at the window, which shattered, letting in the stormy night. Then he turned and splintered the door with a powerful kick. He stepped into the corridor, past the cringing servant, past the impassive Imperial messenger, over the dead mate of the dead General, and down the corridor toward the stairway, heaping curses upon Aged Oak the entire way.

Smashing anything in reach, kicking doors open and terrorizing the other occupants, Seeking Sword called down the wrath of the Infinite to plague the Oak Family and all its descendants. In the vaulted antechamber, the Bandit slammed opened the main door and paused on the threshold for a full minute.

"Anyone who questions the Lord Heir dies on his blade!"

Into the rainy night he went.

Chapter 2

T HE GATHERING of Power was neither a linear nor a static process. Like the growth of bacteria in a closed environment, power grew and declined in erratic cycles. The year Guarding Bear formally relinquished all titles and the year Spying Eagle became Sorcerer Apprentice, 9308, was a peak year for the Gathering. Not until ten years later, however, did power again coalesce. In 9318, the Heir launched his assault on the Windy Mountain bandits. After this tremendous discharge, the members of the Gathering dispersed widely, and five years passed before power gathered again. In 9323, with the assassination of the Commanding General Aged Oak, the Gathering began for the final time.—*The Gathering of Power*, by the Wizard Spying Eagle.

* * *

Wincing, Flaming Arrow slowed to another stop on the Nest-Bastion road, his breathing rough from exertion and his whole body aching. His hood pulled far forward, he stepped off the road, wondering where he was.

The road was nearly empty of traveler and muddy from rain, the footing treacherous. Flaming Arrow felt so tired, and hurt so much, that he wanted to curl up in his cloak beside the road and sleep forever. When he'd left Emparia City at noon with only his servant Cub in attendance, he'd promised Soothing Spirit he'd travel slowly. He'd expected to arrive in Bastion at dawn. Now, he doubted he'd arrive before noon.

Earlier on the journey, near sunset, just outside Nest, his servant had fallen badly and had broken his leg. The Heir had carried Cub back to Nest, to the nearest medacor's office, and then had gone on alone.

For a man of his position to travel alone was unthinkable. Usually, he had the obligatory contingent of guards. Usually, he was an invincible swordfighter. Usually, he had nothing to fear from the citizens of the Eastern Empire.

On this journey, though, he wished now that he hadn't ordered his honor guard to stay behind. His abdomen hurt like the Infinite, each breath aggravating his pain, each step shaking the tender muscles and organs.

Aged Oak had pulverized him.

Flaming Arrow couldn't have swung a sword even to save his own life. Five years ago, he would've been able to walk unarmed anywhere in the Empire. Now, he needed guards and arms. With the Bandit's help, the Heir had lost the exalted reputation he'd enjoyed after assassinating the five bandit leaders.

"But he that filches from me my good name robs me of that which not enriches him and makes me poor indeed," the ancient playwright, Shaking Spear, had once said.

The Bandit had eroded the Heir's reputation until it was no better than mud on the path. He guessed that the Bandit was sick in his hatred of his double across the border, who'd killed his mate's father and ruined his life. The Bandit will do anything to obtain the Northern Imperial Sword, the Heir thought. The man is unscrupulous.

A pity no one ever found the Northern Heir Sword. The last Northerner, Lofty Lion, had died in the dungeons of Emparia Castle after attempting to assassinate Flying Arrow—without revealing where he'd hidden the Heir Sword. With him had died the bandits' hope of building the Northern Empire anew.

Why the Bandit continued to act as if he were the Northern Emperor was beyond Flaming Arrow's comprehension. The Bandit's sullying his reputation was both revenge and an effort to acquire the Northern Imperial Sword—a Sword useless to everyone.

The day before, from his bed in the infirmary of Emparia Castle, Flaming Arrow had asked his father to give Seeking Sword the Sword he sought.

* * *

"No!" Flying Arrow barked, glaring at him.

"Infinite blast your stubborn soul! Why not?" Flaming Arrow cursed. He breathed deeply to compose himself. "*That's* the reason the Bandit's trying to destroy my reputation," he said calmly. "*That's* the reason he's trying to isolate the Eastern Empire: He's sending ambassadors both west and south, but not here. He helped the Western Empire when famine struck. He captured all those Southern expatriates when Stalking Jaguar succeeded his father. He refused to help us when the River Placid flooded everything between here and Cove. He says he'll recognize the Eastern Empire when you acknowledge his sovereignty and give him the Sword."

"I fought *hard* to get that Sword," Flying Arrow replied. "I won't give it up! Besides, he's a despicable Bandit. Like all bandits, he wants to destroy our ancient society and those of the Western and Southern Empires as well! Everything he does violates tradition! Everything! I refuse to legitimize his sovereignty in any way—especially *that* way!"

Four inches taller and fifty pounds heavier than Flying Arrow, Flaming Arrow gazed at his father standing above him from the foot of the infirmary bed. They both knew the Heir could dominate him in any kind of fight, regardless of weapon.

He knew his father was right, though. The Bandit's government in almost every way mocked political structures elsewhere. The apostate Emperor Sword had even made talismans explicitly legal—threatening the sovereignty of the Swords.

My father's being right doesn't correct the problem, the Heir thought. As usual his father would avoid decisive action on some pretext and wait for the situation to resolve itself. Flaming Arrow knew his father was the worst of all Emperors Arrow. Five years ago, just after Lofty Lion's assassination attempt, the Heir could have usurped the throne. Instead, he'd chosen to support his father's recovery from his injuries, knowing he lacked enough experience to be Emperor. Now, he wondered if he should have usurped the throne from his father.

Not that he *is* my father, Flaming Arrow thought, knowing Flying Arrow's quiver empty. The ignominy of bastardy was one of the many shames he endured because of this man. So many shames and most of them for so little reason! Infinite blast you! he thought, staring at him.

"You and I call him the Bandit, Father, but his name to everyone else is the Emperor Sword. When you failed to find the Heir Sword, you failed to conquer the Northern Empire. Give him the Sword, Father."

"No, I told you! Impudent little runt, I ought to disinherit you for your insolence! I *won't*! I've decided!"

Wanting to goad him into disinheriting him, Flaming Arrow stared at his father, hating him and hating being his heir. What he mostly hated was his own impotence: He was powerless to do anything about the Bandit. Of everything he'd endured in his life, the worst was the infuriating knowledge that if he lifted a pinky to harm the Bandit, all four Empires would decry him a warmonger.

So instead of goading his father, he acquiesced. "All right, Lord Emperor," he said caustically. "It's your Sword and your Empire. You know what *I'll* do with it the moment I succeed you."

"Oh? What's that, Lord Emperor Heir?"

Flaming Arrow smiled. "Turn off the light as you leave, would you, Lord Emperor? I want to sleep."

"Stubborn bastard," Flying Arrow muttered loud enough for his son to hear. Turning, he limped from the room.

Flaming Arrow turned off the light himself.

* * *

Flaming Arrow turned back to the road, rested now. His pace slow, he resumed his trek across the Empire, silently blessing his mentor Guarding Bear for bequeathing him the Caven Hills.

Five years ago, the old retired General had lost his sanity upon the death of his mate, the Matriarch Bubbling Water. Mates who'd been together as long as they usually died within hours of each other, sometimes moments.

Guarding Bear *had*n't died, though. His loss of sanity *had* invoked his final testament, as provided for by law. To everyone's surprise, his testament specified that his prefecture go to the Heir Flaming Arrow and his immense wealth to his only surviving son Rolling Bear.

Privately, Flaming Arrow had struck a deal with Rolling Bear, not wanting to incur his enmity over the Caven Hills, which rightly should have gone to him. Flaming Arrow had proposed that Rolling Bear manage the prefecture in the Heir's name. Upon succeeding Flying Arrow as Emperor, Flaming Arrow would reaffirm the Bear Patriarchy's hereditary claim.

Rolling Bear, having a jovial disposition that weathered all storms with equanimity, had smiled at Flaming Arrow. "Enmity? I could never bear you enmity, Lord Heir. Besides, Rippling Water wouldn't like her brother and her mate to be mad at each other, eh? She'd squash our heads together."

Flaming Arrow had laughed, nodding.

Wincing, Flaming Arrow loped through a drizzle along the Nest-Bastion road, his ribcage hurting with each breath.

He was grateful Guarding Bear had bequeathed him the Caven Hills. With a source of income independent of Flying Arrow, with a whole prefecture to retreat to when he needed to retreat, with a home in each Emparia Castle, Nest and Bastion, Flaming Arrow was nearly impervious to his father's tyranny. During the last five years, he'd found these sanctuaries necessary on several occasions. He'd never allowed the hostility between himself and his father to become open.

Despite the Heir's every attempt to reassure the Emperor that he didn't want the throne and wouldn't try to usurp it, Flying Arrow refused to believe otherwise. For instance, after his manhood ritual, Flaming Arrow had encouraged Spying Eagle and Healing Hand to do everything they could to restore the Emperor's right brain. The two Wizards had worked for almost a year, the Heir openly applauding their every success, however minor. When they'd repaired the right hemisphere to the point where the Emperor had full sensorimotor control except for a slight limp, the Heir had asked Flying Arrow to reward them for their efforts.

Grudgingly, the Emperor had, but had also become more suspicious than ever, restricting the duties of the Sorcerer and the Medacor Apprentice. The Heir wondered at his father's senseless ingratitude.

Flaming Arrow trudged up a hill, his sides hurting.

Privately, Spying Eagle had told Flaming Arrow that he didn't enjoy taking orders from the Emperor, that some orders were so distasteful he refused to carry them out.

That had been four years ago. Spying Eagle had since abdicated his position. Flaming Arrow didn't know all the details, not having been at the castle for the confrontation. He knew enough about the two men to guess what had happened, though. Angry that the Sorcerer refused to obey some order, the Emperor ordered Spying Eagle to begin training a Sorcerer Apprentice whom he, the Emperor, selected. After interviewing the Wizard Delving Thought, Spying Eagle refused to train him. Flying Arrow lost his temper. Spying Eagle resigned, and Delving Thought became the Sorcerer. Now Spying Eagle lived in Emparia City, a private citizen, practicing his profession as he had twenty years ago, independent of all political affiliation. Flaming Arrow often went to see his friend.

Healing Hand had also left Imperial service, but not because of any open difference of opinion with Flying Arrow. The Imperial Medacor Soothing Spirit was one hundred twelve years old and showed no signs of flagging. Being more than capable of caring for the castle denizens, the elder man simply didn't need Healing Hand's skills. Flaming Arrow knew too that his father thought the blond-haired Medacor too closely allied with the Heir. Such hostility, however subliminal, wouldn't escape the Wizard-medacor's notice. Two years after Flaming Arrow's manhood ritual, Healing Hand had quietly resigned.

No one was sure of Healing Hand's current whereabouts. He'd told his mother and sister where he'd be, but had asked them not to disclose that information unless someone urgently needed to find him. Knowing the medacor's spiritual nature, Flaming Arrow guessed he'd gone to a retreat somewhere for reflection and meditation.

So, in the last five years, Flaming Arrow had lost two of his three allies inside Emparia Castle. Flaming Arrow didn't include his mother, the Imperial Consort, among those allies. He saw Flowering Pine so rarely, and usually in circumstances so obstructive to intimacy, that he regarded his mother as one person among thousands whom he hoped one day to know personally. Somewhere deep inside he knew he ached to have more than a passing acquaintance with her. Long ago he'd resolved to abide by her wish to have only that. Now, only a dull ache remained.

Therefore, the only person at Emparia Castle who remained unswervingly loyal to him was Aged Oak. That the man had pummeled him mercilessly was simply proof of his loyalty. The Prefect of Cove and Commanding General of the Eastern Armed Forces was a complex man acculturated by the society in which he lived to hide his true feelings behind a facade of indifference and truculence. Anyone of his station who expressed feelings even hinting at vulnerability was weak and soon lost that station. Flaming Arrow knew that Aged Oak had the highest respect for him—and loved him, an admission torture couldn't extract.

Running slowly through the rain, Flaming Arrow wondered if he should give his father a pummeling he'd never forget. The Heir laughed aloud, thinking it a strange way to express loyalty.

After Flaming Arrow's every attempt to elicit Flying Arrow's trust, the Emperor became even more suspicious than before. Perhaps I shouldn't even try, he thought. Perhaps he distrusts me because I try so hard to be trustworthy. Intuitively, he knew he was right. He reflected how rotten their society was to regard a man's motivations as the antithesis of what they actually were. To gain his father's trust he'd have to abandon his attempts to gain it. Ridiculous!

Cresting a hill, Flaming Arrow winced and slowed to a stop, his consciousness swimming in seas of pain, sparkle clouding his vision. Through the rain he saw the crossroads ahead. He was making better time than he'd thought. Crossing the Nest-Bastion road ahead was the Burrow-Eyry road. Set back from the crossroads was a small stone structure. A combination refectory and hostelry, the main part of the structure was underground, the weather torrid during summer.

While the prefecture itself extended all the way to Nest, the geographical region known as the Caven Hills began beyond the

Burrow-Eyry road, the entire region studded with hills so steep they were almost inaccessible. Flaming Arrow dreaded the next leg of his journey. Usually, the hillsides didn't bother him. With his injuries he knew he'd hate every grueling climb.

He considered stopping at the hostelry, where his uncle Flaming Wolf was proprietor. Having not eaten since noon, Flaming Arrow turned toward it.

He hadn't seen his uncle in over a year, their association secret. Very few people knew that Flowering Pine was the daughter of Brazen Bear. Most people needed only a glance at her brother Flaming Wolf to guess: He looked exactly like the deceased, younger Bear.

Years ago, Scowling Tiger had implicated Brazen Bear in a plot to assassinate Smoking Arrow, the sixth Emperor Arrow. His trial and execution had rocked the Empire. Everyone had liked Brazen Bear. Few people had really believed he was a traitor, despite Scowling Tiger's proof that he'd associated with the Broken Arrows. In the end he'd died, executed for treachery.

Walking slowly toward the building, Flaming Arrow wondered how different history might have been if Brazen Bear hadn't mated Fleeting Snow. Because, as everyone knew, their mating had provoked Scowling Tiger to produce the evidence that had eventually spawned a civil war between the Bear and Tiger Patriarchies, resulting in the violent expulsion of Scowling Tiger and all his allies from the Empire. Those had been terrible times for the East.

Years ago, Guarding Bear had told Flaming Arrow how to contact the Broken Arrows, the ancient resistance movement to Arrow Sovereignty. Upon becoming Prefect of the Caven Hills, he'd purchased the hostelry and made Flaming Wolf the proprietor, wanting his uncle to have as good a geographic location as possible.

Flaming Wolf was Flaming Arrow's Broken Arrow contact.

The Heir pulled sword and sheath from his right side and secured it to his left, then pulled his hood far forward. Putting his right palm over the diamond on the Heir Sword pommel, Flaming Arrow pushed open the door and stepped into the building. Opposite a circular stairwell was a counter, behind it a man who looked nonchalantly toward him.

"A room, please, with a private bath."

Standing, the man tried discreetly to peer at his face. "Will you be needing servants to help with the bath, Lord?"

"No," he said too sharply, regretting it immediately. "No, I won't need servants. A meal, however, if you have it."

"We do, Lord. Any other victuals for your pleasure, Lord?"

Courtesans, he thought. "No, I don't have energy for your victuals. I'd like to speak with the proprietor here, if I may."

"I'll see if he's available, Lord …?"

"Chameleon. Have the meal delivered to my room, please."

"Yes, Lord Chameleon. Five taels please, Lord."

The price was usurious. He didn't complain. With his left hand—his right remained on the pommel—he dug into the purse attached to his belt, pulled out a ten-tael coin and tossed it on the counter. "First I'll bathe. How long until the water's hot?"

The man snatched the coin off the counter and replaced it with a five-tael piece. "It's already hot, Lord. We keep a cistern that way. Filling the bath will require a few minutes. While you're waiting, Lord Chameleon, shall I check whether the proprietor is available?"

"Please, yes." With his left hand he pursed the five-tael coin.

The man turned to issue orders to subordinates. Flaming Arrow turned toward the stairwell, hearing sounds of revelry from below. In addition to being a brothel, it served alcoholic beverages and presented other entertainments. He hoped, if he chose to sleep, that the revelry wouldn't be so raucous as to keep him awake.

"The proprietor will meet you at your room, Lord. Three floors down, last door on the left. Thank you for your patronage, Lord Chameleon."

Nodding, Flaming Arrow descended.

The first level below ground was the source of revelry. From a dimly-lit, smoke-filled room, vague faces peered toward him as he descended. The next level was more quiet and contained what looked like private rooms. A young woman stepped from a room, adjusted her robes, touched up her coiffure, saw him and gave him an enticing smile. The makeup caking her face defeated any allure it might have added. "A pittance for my pleasures, Lord," she said, striking a pose.

Shaking his head, he descended to the third level. He counted three more levels below his and entered the corridor. At the end was a stout oaken door. Entering, he bolted it behind him.

Through a doorway opposite the entrance came the sounds of flowing water. Investigating, he saw that a pipe jutting from the wall poured steaming water into a deep bath. An excretory stood against another wall. Gratefully, he used it, then stepped to the sink to wash.

After pulling off his sodden clothes and carefully hanging his eight-arrow robe, Flaming Arrow began to lather himself. The bath almost full, the water stopped by itself. Just then he heard a knock. Picking up his sword, he went to the door, unbolted and opened it.

"Lord Chameleon, you—" Flaming Wolf gasped upon seeing him.

Flaming Arrow silenced him with a finger across the lips and gestured him to enter, then closed and bolted the door behind him.

"Lord Heir, I had no idea," he said, bowing.

"We can talk while I bathe, Lord Wolf."

The peasant didn't merit the title, but the Heir liked and honored Flaming Wolf. The two men repaired to the excretory-bath.

Flaming Arrow began to scrub himself. "Are you licensed to operate a brothel here, Lord?" The nominal Prefect, Flaming Arrow technically approved and licensed all business establishments. In actuality, Rolling Bear administered the Caven Hills.

"I, uh, submitted the request in writing. That was six months ago, Lord. I haven't heard a word. I'm paying all the appropriate taxes. So are the courtesans, of course."

"Probably need to bribe a few bureaucrats before they'll approve your request. I didn't come here to harass you about that. Actually, I didn't know I'd be coming here. I was on my way to Bastion and decided to stop. Since I'm here, though, I want to ask something from you."

"This is quite a detour if you're going to Bastion. And how did you get here so fast?" Flaming Wolf asked, looking puzzled. "You can ask me anything, Lord Nephew, you know that."

Detour? Flaming Arrow wondered, frowning. "You've still got Broken Arrow contacts, don't you?"

"Uh, well, uh—"

"Listen, Lord Wolf, if I wanted your head off your shoulders, I'd only need to point out that you're Brazen Bear's son, eh? I don't. I need to request something of them." Flaming Arrow gingerly bent to wash his legs. His sides screamed in protest, where blue-black bruises blotched the skin.

"Aged Oak really beat the Infinite out of you, eh?"

"Indeed. Will you pass my request along to them?"

"I'll do what I can, Lord. Uh, many of them don't trust the leader anymore. Their internal divisions are about to split them into several factions."

"Oh? What happened?"

"Breaking Arrow may have defected to the enemy."

Flaming Arrow looked at the man. "He vehemently opposes Flying Arrow and actively supports me, eh? As we all know, my father has an empty quiver; hence, I'm no more Arrow than you are Wolf." Flaming Arrow filled a bucket with bathwater and doused himself to rinse off the soap.

"True, Lord, but you bear the name, and are therefore the enemy."

"I'm more than a name. I can understand the thinking, though, especially given the way the Bandit's assassinating my reputation. Well—" A knock on the door interrupted him. "That's probably my food. Would you get it?"

"Certainly, Lord." Flaming Wolf stepped through the doorway.

Putting his sword within easy reach, Flaming Arrow eased his bruised and battered body into the nearly scalding water and sighed gratefully, relaxing and looking toward the doorway.

Flaming Wolf returned, bearing a platter. "The house specialty, Lord. Roast pheasant, baked potato, cranberry sauce, spinach with a cheese sauce. I've asked for the best house wine, which should be here shortly." He set the platter beside the bath within Flaming Arrow's reach, then found a wooden stool and sat. "What did you want me to ask the Broken Arrows?"

"To leave the Lord Oak alone." Hungrily the Heir began to wolf down the food.

Flaming Wolf frowned. "I don't understand, Lord."

Through a mouthful of food, he said, "I want you to ask them not to assassinate him for beating the Infinite out of me."

"Uh, er, well, uh…"

Flaming Arrow didn't like the look on the other man's face. He chewed quickly and swallowed. "What is it? Did something happen?" A sickening feeling settled into his stomach.

"You don't know?"

"No, I don't. I left Emparia City at noon, stopped in Nest just before dusk because my servant fell and broke his leg, and haven't talked to anyone since. What happened?"

"Oh, that's right. Forgive me, Lord, I forget that you can't consult the flow. The news came to us just after sunset, Lord

Heir. Someone assassinated the Lord General Aged Oak." Flaming Wolf watched him carefully.

Oh, dear Lord Infinite, Flaming Arrow thought, biting his lip. He didn't want to ask, yet he knew he had to. "Who killed him?"

Frowning, Flaming Wolf said, "You *did*, Lord."

Chapter 3

I N BUILDING the Northern Empire anew, the Emperor Sword abandoned many of the social customs and political traditions common to the other three empires. While his initial motivation may have been to circumvent the established accession procedure, many of his innovations were entirely practical, others completely extemporaneous. Consider for instance the invention of the psychic-flow projector, a talisman that quickly became indispensable to Seeking Sword. Its invention generated numerous complaints, which then prompted him to promulgate a law explicitly legalizing talismans. The record we have of his life indicates he didn't *plan* to legalize them. He simply responded to the complaints. Of such insignificant events history is often made.—*The Fall of the Swords*, by Keeping Track.

* * *

Into the rainy night Seeking Sword ran, pleased to have stabbed Flaming Arrow's reputation again, hoping it was the killing blow. Then he remembered one of Leaping Elk's admonitions: "Never at another's misfortune pleased be. Same to you happen, eh?"

Reaching the edge of Cove on the Emparia City road, Seeking Sword ducked into a copse of trees. He pulled a cloak from his pack and donned it, wearing the hood far forward. Removing the imitation-diamond cover from his sword, he returned to the road and continued westward.

Now he'd committed himself. During the last five years, he'd chipped away at Flaming Arrow's reputation gradually. Always before he'd chosen targets of lesser importance, wanting the consequences inconsequential, knowing that the opprobrious acts had to build gradually for a credible discrediting. If Seeking Sword had immediately assassinated the retired General Guarding Bear, no one would've believed Flaming Arrow capable of such a perfidious act.

So Seeking Sword had increased the degree of depravity slowly.

When he'd heard that Aged Oak had physically assaulted Flaming Arrow, Seeking Sword had known his chance had come. For the last year, he'd waited for an opportunity similar, seeking some way to deliver the killing blow to the Heir's reputation. He'd told his lieutenant Slithering Snake what he planned.

"That's insane, Lord!" the sectathon had protested.

"It's perfect!" he'd replied, knowing his plan flawless.

"How the Infinite will you get past his guards?"

"Simple. The Heir Flaming Arrow wishes to speak with the Lord Oak alone. I'll think of something so they won't get suspicious. I'll need your Broken Arrow contacts in Cove. The assassination has to take place at the proper time, eh? I'd guess Flaming Arrow will leave the castle as soon as he's fit. About six hours afterward is when I'll assassinate Aged Oak."

Slithering Snake had nodded. "Hopefully, Lord, the Heir will leave the castle openly, so the flow will carry the news, eh? What if he doesn't? What if he leaves clandestinely?"

Seeking Sword had frowned in thought. "Ask one of your contacts in Emparia Castle to send a messenger to Cove. Then my timing will be perfect."

Slithering Snake had nodded, smiling.

Now, the deed done, Seeking Sword traveled through a heavy downpour along the Emparia City road, pleased it'd been so easy. Shortly before dusk the day before, a Broken Arrow courier had arrived from Emparia City. Seeking Sword had walked through Cove toward the House of Oak. Gaining entrance hadn't been difficult. A servant had led him toward the General's offices. Along the way the Matriarch Shading Oak had intercepted them. After a polite amount of conversation, she'd led him the rest of the way.

He'd forgotten about the mate-empathy link, however, and felt sad that the moment the General had died, so had his mate of fifty years, mates often dying with such proximity.

The Wizard-medacor Easing Comfort had explained the phenomenon to him. "Mates—whatever their disposition—develop an interdependence. The longer their mateship, the deeper that interdependence, eh? There is a psychological predisposition to dying when one's mate does—simply the belief that the surviving mate doesn't want to live without the deceased. It's also psychic, though. When one mate dies, the other experiences a psychic backlash, an implosion, you could call it. In the prefrontal lobes, the neural-psychic interface assemblies—networks of neurons that generate and interpret psychic energy—suddenly drain of energy. Depending on many factors, it can be fatal."

Seeking Sword hadn't anticipated that Shading Oak might also die, and felt terrible. On a spiritual level of his being, the Bandit sought peace, remembering Leaping Elk's admonition not to rejoice at another's misfortune.

When, five years ago, he'd first proposed his plan to assassinate Flaming Arrow's character, Leaping Elk had expressed no public objection. Privately, he'd admonished Seeking Sword to be careful. "Action gradual bad be, so gradual your character also erode, eh?" the Southerner had said.

At the time he'd given his mentor's words little thought. Now however, he understood. In assassinating the Heir's character, the Bandit needed to insure that he didn't sacrifice his dignity or morals.

When Seeking Sword had left the Northern Empire, Leaping Elk had been sick and near death. The Bandit hoped to return and see him one more time, respecting and loving the old black man as he might a father.

Twenty years ago, the old Southerner had all but adopted Seeking Sword. His mate Fawning Elk had given him suckle. His lieutenant Slithering Snake had been his weapons instructor. Other band members had taught him and nurtured him at Leaping Elk's direction. The black bandit had been everything to him that Icy Wind couldn't, a father in substance if not name. Seeking Sword was and would eternally be grateful.

His moccasins splashing in mud, Seeking Sword ran westward.

When he'd begun to forge the Northern Empire anew, the Bandit had found Leaping Elk's experience and knowledge invaluable. While the social and political systems of the other three Empires operated on primogeniture, their prefectures semi-independent and hereditary, no such structure existed in the Northern Empire. In deciding how to establish the Northern Prefectures, Seeking Sword had heeded Leaping Elk's warning about the pitfalls inherent in primogeniture.

Pitfalls with which Leaping Elk was intimately familiar.

The first-born son of the Emperor Scratching Jaguar, Leaping Jaguar had been ill suited to succeed his father, while his younger brother had seemed born for the position, having an aptitude for government. Only through elaborate subterfuge had the two brothers arranged for Leaping Jaguar's disinheriting and Snarling Jaguar's investiture. The Southern Empire had gained an Emperor far more sagacious than it would've other-wise had. The subterfuge had cost Leaping Jaguar his home.

Therefore, instead of making the prefectures hereditary, Seeking Sword had set up a meritocracy, mandating that applicants compete for all civil service positions through a battery of tests, the final results computed on a weighted combination of test scores and previous experience. Emperors in the past had tried this tactic and had failed in the face of resistance from the aristocracies. The Northern Empire, however, had no aristocracy. They were all bandits equally. Thus he'd easily implemented the system of civil service testing.

In addition to testing, the Bandit had required that every civil servant retire from that position after ten years, when new applicants would test for it. To prevent a glut of open positions and a flurry of testing every ten years, Seeking Sword had staggered the terms of office so at each new year a tenth of all bureaucracy positions came open.

These regional bureaucracies reported directly to the central governing body of the Northern Empire, the Council of Swords.

In addition to civil service, Seeking Sword had created a new position granted on the sole basis of honesty, the position of *Duce*. He'd first created the position five years before, while the Eastern Armed Forces still harried the western Windy Mountains. A *Duce's* one responsibility was simple: That he or she tell the Emperor what he or she thought, another idea anathema to social and political structures extant in the other Empires. The other Emperors, and many of their subordinates, often killed the messenger when they didn't like the message. Seeking Sword refused to surround himself with sycophantic advisors telling him only what he wanted to hear, and had created the *Duces* to insure that that didn't happen. Most of the Duces attended the Council of Swords.

The only structural resemblance that his government bore to those of the other Empires was the Matriarchies. Seeking Sword had asked Leaping Elk's mate of twenty years to organize the female voice. Fawning Elk had established the genealogy of every female in the Northern Empire, had linked together a thousand tiny Matriarchies into thirty larger ones. These Matriarchs met on a regular basis and sent five representatives to the Council of Swords at Seat.

Composed of three different groups—the Prefects, the Matriarchs and the *Duces*—the Council of Swords convened at Seat every three months for a maximum of two weeks, at the end of which they scrapped any unapproved legislation by default. In addition, the amphitheater where they convened was open to any resident of the Northern Empire. Foreigners, if they sought permission, were usually welcome as well.

In the Northern Empire, a meritocracy had replaced the ancient feudal structure. In the other Empires, sociologists composed the eulogy of feudalism, which amused Seeking Sword. His experimental bureaucracy enraged the nobility of the other three Empires. None of them liked the implied threat to their social positions and political structures. Seeking Sword's government and the society it governed blurred the distinctions between peasant and noble, warrior and farmer, man and woman, because any citizen could take the tests and any citizen could voice their concerns in the Council of Swords. The nobles of other Empires, despite the threat posed by the meritocracy, were powerless to stop Seeking Sword.

The Bandit peered through the pouring rain, looking for a landmark. Since he was without the slightest trace of talent, and because levithons couldn't lift him, he usually crossed the River Placid by boat. His paddling a boat across the river usually provoked outbursts of laughter from his companions. Boating across was easier than swimming, especially during spring runoff, when the river was a frothing torrent. Two days ago he'd paddled his canoe across the river and had concealed it in the brush on the north side of the levee, noting the landmarks on the south, for which he now looked.

There! An abandoned farmhouse with its back to the levee marked the place. In the flood two years ago, the water had driven thousands of families from their homes and had washed away several hundred dwellings. Whoever had lived in this farmhouse had never reclaimed it, the land around it fallow.

Seeking Sword checked the road both east and west, saw no one else through the dark and the rain, and quickly sprinted toward the farmhouse. Skirting it, he climbed the levee, then oriented himself and began to descend through the thick, luxuriant ferns on the other side. Their leaves saturated his already-soaked blue and white robe. He stepped between two saplings toward a cottonwood, at the base of which he'd hidden the canoe, between thick ferns.

He couldn't find it.

Ten feet long and three feet abeam, he doubted he was looking in the wrong place. Even so, he stepped down to the water's edge and compared that point of view with what he remembered. This was the place. He climbed toward the cottonwood again. His canoe wasn't here.

Infinite blast it, he thought, glancing at the river. He was a good swimmer. The river swollen with rain, he risked drowning if he tried to swim the swirling torrent with his accoutrements.

Climbing to the levee top, Seeking Sword looked left and right, hoping he was merely looking in the wrong place. He saw he wasn't. On either side of the single cottonwood was mostly empty river bank. He remembered choosing this place, this tree, because it'd looked like the only place along this stretch of river with foliage thick enough to offer concealment.

Blast! he thought.

Sighing, he turned westward. Months ago, he'd secreted another canoe just east of Emparia City. He hadn't planned on using it, having arranged to meet Slithering Snake near the old

Tiger Fortress once he'd assassinated Aged Oak. Now he had no choice. Slithering Snake would have to wait. The Commander of Seeking Sword's elite cadre would understand.

Loping along the muddy levee top, the Bandit quickly settled into the same ground-eating pace. He guessed that the time was near midnight and that he'd arrive at the nearly empty fortress after dawn. The Bandit hoped Slithering Snake would wait for him at the fortress, instead of coming across the border to look for him.

Five years ago, the Tiger Fortress had housed fifteen thousand bandits. Now, the upper levels sealed, silk and clothing factories occupied the three levels still in use, the only warriors a small border outpost of a thousand. The heyday of the Tiger Fortress was past. Soon after mating Purring Tiger, Seeking Sword had declared raids across the border illegal and begun to move the center of government to Seat.

Since mating five years ago, he and Purring Tiger had both worked long and hard to bring forth upon the empty lands a new Northern Empire. Along the way they'd both begun to understand the differences between the Empires they each wanted to create. She wanted a society divided by income, position and birth, and one that rewarded obedience and ruthlessly punished dissension. He wanted a class-less Empire in which the citizens were relatively equal, highly mobile, and intricately involved in the governing of their Empire. Since these differences had emerged, they'd grown apart. Seeking Sword hadn't felt close to Purring Tiger for a long time.

Trudging through rain, the Bandit slipped into a meditative state in which the rigors of travel no longer reached his conscious mind. Despite his lack of talent, Seeking Sword had developed several techniques to alter his perception of the demands travel made on his body, techniques that Easing Comfort had said were similar to a Wizard's rearranging of brain cells.

* * *

Emerging from his meditative state, the Bandit saw the lights of Emparia City ahead, glowing on the undersides of clouds. He began to search for the landmark near which he kept a canoe. Across fallow fields to his left he saw the pyre grounds, a round coliseum where the Empire gathered to burn its dead. Slowing, he looked along the banks of the river below him.

He saw the two cottonwoods and descended toward the river. The canoe was still there.

He sighed, relieved that he wouldn't have to swim the torrent.

Lifting the canoe, he carried it to the water, pulled the paddle from its sling, and pushed off from the south bank.

Paddling nearly upstream, Seeking Sword fought the current to get across. The river swift, he landed much farther downstream than usual. Now, he'd have to carry it upstream to the place he usually concealed it. Pulling the canoe from the water, he lifted it over his head.

Laying on the grassy levee-side was an odd looking stick, half concealed by grass and darkness. It looked too smooth and polished and straight to be an ordinary stick. He put down the boat and stepped toward it. On closer inspection, he saw it was a staff. My father's staff? he wondered and picked it up without thinking.

Nodding at the sentries, Seeking Sword squinted in the bright morning light. He stepped between the twin towers standing sentinel over the northern entrance of the Tiger Fortress. How did I get here? he wondered. Disoriented, he felt strange, as if intoxicated. His whole body hurt for some reason, particularly his trunk. His ribcage hurt so badly, he could barely breathe.

Slithering Snake came loping toward him and slowed, grinning ecstatically. "Infinite be with you, my friend."

"And with you," the Bandit replied, looking around wide-eyed. He put his hands to his aching sides.

The larger sectathon gave a crisp bow and fell in step beside him.

Seeking Sword nodded, wincing.

"Your performance was a great success, Lord Emperor Sword. You nearly brought down the house. Only minutes ago, Flying Arrow summoned the Heir to the castle to face an inquest for the murder of the Lord and Lady Oak."

"Eh?" he asked, puzzled.

"Don't you remember?" Slithering Snake asked, looking baffled.

"Oh, yes, yes, I do. I just…" He shook his head, trying to remember something, and failing to remember what he wanted to remember.

"Well, you don't seem very excited. Where'd you get the staff? It looks like your father's."

The Bandit looked blankly at his friend. "What staff?"

"Has the Infinite addled your brains?! The one in your hand!"

First Seeking Sword looked at his empty left hand, then at his right, which held a long, slim, polished length of carved wood. Where had he gotten it? It looked familiar, very familiar. He shook his head, puzzled.

"I'm sure it's your father's," Slithering Snake said softly. "Lord Sword?"

"Eh? What is it, my friend?"

"I want you to come with me, all right? I think Easing Comfort is nearby. I want you to lie down until he gets here."

"Why, Lord Snake? I don't understand."

"Something has happened to you that … concerns me. Would you just do as I ask? This way, all right? I've secured you lodgings so you can sleep. You've been awake and traveled all night and you need your sleep, eh? Come with me, Lord Emperor Sword."

Complacently, the Bandit obeyed, puzzled but trusting his friend. Together they entered the fortress and quickly found the dwelling on the third level.

"The bedroom's in there, Lord. Go on. I insist. No, you can't bathe. I want you to undress and try to sleep, eh? I'll scratch together a quick meal and bring it back in a moment." Slithering Snake left the room.

Seeking Sword did as the other man bade him, not understanding. His thoughts were hazy and leaden, his body weary and aching. He didn't notice that he held the staff while he undressed, nor that it was still in his hand when he lay down. The bed felt very comfortable. Seeking Sword slept.

* * *

"Lord Emperor Sword?"

He opened his eyes and blinked a few times until they focused on the face of the Wizard-medacor Easing Comfort.

"Do you know where you are, Lord?"

He looked around. A blanket covered him to the chin. Dimly, he remembered arriving at … "The fortress, right?"

Easing Comfort nodded. Behind him was Slithering Snake and Flashing Blade, the two men wearing the purple and green robes of the Emperor Sword's elite cadre.

"What did you do yesterday, Lord Sword?"

"The flow ought to have told you that by now, Lord Comfort."

The medacor smiled. "I want to know if *you* know."

"I assassinated Aged Oak."

Slithering Snake and Flashing Blade sighed, and Easing Comfort glanced over his shoulder at them. All three men looked very, very relieved.

"What's with you three?" Seeking Sword asked. "You act as if the Infinite has blessed me." He struggled to sit up and found that a staff was in his way. The blanket fell from his upper body.

"Your sides!" the medacor said.

Blue-black bruises blotched Seeking Sword's skin from navel to nipples.

"Looks like someone beat the Infinite out of you, Lord Emperor," Flashing Blade said. "Don't they hurt?"

The Bandit realized then that he was in pain. Nodding, he winced, saw he still held the staff, then extended it as if to hand it to the medacor.

"No!" Slithering Snake said sharply. "No one's to touch it!"

Seeking Sword frowned at him, then at Easing Comfort, who'd backed away, as if afraid of the staff. "He's the one you should concern yourself with, Lord Comfort. The Infinite has blessed *him*, not me." He sat up in bed and looked around the room for his clothes. Someone had taken them. His sword and other accoutrements hung from pegs on the wall behind Flashing Blade. Seeking Sword put the staff on the bed behind him.

"It's Icy Wind's staff. Have you forgotten, my friend?" Slithering Snake asked. "After your father almost assassinated Flying Arrow, several Arrow Warriors tried to pick up the staff. Don't you remember?"

Dimly, he remembered something. "What happened to them?"

"They died, Lord Sword."

He regarded it in on the bed. Throughout his childhood, he'd always feared it, never knowing when Icy Wind would use it on him. He didn't fear it now. "It's a talisman, isn't it?"

"Like most talismans," Easing Comfort said, "it kills all but its rightful wielder."

"Then I must be the rightful wielder, eh?" He laughed, knowing how ridiculous his having a talisman was. Bereft of a single psychic talent, Seeking Sword needed no talisman, didn't want one, had no use for one.

"Not likely, Lord Sword," Flashing Blade said. "Sorcerers tailor all talismans for specific people. Only Heir Swords adapt to different people. When a talisman's wielder dies, usually no one else can wield it. The Heir and Imperial Swords are the exception, of course."

Seeking Sword nodded, smiling. Fearlessly he picked up the staff. "What do you want me to do with it? I can't just leave it lying around."

Easing Comfort wrinkled his brow, his gaze upon the staff. "It isn't blocking my probe. Its circuits appear to have been disabled." He reached out his hand.

Seeking Sword gave it to him.

Easing Comfort gave it back, unaffected. "Disabled."

"He had it when he got here," Slithering Snake said. "And he didn't know it was in his hand."

The blond brows of the blond medacor crept up his forehead.

"I need another talisman," Seeking Sword said. "Anyone have one? Does anyone in the Northern Empire have one?"

Slithering Snake peered at him. "Do you think to pit yourself against a talisman?"

"I think I'm impervious to talismans. We've no way to test that, eh? Well, I'd like to find a safe place for my father's staff. Then I want to leave for Seat and see the Lord Elk. Is he still with us?" he asked the pyrathon.

"Yes, Lord," Flashing Blade said. "He's asking for you."

"How bad is he?"

"Very sick, Lord Emperor."

"All right. I'll take the staff with me for now."

"First you'll let me treat your wounds, Lord Sword," Easing Comfort said, stepping forward implacably.

"Of course, Lord." Seeking Sword watched while the medacor placed his large wrinkled palms on his bruised sides.

At the medacor's touch, the pain diminished. The bruising looked no better.

"Odd—did a medacor treat you already, Lord?"

He shook his head. Five years ago, he'd discovered that beneficent talents such as healing worked on him but maleficent talents didn't, something that baffled everyone. "I don't even remember how I got hurt."

Easing Comfort frowned. "Do you remember when? If you got injured before you assassinated Aged Oak, I doubt you'd have been able to swing a sword, much less travel all that way. See these?" the medacor asked, pointing. "Those are the oblique muscles. With the extent of your bruising, even after treatment, you'd still be unable to swing a sword."

Seeking Sword tried to think. "I don't remember, Lord."

Easing Comfort turned his head to look at Slithering Snake.

"Lord Snake, Lord Comfort," the Bandit said. "Tell me what you're discussing please."

The sectathon frowned. "Lord Sword, your injuries look like those Aged Oak inflicted upon Flaming Arrow."

"Are you sure, Lord Snake?"

"Yes, Lord," he replied. "I do have spies in Emparia Castle."

Seeking Sword nodded, not knowing what to think. Sighing, he looked at the medacor. "Thank you, Lord Comfort. I appreciate your help and hope I didn't inconvenience you. Infinite be with you."

"Treating you was a pleasure, not an inconvenience, Lord Emperor Sword." Easing Comfort bowed. "Infinite be with you all," he said, leaving.

Seeking Sword sighed, deeply perturbed. Nothing I can do about it now, he thought. "That meal you promised me earlier, Lord Snake? A bath while I eat."

"The bath's in here, Lord," Slithering Snake said, gesturing the Bandit to follow him. In the hot bath, Seeking Sword relaxed.

Stepping into the room, Flashing Blade watched him a moment, then said, "Yesterday's storm washed out the east-west road in ten places, Lord Emperor."

"Ten?" he said, alarmed. Each year the road washed out in at least as many places, but never during one rainstorm.

The pyrathon nodded. Small, brown-haired and approaching sixty years, Flashing Blade still had the fastest sword in the Northern Empire. "We spend too much time every year repairing the mountain roads, Lord."

"I agree. Any suggestions?" he asked.

Slithering Snake brought in the meal.

Hungrily the Bandit began to wolf down the food.

Flashing Blade frowned. "I don't have any, Lord."

Through a mouthful of food, he said, "I don't either."

Suddenly, both the sectathon and the pyrathon spun to look north.

He didn't like the look on the other men's faces. He chewed quickly and swallowed. "What is it? Did something happen?" A sickening, familiar feeling settled into his stomach.

Closing his eyes and bowing his head, the large sectathon seemed to shrink. "The Lord Infinite has taken our friend the Lord Leaping Elk beyond."

Chapter 4

EDACOR, WIZARD, warrior, priest. By the year 9323, Healing Hand had explored his abilities to their limit. It seemed there was nothing of which he was incapable. Despite all his accomplishments, he was a likable human being as well. One would expect that a person of such merit and talent might so exalt him or herself that he or she would not feel bound by social convention or even by simple regard for the needs and feelings of others. Yet Healing Hand had more care and consideration for others than personal ambition. He was in the simplest of terms an exemplary human being.—*Wizard and Medacor*, by the Matriarch Rippling Water.

* * *

It was indeed his father's staff—and a talisman.

The electrical circuits tried to lance his brain with a bolt of heat. He fended it off. Then they tried to delve into his mind and kill his spirit. He easily deflected the energy. The circuits tried to encroach upon his brain, to change the structure of his prefrontal lobes. His talent held fast and blocked the attempt. The staff appeared to change shape, becoming flexible and wrapping itself around his neck to choke him. He knew it manipulated his visual cortex to create that illusion. It was still a straight, wooden staff. Stubbornly, the circuits tried to lance his brain with a bolt of heat. Fending off the bolt, he realized the circuits would continue their attempts to kill him. Then they tried to delve into his mind and kill his spirit.

Turning aside the energy, he reached into the circuits with his mind and mapped them. He found a circuit that interpreted commands issued by someone with a specific psychic signature, an odd structure for a talisman. The Wizard appeared to have designed the circuits to obey both the talisman wielder and designer. Emulating one of the signatures, he ordered the staff to cease.

He looked around in the darkness. The clouds above raveled under a bright moon. The rain had ceased.

He stepped to the canoe and lifted it, then set off westward.

A half-hour later, he reached a tangle of blackberry bush that extended nearly to the water's edge. He set down the canoe and slid it underneath vines, where he'd hollowed out a hiding place. He tied the canoe to a vine, in case the river rose, then scrambled up the bank, staff in hand.

From the levee-top he could see the reflected lights of Emparia City to the southwest, which, for some reason looked too bright to be merely electrical lamp-light. He saw an orange tint to the light, as if something burned. Looking north, toward Burrow and the Tiger Fortress, he saw reflected amber light as well. What's burning? he wondered.

Descending the north side of the levee, he set a grueling pace through night-time, rain-wet forest and quickly entered a meditative state in which his spirit detached from his body.

Two hours later, he returned to his body and saw he approached Burrow. Smelling smoke, he wondered whether to detour. He decided not to, wanting to see for himself what he suspected.

He entered Burrow at a loping run. On the avenue ahead, he saw the bright glow of burning building, black smoke billowing into the sky. The denizens ran in and out of the lesser streets. One man ran naked past him, screaming incoherently. Approaching the garrison, he saw that the warriors surrounding it made no effort to stop the pillaging. He turned off the main avenue and skirted the garrison on side streets. He loped past a building engulfed in flame, so hot he squinted and shielded his face. A structure on the corner was a collapsed ruin, as if a giant fist had smashed it flat. A woman, rage mutilating her face, lunged at him with a knife. With the staff, he knocked it from her hand then tripped her up and sent her flying. She didn't get up. He didn't stop to find out why. Reaching the east-west road, he crossed it into forest, relieved to be leaving the mayhem behind.

Rioting in Burrow.

Settling back into his meditative state, he took only brief note of the changing landscape, which became progressively more hilly. The sky grew pale in the east. Mountains marched southward past him, the bare mountain ahead his destination. He reached its base and made his way around it, reaching a muddy road. The sun blazed upon the day, chasing away the chill of night. He saw the twin towers ahead. He slowed as he approached them, throwing back his hood, seeing the two sentries between the towers.

* * *

Suddenly awake, Flaming Arrow abruptly sat up in bed and looked around, disoriented. The room looked familiar. Then he remembered the night before, and wished he hadn't.

The night before, Flaming Wolf had told him that Aged Oak was dead and that he, the Heir, had killed him. For a few minutes, Flaming Arrow had just soaked in the bath, in a stupor of shock and disbelief. Then he'd begun to cry. He vaguely remembered that his uncle had helped him to bed, then left. The great racking sobs, which would've hurt his gut even without his injuries, had felt unbearably painful. Flaming Wolf had returned with a bottle of strong alcoholic beverage and a woman of gentle disposition. He'd told Flaming Arrow that she was his for the night, and that he trusted her. "Even if you don't fornicate with her, it's still important for you to have someone with you." Flaming Arrow hadn't disagreed, unable to speak. She'd held him while he wept, serving him glass after glass of the most foul-tasting beverage he'd ever tried. It'd warmed his insides and cooled his grief. Eventually, he'd slept.

Now, the courtesan slept soundly beside him. He got up to use the excretory, not waking her. He noticed then that his physical pain was gone. He looked down.

What happened to all my bruises? he wondered, seeing not one.

His urine chattering against porcelain, he tried to understand what had happened to the bruises. He remembered how they'd felt and looked last night. Now, he had none left. Did a medacor treat me in my sleep? he wondered. Soothing Spirit, when treating him the day before, had said after repairing all the tissue that his sides would still be sore and discolored.

He stepped away from the wall and swung an imaginary sword. No soreness at all. He stepped into the other room and pulled his sword off the wall hook. He swung gingerly. Still no soreness. He felt as fit as he ever had. Checking for nearby objects and grasping the sword firmly, Flaming Arrow swung with all his might.

Not a whisper of pain.

What happened to all my bruises? he wondered.

The courtesan still slept and didn't wake even when he sat roughly on the bed. Shrugging, he went to look for his clothes. In the bath he found a fresh loincloth and pair of moccasins. Gratefully, he put them on, then pulled a fresh eight-arrow robe from his pack, where he then put his soiled robe and cloak, now dry. Securing his weapons belt around his waist, he tied the sword sheath to his belt. Feeling more fit than he had since the beating, he stepped into the other room.

She still slept. He couldn't remember if he'd fornicated with her. Knowing it unimportant, and that he'd become very intoxicated, he shook her, wanting to know her rates so he could pay her and leave.

She still didn't awaken.

Odd, he thought, shaking her harder.

No response. Her breathing soft and regular, he knew she was alive. Why can't I wake her? he wondered. He tried again, and again got no response. He couldn't wake her no matter what he did. He carefully lay her back on the bed, frustrated, and placed a five-tael piece between her breasts. Turning, he left the room.

He ascended the circular stairwell to the first level below ground, where the revelry last night had been so loud he thought it might keep him awake. Strewn around the room were bodies, most in chairs, some laying across tables, some on the floor. They all looked as if they'd drunk themselves into a stupor. He entered the room and looked closely at one. Sleeping soundly, he saw. Putting the man more comfortably on the floor, Flaming Arrow guessed from their positions and the uniform depth of sleep that something or someone had *put* them all to sleep.

He left the room and ascended. Even the clerk was asleep at the desk.

He stepped outside and squinted at the morning brightness. Shielding his eyes, he looked toward the crossroads. He saw several travelers, but fewer than usual, having often traveled the Nest-Bastion road. Some of them looked toward the Heir, their expressions hostile. From the intersection confluence appeared Flaming Wolf, who began to walk toward him.

"Infinite be with you, Lord Heir."

"And you, Lord Wolf." He nodded at the other's obeisance.

"What's wrong with the shields?" Flaming Wolf pointed at the hostelry.

Flaming Arrow shrugged, knowing his uncle had forgotten again that he didn't have talent.

"Oh, that's right. Forgive me, Lord, I forgot. Did the clerk tell you what's on the flow before he fell asleep?"

"No, he didn't."

"Well, blast it. I told him to inform you if it was important. Infinite knows, this is important!"

"You don't live here, Lord Wolf?"

"Absolutely not! I'd be up all night with the carousing and the interruptions and every patron's wanting to see the proprietor. I tried it, Lord, and found it impossible. I live a mile or so toward Eyry." He gestured vaguely southward. "Anyway, Lord, you won't like what's on the flow. Rioting in Burrow, Nest, Eyry, Crag, Emparia City and of course Cove."

"That's every major city but Bastion!" He remembered he'd dreamt of rioting in Burrow, and frowned.

"Most of the smaller towns, too, Lord. The worst part is that all the riots look spontaneous. The Broken Arrows didn't start them."

Flaming Arrow felt dismayed. "Not even those discontent with Breaking Arrow?"

"Not even them, Lord, although they probably joined the riots afterward. Anyway, the Lord Emperor announced about ten minutes ago that you're to return to Emparia City to face possible charges of murder."

A hole opened in his gut and he fell into it. Flaming Arrow stepped away, his gaze vacant, his shoulders sagging. He wondered: Is this the Emperor's artifice to dampen the flames of discontent? Will I face an inquest?

Initially, he decided, Flying Arrow's announcement was an artifice, because until the Emperor restored order, Arrow Sovereignty lay endangered. Flaming Arrow knew that if the riots remained unquelled, he'd stand trial. Furthermore, if the insurrection continued, Flying Arrow would arrange a guilty verdict. The only justice in the Eastern Empire was Flying Arrow's justice. When something threatened his Sovereignty, he prosecuted until he'd quashed that threat with any available means.

The threat, or the perceived threat, was Flaming Arrow.

"I'll be back in a moment, Lord." Flaming Wolf bowed, entering the hostelry.

Flaming Arrow felt tempted to follow, to see if his uncle would succeed in waking anyone inside. Instead, he stared toward the crossroads, wondering what to do. The ache of Aged Oak's death was bearable now. Now he could think through his decision.

The Bandit had assassinated the Commanding General of the Eastern Armed Forces while impersonating the Heir. Last night, Flaming Wolf had told him what the Bandit had said after the assassination. Flaming Arrow knew, because of the rioting and because people were people, that many citizens believed the Heir had killed the General. The Emperor's summons indicated that he might also believe it. They can all believe what they want to believe, Flaming Arrow thought. Unless they execute me for murder, their beliefs don't matter right now.

Dreading the endless legal proceedings, he wondered how long they'd last. He felt as if he'd spent most of the last five years in one court or another, listening to endless testimony and questioning. At least my father will dispense his warped justice quickly, Flaming Arrow thought.

He needed to decide what to do about the Bandit afterward. Since he was the Heir, and as such a representative of his Empire, he couldn't cross the border to assassinate the Bandit. The other Empires would construe such an action as unprovoked aggression against a sovereign, if unsanctioned, Empire.

Then he questioned his thinking: Why do I want to kill him? How could I forget what Probing Gaze said to me? "Vendetta is a cruel gauntlet that enslaves both the agent and recipient of vengeance under the scourge of strike and counterstrike and alternately flogs both agent and recipient onto more severe retaliation with the whip of hatred and intolerance, each laying lashes upon wounds barely healed, further fomenting the spiraling cycle of reprisal, until the original transgression is a forgotten blur and the requiters resemble raw masses of flayed flesh, the gauntlet rarely killing early," the sectathon had said in a garrulous moment.

Thanking the Infinite for giving him such teachers, Flaming Arrow wondered what Guarding Bear would do. Then he laughed aloud. For forty-five years, the old General and Scowling Tiger had danced the deadly dance of vengeance. In the end Scowling Tiger had died and Guarding Bear had lost his sanity.

What will *I* do? he wondered, looking toward the crossroads.

He'd go to Emparia City. That much was certain.

He saw a flash of turquoise and wondered if his mate Rippling Water had traveled here from bastion.

Just then, someone on the Burrow-Eyry road shouted, "You despicable bastard!"

Flaming Arrow couldn't see who it was and shrugged it off, feeling sad that another ignorant soul chose to hate him for something he hadn't done. A moment later, travelers scattered from the road. Metal flashed, strangling a scream. Rippling Water pulled her sword from the body and nimbly hacked off the head.

"We all know the Bandit assassinated the Lord General Aged Oak! Don't we?" she yelled at no one in particular, and at everyone. She yanked off the sash and wiped her blade, then sheathed it and walked toward him.

He tried not to smile.

Muttering under her breath, she stepped into his arms and hugged him tightly.

He hugged her and held her.

Stepping back, she looked at him and shook her head. "What will you do, my love?" she asked, as though continuing a conversation interrupted moments before. They hadn't seen each other for a week.

"Go to Emparia City, my love," he replied.

She glanced at the sky. "About *him*!"

Smiling, he shrugged. "I haven't decided."

She nodded. "Will you retaliate finally?"

He'd often told her that the Bandit had done nothing that merited retaliation. Now, despite wanting to avoid its vicious cycle, he knew he needed to do something. The ancient principle of *lex talionis* was the root of their government, and the law of retaliation was the soil in which their culture had grown. That didn't obligate him to live by the principle, not when it meant that he, his family and all his friends might become the Bandit's target. No, he wouldn't seek revenge, but he did need to seek resolution.

"I think the Bandit has repaid me the injury I inflicted upon him five years ago," Flaming Arrow said carefully. "Here, I want it to end."

She laughed, incredulous. "Try to tell that to a bandit!"

"I will," he replied, thinking the suggestion perfectly reasonable.

Puzzled, she looked at him, glancing at the sky again. "At least the Lord Emperor hasn't disinherited you, eh?"

Nodding, he gathered her to him. "I missed you."

"I missed you. I want you to know I love you. I don't under*stand* you sometimes, Flaming Arrow, but you could throw away that blasted Heir Sword and I'd love you still."

"I know," he whispered, cradling her face between his palms. "I love you too." He kissed her. "How are the children?"

Their son Burning Arrow was four and their daughter Trickling Water was three. Both were bright, lively, talented children—a miracle of the Infinite, considering their father didn't possess even a trace of psychic power.

"They came home from their psychics instructor last night and said he called you a 'bad man.' I went to talk to him, and told him he could teach them psychics. If he mentioned the subject of Imperial politics again, I'd find another instructor. Thankfully, he agreed, or I'd have gutted him."

Flaming Arrow laughed, hugging her.

Flaming Wolf stepped from the hostelry and bowed to them both. "Lady Water, Infinite be with you. What happened last night, Lord?"

"I don't know, Lord Wolf," Flaming Arrow replied. "When I woke, everyone else was asleep. I couldn't wake them no matter what the Infinite I did."

"Eh?" Rippling Water said, frowning.

"Everyone but a Wizard," Flaming Wolf said. "He's in there now, waking everyone up. He said someone put them all to sleep by converting something in their blood, said the energy didn't affect him because he's a medacor and—"

"Oh? Does he have blond hair?" Rippling Water asked.

"How did you know?"

She glanced at Flaming Arrow. They both stepped past Flaming Wolf and into the hostelry. His back to the door, the Wizard was treating the clerk. He wore the black robes of a priest. At his side was a sword that looked incongruous on a man of the Infinite. He finished and turned around. "Infinite be with you, Lord Heir, Lady Water," Healing Hand said placidly, as if he'd seen them yesterday.

Grinning, Rippling Water put her arms around him and hugged him tightly, then Flaming Arrow pushed her aside and did the same. "Why are you here? I thought you'd be on some mountain-top, giving advice to the spiritually bereft."

Healing Hand laughed. "That's exactly the wrong place to go for enlightenment, Lord. I was on my way home to see my mother and sister. You're going to Emparia City too, eh? Well, then, shall we?"

"Why the black robes, Lord Hand?" Rippling Water asked as they stepped from the hostelry.

"The Infinite has initiated me into its mysteries, Lady. I'm a priest now." The sun glinted in his wheat-blond hair.

"Medacor, Wizard, warrior, priest—what next, Lord Hand?"

"I don't know how the Infinite will bless me next, Lord Heir."

Flaming Wolf was just returning from the Burrow-Eyry road. "Someone killed a peasant over there," he said.

"Oh, how terrible!" Rippling Water said in mock distress.

The Heir grinned. "Thank you, Lord Wolf, for all your help, eh? Walk with the Infinite," Flaming Arrow said, nodding to acknowledge the other's obeisance. His uncle exchanged bows with the other two, and the trio walked toward the Bastion-Nest road.

On the way to Nest, Flaming Arrow found he could travel at his usual pace, as if Aged Oak hadn't pummeled him at all. He told them both about his dream, and about what he'd found when he woke.

"That doesn't sound much different from what happened five years ago, Lord," Healing Hand said. "If the Bandit assassinated the Lord Oak, he might have been in exactly the place you described. Do you know anyone in Burrow who could look for the canoe?"

"I wonder what Probing Gaze is doing," Flaming Arrow said.

"Last I heard," Rippling Water said, "he still lived in Emparia City. Let's stop on the way to the castle, eh?"

Flaming Arrow nodded. Five years ago, the sectathon Colonel Probing Gaze had assisted him in his manhood ritual. The Heir hadn't seen him since. Flaming Arrow guessed that the bandit expert had found himself without a vocation.

"Did he retire after the Lord Emperor Sword made raids illegal?" Healing Hand asked.

The question jolted something inside Flaming Arrow. Healing Hand had retired from his position of Medacor Apprentice. Spying Eagle had resigned as Sorcerer. Two years before the Heir was born, Guarding Bear had retired from all positions except Prefect of the Caven Hills.

What had they each gained by retiring?

Chapter 5

THE PSYCHOLOGY of Swords themselves ended their nine-thousand year reign. The tendency in people to identify and emulate figures of authority is strong. Hence, when an object becomes the literal and figurative source of authority, the society governed by that authority reflects the values embodied by that object. One value that the Swords embodied was dominion over others. Investing a weapon like the Swords with such absolute authority condemned civilization to a nine-thousand year history of bloodshed and violence. What continues to puzzle historians today is that the sovereignty of the Swords lasted so long.—*The Fall of the Swords*, by Keeping Track.

* * *

"Listen, my love," Leaping Elk said. "I don't know if Seeking Sword will return in time, so I need you to tell him something for me."

In the refectory of the home Seeking Sword had given them four years ago, Fawning Elk looked up from her plate.

Across from her, Leaping Elk ate heartily despite the cancers eating him.

"You've plenty of time," she protested, looking at him. The thought of his dying filled her with fear.

Seventy-five years old, completely gray, wizened like a prune and full of life despite being full of death, Leaping Elk smiled at her. He shoveled another forkful into his face. "Perhaps I've plenty of time—perhaps not," he said, speaking with her in the Southern tongue as always. "I wielded the Southern Heir Sword before my father disinherited me. Remember the day Seeking Sword joined the Elk Raiders? He tried to give me his sword. I refused it—to say it more accurately, it refused *me*. You know how Seeking Sword's father was once Lofty Lion? Well, he named his son appropriately."

"I know," she replied, "He seeks the Northern Imperial Sword." The Sword won't do him a lion's turd worth of good, she thought.

"Well, everyone assumes now that the Northern Imperial Sword won't do him a lion's turd worth of good, eh? They're all wrong."

"Eh? Are you Infinite-blessed? The Northern Heir Sword's been missing so long, we haven't an Infinite's chance of finding it."

"*You're* wrong!" Leaping Elk said. "I know what an Heir Sword looks like. I know what can be done with its psychic tools. Those psychic storms five years ago were an example. I want you to tell Seeking Sword that he wields the Northern Heir Sword."

Fawning Elk put down her fork and stared at him. She shook her head and picked up her fork. Then she put it down again and sat back in her chair. Then she leaned forward to say something—and said nothing. Then she picked up her fork, and put it down again.

"You'll tell him when the time is right?" Leaping Elk asked. "Good, thank you, my love." He took another bite. "What'll you do when I'm gone?"

She didn't answer, stunned by his revelation.

* * *

Leaping Elk doubted she'd heard the question.

He knew she'd be safe after he died. Seeking Sword considered her the only mother he'd ever known. Her positions on two of the Bandit's councils would insure that she continued to have a purpose in life. The terrible tragedy that had befallen Trickling Stream more than twenty years before still haunted Fawning Elk. His impending death would remove one of the stanchions supporting her now. He sincerely hoped she didn't grieve too long, loving her and wanting her to be as happy as she could. He knew Fawning Elk was resilient. A person of less strength would've slit his or her belly long ago. She wouldn't immolate herself upon the flames of his pyre, as many a disconsolate widow did. Nor would the strength of their mate-empathy link kill her, because they'd mated only twenty years ago. Leaping Elk fully expected the beautiful woman across from him to live a happy purposeful life after the Infinite called him onward.

That won't be long now, the black bandit thought. He felt the presence of the Infinite over his shoulder and hoped the Emperor Sword could return to Seat to see him one last time.

After Seeking Sword had ordered peace, change had followed. Leaping Elk and his family had moved north to Seat, where life had treated them well. Although he held no official position in Seeking Sword's government—after retiring from his position as *Duce*—Leaping Elk had often participated in the conception and inception of its institutions. Minister without portfolio, Leaping Elk therefore acted with only the restraint of his conscience, a freedom Seeking Sword would never have. Years ago, Leaping Elk had thought he'd never see the Northern Empire reborn. He knew now he was watching it take its first breath. The Imperial Sword was just a formality.

Seeking Sword's genius still bedazzled Leaping Elk, even now, five years after the Bandit's unbelievable announcement. Declaring the raids illegal had been beyond the imagination of every single bandit in the empty northern lands. It'd simply not occurred to anyone that if the raids stopped, the Empires would leave the bandits be and would tacitly support anyone who enforced peace.

Seeking Sword enforced it ruthlessly.

Guaranteeing the northern lands a long respite from the threat of invasion still hadn't satisfied the Bandit. Sending relief shipments of food to the Western Empire and negotiating a treaty of non-aggression had etched in stone a long prosperous relationship with the Western neighbors. Capturing the refugees of succession from the Southern Empire and offering to extradite the expatriates had legitimized Seeking Sword's rule by the respect he'd shown for other Emperors. The message to the other three Empires was clear: The Emperor Sword would return criminals to their native countries. The northern lands were no longer a haven for fugitives.

With the Eastern Empire, however, Seeking Sword stood intransigent. When a flood devastated nearly every town along the River Placid from Emparia City to Cove, Seeking Sword had refused to commit a single tael to the relief efforts. He'd stated publicly he'd happily send supplies and labor if Flying Arrow gave him the Imperial Sword. When the embezzler Foraging Puma crossed the border with a million taels filched from Flying Arrow's coffers, Seeking Sword put him to death and confiscated the money. He'd stated publicly he'd return it if Flying Arrow gave him the Imperial Sword. On immigration, Seeking Sword established an open-door policy, provided the individual wasn't a fugitive. People from the Southern and Western Empires emigrated freely. Northerners politely turned away each Eastern immigrant twice. The third time they died. In trade, Seeking Sword encouraged any bandit to import or export any noncontraband product from or to any place—except the Eastern Empire. In diplomacy, Seeking Sword had sent representatives to the Western and Southern Empires to negotiate an exchange of ambassadors, deliberately excluding the Eastern Empire.

Of the many ways to isolate the Eastern Empire, the fastest and surest was an unwarranted act of aggression. Seeking Sword's precious peace, his respect for the laws of the other Empires, the treaties he'd negotiated and the good relations he'd cultivated, had legitimized the Bandit's sovereignty in ways that even an Imperial Sword couldn't. Ordinary people across the continent said Seeking Sword was more philanthropic than the Matriarch Water. The General Sword had usurped the General Bear's place at the right hand of the Infinite. The Bandit had grown more face than the Heir. The Emperor Sword had earned the same respect automatically given to the other three Emperors. In the face of all these factors, any act of aggression against the Northern Empire would likely bring the condemnation of most the people in all four Empires. The Bandit was trying to provoke the Heir into just such an act.

Somewhere a door slammed. Leaping Elk saw his mate's half-empty plate across the table—but no mate. Mystified, he rose and went to look for her. He looked into his son's bedroom, knowing it empty. Rearing Elk was a member of the delegation Seeking Sword had sent south to negotiate the exchange of ambassadors.

Leaping Elk looked at the bed. Without thinking, he lay down.

On his son's bed, he drifted into a consciousness somewhere between waking and sleeping, where pain didn't follow and the weight of his ancient body lifted. Thence, he saw all the waves of time.

He cried out at the anarchy that threatened to overwhelm humanity. Fewer than a quarter of the futures that might evolve within the next ten years contained peace and prosperity. Trying to distinguish the factor that predetermined anarchy, he saw that the absence of the Swords caused upheaval in most of the futures. He also saw that talismans were no longer pro-scribed, the laws repealed, freeing the psychic disciplines from their nine-thousand year cages and unleashing an anarchy all its own. Searching far into the peaceful futures, he saw that in a hundred years perhaps a third of them were anarchy as well, but that not a single future contained the Swords. Not one future. Leaping Elk couldn't conceive of a society not governed by the Swords.

Another talisman loomed large in the future, one not limited as the Swords were. He remembered the waking prescient vision he'd had a few days after the Arrow Twins were born. "They will put down the sword and pick up the staff," he'd said. The new talisman was a staff, not a sword, a symbol of aid, not of war. Those wielding the staffs wouldn't be as susceptible as to neurological disorders. A benefit insignificant compared to the pervasive effects of the staffs on civilization itself.

Far in the future the societal changes resulting from the staffs as scepters would be profound. Few people realized the la-tent, subconscious effects when a sword represented authority. Thank the Infinite, the investiture of the staffs with comparable authority would enable civilization to grow beyond the stric-tures imposed by the Swords. The staffs would impose their own strictures, their own values, but ones not as narrow or destruc-tive.

Leaping Elk saw all this and felt boundless hope and joy.

Then he wondered why the Infinite had shown him the fu-tures.

"Come, my child," a gentle voice said, "I'll tell you why."

He went willingly, gratefully. Outward he soared.

Looking back, he saw his mate enter his son's bedroom and shake the body he'd inhabited for three-quarters of a century. Leaping Elk said farewell to Fawning Elk and turned to join the Infinite.

* * *

Before she touched him, she knew he was dead.

Fawning Elk shook his shoulder anyway, just to confirm he was irrevocably gone. A distant voice so like his own emitted from nowhere and everywhere and whispered farewell. Shivering, she sat beside the bed, put her head on his arm and wept disconsolately.

How long she wept there she didn't know.

At some point, her seventeen-year old daughter, Frosty Elk, helped her to her room so they might prepare the body for the pyre. Her daughter made sure she was comfortable, then left her in the darkened room.

Fawning Elk recalled the highlights of her mateship to the man who'd always called himself "humble bandit." To others he might have been an Heir disinherited, a traitor, an exile, a foreigner—but not to her. The Leaping Elk she'd known was a man realistic about his limitations, who lived within them, who didn't aspire to be anything beyond them.

Fawning Elk remembered a conversation that exemplified Leaping Elk's lack of pretension:

"Lord Elk," Seeking Sword said. "Now that I have room to maneuver, I'll be setting up a complete government. I want you in it. What position do you want?" The Emperor Sword had declared an end to the raids months before—and had spent most of that time convincing the other bands to obey the new laws. The bands he couldn't convince he'd expelled from the Empire.

"Humble bandit good position now have," Leaping Elk replied.

"You don't *have* a position, Lord Elk!"

"That good position."

Seeking Sword shook his head. "Commanding General of the Northern Armed Forces, Lord Elk. Do you want to command my armies?"

"No, Lord."

"Prefect of the northwestern provinces?"

"No, Lord."

"Which prefecture do you want? Just name it."

"Four wall of home, Sword Lord."

Seeking Sword grimaced. "Ambassador to the Southern Empire?"

Leaping Elk laughed disdainfully, shaking his head.

"What *do* you want, by the Infinite?"

"Humble bandit what have want, Sword Lord."

The Bandit pulled his hair and roared theatrically. Eventually, Leaping Elk convinced Seeking Sword that he wanted nothing more than what he had. Only at Fawning Elk's insistence had Leaping Elk, she and their children moved from the dank, musty fortress to the new city of Seat, where Seeking Sword had insisted they accept this house as a gift, where for three-and a half years, they'd lived.

During that time, gradually, the administrative center of the Northern Empire had also moved from the fortress to Seat, where a curious phenomenon had developed. The amphitheater in which the Council of Swords met was open to all bandits at all hours. While Generals, Prefects, Matriarchs and *Duces* discussed sensitive issues and promulgated laws, the bandits in the spectator galleries might comment, cheer or jeer. Very quickly, ordinary bandits who should only have observed the legislative process began to influence it.

Leaping Elk discovered soon after they moved to Seat that attending the legislative sessions was a pleasant and constructive way to pass the time. One day, however, guards turned him and everyone else away, saying that the Council of Swords had closed the meetings. Leaping Elk went to find Seeking Sword.

"What?!" the Bandit exclaimed when the Southerner told him what had happened. "When those in power seek to conceal their doings or to preserve their power at all costs, the time for revolution has come."

Seeking Sword went to find two of his elite cadre, warriors whose absolute and unswerving loyalty to him had earned them the privilege of wearing the purple-and green single sword insignia. The Bandit took them to the amphitheater and ordered the doors to remain open and the amphitheater to remain accessible to all bandits always. The doors stayed open.

Fawning Elk remembered how her mate had harassed government officials without respite—yet without malice. Of every five laws promulgated in the last three years, at least one bore the distinctive mark of Leaping Elk's wisdom. For a simple man who'd wanted nothing more than what he had, the former Heir, expatriate Southerner, and reviled traitor had found a home and a place for himself, and had been instrumental in helping the Bandit re-establish the Northern Empire.

Fawning Elk felt honored to have known him. She wanted to join him. She slowed her heart.

"Mother?"

Blast, she thought, restarting her heart. "Yes?" The room was now dark. Hours had passed without her noticing.

"Mother, the Lord Emperor Sword is here to see you."

"See that he's comfortable, please. I'll be there in a moment," Fawning Elk said, sitting up. The room was pitch black but for the glow of the central room lights seeping under the door. The family servant bustled in, turned on the lights, led her to the excretory-bath and repaired her face. She began to fuss over Fawning Elk's hair. She pushed her away. "It doesn't matter."

Walking toward the central room, feeling pensive and sad, she wondered why the Bandit had come so quickly.

He stood as she entered, stepped up to her and enclosed her in his arms. She began to cry, holding him tight. Gently, he loosened her hold a little, as if he were in pain.

When, a long time later, only salt remained of her tears, she said, "You needn't have come."

"I wanted to be here. You forget sometimes that you're the only mother I've ever known."

"I do forget," she murmured, laying her cheek against his chest. Beneath the Northern-made silk of his purple-and green robe, she heard his heartbeat, and felt comforted.

"Your future concerns me," he said. "Even in your happier moments, I've seen the shadow on your soul. I know you're a daughter of the Water Matriarchy, Trickling Stream. I know your past hides in that shadow. Your future concerns me, because your past is opaque. I need to know more."

Nodding, she pulled away and turned her back to him, wondering whether to tell him the truth about herself. What about his sword?

For now, she thought, I'll just tell him about me.

Sighing, she began. "Twenty-one years ago, the Emperor Flying Arrow executed my mate Tumbling Pigeon for failing in his duty. All three of my sons died with him. I no longer wanted to live." Turning around, Fawning Elk looked at him. "The Lady Matriarch Bubbling Water in her infinite wisdom ordered me to live, impregnated me with Snarling Jaguar's child, and gave me as mate to Leaping Elk. He helped me through the worst of my grief. When Rearing Elk was born, I found reason to live. Of course, you needed someone to breastfeed you, too. In caring for you both, I put aside my grief. That's the shadow you've seen. In my deepest heart, I still want to die."

As her grief took her again she felt his arms around her.

Later, when her grief had lifted, she said, "The Lady Matriarch gave me to Leaping Elk in return for his shifting of loyalty at the proper time. That time never came and now his obligation, and mine, are empty."

He nodded, cradling her. "If you really want to join the Infinite, it'd be an honor to help you onward. First I'd like you to listen."

"All right. I'll listen." She doubted she'd change her mind.

"Men don't build empires alone. Women such as yourself are vital. I'll need every resource at my disposal to get that Sword and rebuild the Northern Empire. I'd like your help. I won't promise you anything, because a person who wants to die doesn't have incentives. I can only ask."

Puzzled, she searched his face. "What about my children?"

"Whatever your answer, we'll take care of them. I thought you knew that. I couldn't do any less for my brother and sister, eh?"

She nodded. "I wasn't thinking. What if the Matriarch Rippling Water orders me to kill you?"

"I hope she knows we'll all benefit more by having an emissary, eh? Listen, Mother Elk, I want you to think about your decision. You can give me your answer any time after the funeral."

"Not before?"

"You won't have given it much thought if you tell me before, eh?"

"The Infinite *has* addled my brain. All right, Son Sword, I'll think about it."

"Good." Seeking Sword kissed her on the forehead and hugged her once more. "By the way, the Empire has scheduled Aged Oak's funeral pyre for sunset in two days. With your permission, I'd like to have the Lord Elk's then too."

"That's being downright insolent, Lord Emperor!"

"Exactly, Lady."

"Permission granted!"

They shared a laugh of pathos. "I'll see you then, if not before. I love you, Fawning Elk. Infinite bless you." Then, like the wind, the Emperor Sword was gone.

She smiled wistfully, wanting him to stay and thanking the Infinite for making the young man part of her life. She felt a moment of pity for Purring Tiger, because Seeking Sword was always on the move and rarely at home.

She was still watching the open doorway when Slithering Snake appeared on the threshold, resplendent in his robes of purple and green, the single sword embroidered into the left breast of the fine silk.

He stepped inside without a word and embraced her. "I'm sorry the Lord Elk's gone, Lady. Five years ago, he asked me to do something when he died. I don't know if this is the appropriate time. I'll ask anyway. You can take all the time you want to answer. The Lord Elk asked me to take you to mate after he died."

Chapter 6

FIVE YEARS after the assassination attempt, the Emperor showed almost no ill effects, despite the death of nearly forty percent of his brain. Healing Hand and Spying Eagle pioneered a tissue regeneration process that earned them accolades from psychological Wizards across the continent. Fetal neurons stop dividing in the womb six months after conception. Neural damage to an adult is nearly always permanent. Healing Hand located the chromosome that controls neural mitosis. Splicing the proper peptide into a single neuron, the Wizards were able to grow four billion new neurons to replace the dead ones on the right side of Flying Arrow's cerebral cortex.

Live neurons don't a functioning brain make, however. Connecting the neural tissue into assemblies that would allow the body and mind to use them was the daunting part of the Wizards' task. Spying Eagle finally suggested that they use the left cortex as a template for rewiring the right cortex. The technique worked so well that the Emperor was almost fully functional. Other than a limp, the only problem to manifest was that, on occasion, Flying Arrow would move his right hand only to find his left engaged in exactly the same motion. A minor malfunction, considering the extent of the initial damage.—*Wizard and Medacor*, by the Matriarch Rippling Water.

* * *

In the eastern audience hall of Emparia Castle, two rapathons watched the inquest and broadcast the proceedings on the psychic flow to the citizenry of the Eastern Empire, the castle shields shut off for the occasion.

In the eastern audience hall of Emparia Castle, the nobility of the Empire had assembled. Most had come to Emparia City for the funeral pyre of Aged and Shading Oak. All wanted to see if the Emperor would indict his own Heir.

In the eastern audience hall of Emparia Castle, wearing rich, seven-arrow robes of blue and white silk, Flying Arrow lowered himself to the dais and glowered at his son like a wrathful, vengeful god.

Flaming Arrow, in his usual coarse, eight-arrow silk robes of the same two colors, humbly bowed to his father, his forehead touching the marble floor.

Above Flying Arrow shimmered an old silk tapestry, blue and white the predominant colors. Seven arrows in a quiver portrayed seven Emperors, each shaft distinct from the others. Woven most recently into the tapestry was an arrow with white glittering wings, representing the present Emperor.

On a tasseled pillow beside him lay two swords. They didn't look important. The sword adorned with a large diamond was the Eastern Imperial Sword, the source of Flying Arrow's political power. The second sword, having a ruby where the Imperial Sword had a diamond, was the Northern Imperial Sword. At Flaming Arrow's side was a third sword, having a slightly smaller diamond, but in other respects identical to the Eastern Imperial Sword. The absence of the Sword needed to complete the set diminished the importance of the other three. Missing, and presumed destroyed, was the Northern Heir Sword, its function to assure the Northern Succession.

Between Emperor and Heir, at the forward corners of the pyramidal dais, stood two stone Arrow sentries, eternally sentinel in their obsidian cages. The statues had been gifts from Guarding Bear.

The silence stretched. Flying Arrow stared balefully at his prostrate son. A full ten minutes passed before Flying Arrow said, "Lord Heir."

Flaming Arrow straightened, his face betraying no emotion at the Emperor's having kept him in the attitude of obeisance for far longer than his station merited. Flying Arrow's delay was an indication already of the Emperor's decision. Often, the Emperor Arrow treated those in disfavor similarly, his petulance incurable.

Since the rioting had abated but hadn't ceased, Flaming Arrow wondered if his father *wanted* the inquest to result in official charges against him. If Flying Arrow thought his son's indictment were necessary to quell the riots, then he'd indict Flaming Arrow.

Rioting in every major city but Bastion had left thousands dead and millions of taels worth of damage. Along the Windy Mountains, the bandits had turned back hundreds of citizens trying to expatriate themselves. Along the southern border, Stalking Jaguar's border patrols had rounded up over five hundred people trying to emigrate. All the rioters and emigrants had only one demand: The disinheriting of Flaming Arrow.

"I, the Lord Flying Arrow, seventh of my exalted lineage, Emperor of the Eastern Empire, Conqueror of the Northern Empire, do hereby declare, on this fifteenth day of the fourth month of the year of the Infinite ninety-three twenty three, that this inquest begins. Do you, Lord Heir Flaming Arrow, eighth of your lineage, prostrate yourself before this court to submit to its findings in the death of the Lady Matriarch Shading Oak and her mate the Lord General, Prefect, and Patriarch Aged Oak, twelfth of his illustrious line?"

"I do, Lord Emperor Arrow." Ritually, he bowed again.

"Do you, Lord Heir Flaming Arrow, acknowledge the sovereignty of this court to exonerate or indict you for the murder of the Lady Matriarch Shading Oak and the Lord General Aged Oak?"

"I do, Lord Emperor Arrow."

"Very well. Have you, Lord Heir Flaming Arrow, selected an advocate?"

"Yes, Lord Emperor," said a voice from the rear of the hall.

Confused, Flaming Arrow turned to see who'd answered for him, wanting to speak for himself.

Healing Hand, robed in black and armed with sword, approached the dais. At twenty paces he bowed. "I'm the Lord Heir's advocate, Lord Emperor Arrow."

Flying Arrow glanced between them. "The Lord Priest Healing Hand states he is your advocate, Lord Heir Flaming Arrow. Is this true?"

Flaming Arrow shrugged, nodding. "It is true, Lord Emperor Arrow."

"The Lord Heir Flaming Arrow has chosen the Lord Priest Healing Hand as his advocate. Bring the first prosecution witness."

Unobtrusively, Flowering Pine entered from the door behind the dais and eased herself to a step just behind an obsidian statue.

Aged Oak's personal servant stepped forward. The man bowed to Emperor, Heir and advocate, then settled himself halfway between the dais and the Heir.

A clerk approached. "For the record, what is your name please?"

"I am Cackling Crow," the servant said.

"Crow," Flying Arrow said, "please describe events on the night of the Lord and Lady Oaks' murders."

"Yes, Lord Emperor Arrow. The Lord Heir Flaming Arrow entered the office of my master, the Lord General Aged Oak, shortly after sunset, and bade myself and the Lady Matriarch Shading Oak to leave them alone. I, uh, I hadn't left the Lord Oak's presence for a week, not since he'd lost his temper with the Lord Heir. The Lady Oak and I went into the corridor, where an Imperial messenger waited. We were there only a few minutes when the Lady Oak screamed and collapsed beside me, dead." Cackling Crow's voice broke. "Through the door I heard breaking glass. A moment later, the door burst apart and the Lord Heir came out. I immediately put my head to the floor. He stepped around me and down the corridor, kicking doors open as he went. When I thought it was safe, I went into the Lord Oak's office and found his body on the floor. Rain was pouring in through the broken window. The Lord Oak's head was missing." Cackling Crow bowed his head, his shoulders shaking with sobs. "He was dead."

Flying Arrow waited for the man to collect himself. "Thank you, Cackling Crow," Flying Arrow said. "You may question, Lord Advocate."

"Thank you, Lord Emperor Arrow," Healing Hand said. "Crow, had you ever met the Lord Heir Flaming Arrow before that night?"

"Yes, Lord Advocate, many times," the servant said, struggling to maintain his composure.

"Before that night, had the Lord Heir ever mistreated you?"

"Uh, no, Lord."

"What was your impression of the Lord Heir before that night?"

"I, uh … Can I state my opinion, Lord?"

"That's exactly what I want you to state, Crow."

"Yes, Lord. I thought he was the nicest man I ever met. When we had that flood two years ago, my daughter drowned. The Lord Heir told me how sorry he was that happened. The Lord and Lady Oak, they told me too, but I see them every day. The Lord Heir, I only saw him five, six times before that, and he said that. It was really kind of him."

Healing Hand nodded. "To summarize then, the Lord Heir extended sympathy in a situation clearly beyond his obligation."

"Supposition," Flying Arrow said. "Strike from the record."

Healing Hand smiled. "To summarize then, the Lord Heir extended sympathy to a peasant with whom he'd had only limited contact. One more question. From what you knew of him before that night, do you think he killed the Lord and Lady Oak?"

Cackling Crow looked up at the advocate and shook his head.

"Let the record state that the witness answered negatively," Flying Arrow said irritably.

"Thank you for your time, Crow. Nothing further, Lord Emperor."

"Very well. Crow, you may go. The court implores you to be ready to testify again, depending on the results of the inquest."

"Yes, Lord Emperor Arrow." Bowing, he retreated.

"The second prosecution witness please," Flying Arrow said.

An Imperial messenger pushed his way forward through spectators. His cheeks each tattooed with the Imperial insignia, the messenger bowed to Emperor, Heir and advocate, then settled back on his haunches.

The clerk approached. "For the record, what is your name please?"

"I am Swift Foot," the messenger said.

"Foot, please describe what you saw," Flying Arrow said.

"Yes, Lord Emperor Arrow. I saw the Lord Heir Flaming Arrow leave a room in which I saw the body of the Lord General Aged Oak, without its head. I saw blood on the Lord Heir's sword."

Flying Arrow waited for the man to continue. Finally, scowling, he asked, "Well?"

"That's all I saw, Lord Emperor Arrow."

"What about his sword?!" Flying Arrow nearly screamed.

"I saw blood on it, Lord Emperor."

Muttering an imprecation, Flying Arrow said through a tight grimace, "The pommel, idiot!"

"Oh, yes, forgive me, Lord. On the pommel I saw a diamond."

"Thank you!" Flying Arrow said, stating his gratitude emphatically. "You may question, Lord Advocate."

"Thank you, Lord Emperor Arrow," Healing Hand said. "Foot, did you see the Lord Heir Flaming Arrow cut off the head of the Lord General Aged Oak?"

"No, Lord Advocate."

"Thank you, Foot. Nothing further, Lord Emperor."

"Foot, you may go," Flying Arrow said. "The court implores you to be ready to testify again, depending on the results of the inquest."

"Yes, Lord Emperor." Puzzled, the messenger bowed, retreating.

Flaming Arrow tried not to smile. Obviously literal-minded, Swift Foot had told the court only what he'd seen.

"The third prosecution witness please," the Emperor said, mumbling audibly.

A small, black-haired, black-robed woman stepped forward. She bowed to Emperor, Heir and advocate, then settled herself on the floor and pulled her sword into her lap.

The clerk approached. "For the record, what is your name please?"

"I am Whispering Oak," she replied.

"The court extends its condolences to you, Lady Oak," Flying Arrow said. "Please describe what you saw."

"Yes, Lord Emperor Arrow. Thank you." She was dry-eyed and stoic, showing not a hint of her grief at losing both her father and mother. "On the night in question, I was asleep downstairs, in a shielded bedroom. The sound of breaking glass woke me.

When I stepped into the corridor, I saw him—" she pointed toward Flaming Arrow "—coming down the stairs."

The Heir saw that her gaze was without malice.

"The witness has pointed at the Lord Heir Flaming Arrow. Proceed."

"He kicked open several doors. I'd have gutted the reprehensible bastard, but—"

"The witness will refrain from using expletives."

Glancing at the Emperor, she looked annoyed. "I'd have gutted the reprehensible bastard, but I know how skilled a swordfighter he is. Instead, I followed him, hoping to ambush him. Unfortunately, his conspirators were following him too. They tried to stop me. After I killed the motherless turds, I tried to catch up to him. I lost his trail. The rotten snake was traveling too fast and escaped. I returned to the bodies I'd left behind and identified one. The gutless traitor was a known subversive in Cove. I found this on him." She held up a ragged silk cloth.

"Strike the expletives from the record and let it show that the Lady Oak is displaying a banner of *seven* broken arrows. Thank you, Lady Oak. You may question, Lord Advocate."

Healing Hand said, "Thank you, Lord Emperor. My condolences, Lady Oak. I'm very sorry your father and mother are dead. Your loss is our loss."

"Thank you, Lord," she whispered, biting her lip.

"When the assailant was descending the stairs, did the person look at you?"

"Briefly, Lord, yes."

"Did the person clearly see your features, Lady?"

"Yes, Lord, I'm sure of it. The corridor was well-lit."

"Have you had much interaction with the Lord Heir, Lady?"

"Yes, Lord. His mate, the Lady Matriarch Rippling Water, is my friend. I'd have even said that of the Lord Heir."

"When this person was descending the stairs, Lady, this person who looked like your friend the Lord Heir, did he recognize you?"

"I don't think so, Lord, no."

"What was his reaction when he saw you?"

"He … I was naked, Lord. I'd guess he was considering whether to rape me."

"Supposition," Flying Arrow said. "Strike from the record."

"How did he look at you, Lady Oak?"

"As if I were a warm, well oiled sheath where he could ensconce his sword, Lord."

"The way the Lord Heir's looking at you now, Lady?"

She glanced at him. "No," she said. One, then another tear trickled down her cheek. "No, Lord, not at all."

"May I examine the banner, Lady?" He extended a large hand.

"Of course, Lord," she said, handing it to him.

He held it up and carefully counted. "Lord Emperor, I ask the court to revise the record. This banner has *eight* broken arrows."

Flying Arrow turned a livid shade of red, looking both embarrassed and angry. "Revise the record accordingly, please," he said.

"In your experience, Lady Oak, what is the significance of seven broken arrows?"

"A banner of seven broken arrows is the pennant of the ancient resistance movement to Arrow Sovereignty, Lord, which sprang into existence during the reign of the second Emperor Arrow. At the time it was of course a banner of two broken arrows. The organization's formal name is the Broken Arrows. In contrast, a banner of eight broken arrows is the pennant of a much more recently formed organization that opposes the Heir Flaming Arrow's accession to the throne of the Eastern Empire. I don't know its formal name."

"To clarify then, Lady Oak, seven signifies opposition to the Lord Emperor, and eight to the Lord Heir?"

"Yes, Lord Advocate, that is correct."

"Thank you, Lady Oak. A minor point: Why were you asleep at sunset?"

"I'd traveled all day from Emparia City, Lord Hand."

"Thank you. Lady Oak, can you tell the court at what time and location you abandoned your pursuit of the man who killed the Lord and Lady Oak?"

She frowned. It looked as if she hadn't expected the question. "Just after midnight, Lord. I think I was forty miles from the crossroads."

"Would you be more specific about your location, Lady Oak?"

"Yes, Lord. I was forty miles east of where the Burrow Eyry road crosses the Cove Emparia City road."

"This was just after midnight, Lady Oak? Very well. Thank you, Lady Oak, and again my condolences." Healing Hand bowed to her. "Nothing further, Lord Emperor."

"Lady Oak, you may go. The court requests you to be ready to testify again, depending on the results of the inquest."

Bowing, Whispering Oak stood and melted back into the spectators.

"Did you bring witnesses, Lord Advocate?" Flying Arrow asked.

"Yes, Lord Emperor Arrow. First defense witness, please."

Flaming Arrow's servant pushed his way through the crowd. He limped forward, bowed to Emperor, Heir and advocate, then settled on his haunches, wincing.

The clerk approached. "For the record, what is your name please?"

"I am the Lord Heir Flaming Arrow's personal servant, Frolicking Cub."

"Cub," Healing Hand said, "please describe where you were shortly before sunset on the day the Lord and Lady Oak died."

"I was traveling eastward on the Nest Bastion road about two miles past Nest, with the Lord Heir. The rain made the road muddy. I slipped and fell and broke my leg. The Lord Heir carried me back to Nest to the nearest medacor's office, then he went on alone toward Bastion."

"How long before sunset was that?"

"About a half hour, Lord."

"How fast were you traveling?" Healing Hand asked.

"Very slowly, Lord. The Lord Heir was still very sore from, uh, the beating. We stopped six, eight times between Emparia City and Nest."

"You stopped? Why did you stop?"

"As I said, because he was sore, Lord."

"He was so sore that he needed to stop?"

"That's right, Lord."

"How did he carry you back to Nest, if he was so sore?"

"I don't know, Lord. It was agony for us both. He got me there somehow. I wouldn't have been able to do the same for him, I'm sure."

"Supposition," Flying Arrow said. "Strike from the record."

"Thank you, Cub," Healing Hand said. "You may question, Lord Emperor."

"Cub," Flying Arrow began, "how long before sunset did the Lord Heir leave you in Nest?"

"A half hour, Lord, like I said."

"Nothing further. You may go, Cub," Flying Arrow said. "The court implores you to be ready to testify again, depending on the results of the inquest."

"Yes, Lord Emperor Arrow." Bowing, Cub retreated.

"Next defense witness please," Healing Hand said.

Flaming Wolf stepped forward, knelt and bowed to Emperor, Heir and advocate.

The clerk approached. "For the record, what is your name please?"

"I'm Flaming Wolf."

Flying Arrow glared at him, a vein at his temple pulsing.

Healing Hand didn't smile. "Wolf, do you know this man?" He pointed at Flaming Arrow.

"I do, Lord."

"When did you last see him?"

"Yesterday morning, Lord, at my hostelry, where he stayed the night."

Flying Arrow looked flushed, as if furious.

"What time did the Lord Heir arrive?"

"Just after midnight, Lord."

"What was his physical condition?"

"He looked like someone had beat the Infinite out of him, Lord."

"Could you be more specific, Wolf?"

"Yes, Lord. He had livid, blue black bruises from his navel to his chest. He was in so much pain he could hardly wash himself."

"You watched him bathe?"

"Yes, Lord. The hostelry offers servants to all clients. The Lord Heir opted not to have them. Likes his privacy."

"Thank you, Wolf." Healing Hand backed away.

"Wolf, are you the son of the Lord General Scratching Wolf?"

"No, Lord Emperor Arrow, although the Lord General was kind enough to give me his name and to treat me like a son."

"Yet he didn't formally adopt you?"

"No, Lord, he didn't."

"Then who's your father?"

"I ... I don't know, Lord."

"Is that your hostelry at the crossroads?"

"No, Lord Emperor, I only operate it."

"Who owns it?"

"The Lord Heir Flaming Arrow, Lord."

"So he coerced you into coming here with the threat of—"

"No, Lord, he didn't," Flaming Wolf interrupted him. "The Lord Heir didn't know I'd be here. The Lord Advocate asked me here."

"Are you the son of the Traitor Brazen Bear?"

"I don't think so, Lord Emperor." Flaming Wolf looked puzzled. "If I am, Lord, then my sister, the Lady Consort Flowering Pine, is a traitor's daughter." He glanced at his sister, who was sitting behind one of the obsidian statues, then looked at the floor.

"Very well, Wolf," Flying Arrow said, his face livid again. "Nothing further. You may go. The court implores you to be ready to testify again, depending on the results of the inquest."

Flaming Wolf bowed and retreated.

"No further witnesses, Lord Emperor Arrow," Healing Hand said.

"Very well, Lord Advocate. Do you wish to make a summation?"

Unobtrusively, Flowering Pine rose and went whence she'd come.

"Yes, I would, Lord Emperor," Healing Hand said, "Thank you. At or around midnight, the Lady Whispering Oak saw the killer of her mother and father forty miles east of the junction of the Burrow-Eyry road and moving toward Emparia City. At or around midnight, Flaming Wolf saw the Lord Heir at his hostelry at the junction of the Burrow-Eyry and Nest-Bastion roads. I'd estimate the two locations are eighty miles apart. In his physical condition, the Lord Heir couldn't have traveled that distance in so little time. Hence, I ask this inquest to find the Lord Heir Flaming Arrow not culpable for the killing of the Lord General Aged Oak and his mate the Lady Matriarch Shading Oak."

"This court grants your request, Lord Advocate," Flying Arrow said, a deep frown on his face. "Lord Heir Flaming Arrow, this inquest finds you not culpable." His face flaming red, the Emperor rose and disappeared through the rear door of the audience hall.

Chapter 7

A T THE Council hall, in Seat, was a projector that translated the flow into visual images. Six Northern Wizards worked on the project for a year, most complaining that the projector violated all the ancient proscriptions against making talismans. Hearing their objections, Seeking Sword promulgated a law that made talismans explicitly legal. In each of the other Empires, where an Imperial Sword was the figurative and literal source of authority, talismans threatened the Emperor's sovereignty. Since the Northern Empire wasn't a talisman-controlled government, Seeking Sword reasoned that their being illegal was counterproductive. The psychic projector was only the first experimental talisman produced by a society that was itself experimental.—*The Political Geography*, by Guarding Bear.

* * *

Seeking Sword gestured at the natural dell amid three hills and looked at Fawning Elk for her opinion.

"It's beautiful, Seeking Sword," she said. "I'm sure Leaping Elk would've loved it." She sniffled a little. Since the death of her mate, she'd cried through nearly every waking hour. She knew she'd cry even more, but she had resolved not to cry in this little time she had with her friend, her son, her liege lord, her Emperor.

She pitied Purring Tiger, the Bandit so rarely at home.

Imperial business so often took Seeking Sword away that when he did come home Purring Tiger frequently asked him never to leave. Soon after officially mating the mother of his child, Seeking Sword had adopted Burning Tiger and changed his name to Burning Sword. Like his father he had flame for hair and sky for eyes. He was a precocious extrovert, charming everyone he met. His sister Stalking Tiger was his antithesis. Purring Tiger had gotten pregnant immediately after mating the Bandit, and had given birth to their daughter nine months later. Dour and taciturn, Stalking Tiger didn't laugh or smile often. Like her mother she had obsidian for hair and fog for eyes. Most people found her unattractive.

To all appearances, Seeking Sword regretted his frequent trips away, obviously treasuring his children, wanting to be at home to share in their growth and learning. Privately, Fawning Elk wondered if he arranged some of his absences. She knew something was profoundly wrong with Purring Tiger. Her affliction deeply disturbed Seeking Sword, the nature of which no one but Easing Comfort knew. Since the tiger had died four years ago in an earthquake, Purring Tiger had become different, obsessed, furtive like her daughter.

Smiling, the Bandit put his arm around Fawning Elk. "I thought you'd like this place. I think I'll make it the Imperial pyre grounds. I'm just sorry I don't have the grounds properly constructed. Of course, the Northern Empire doesn't even have a priest to consecrate it." He shrugged helplessly.

"The Infinite won't care. I'm sure my mate's already safely in Its embrace." She smiled up at him.

"He was a good man. I'll miss him," Seeking Sword said. "Remember when I tried to give him a position in my government?"

She nodded. "We laughed about that conversation for weeks. Didn't he prove helpful despite his lack of position?"

"Perhaps *because* of, eh?" the Bandit said, grinning. "If he couldn't help me himself, he found others who could."

Fawning Elk nodded, lost in her own pensive thoughts.

During the first three years of creating a new government for the Northern Empire, Seeking Sword had worked tirelessly to establish the internal structure. He couldn't have done it all himself, not even with the help of seventy-five thousand bandits. A month after he'd mated Purring Tiger, Seeking Sword had felt so overwhelmed by the task that he'd asked Leaping Elk for suggestions.

"Humble bandit idea have," he'd said. Two weeks later, a delegation from Snarling Jaguar had come north. With the Heir Stalking Jaguar were seven Wizards, siblings all, children of the Matriarch Bubbling Water and the Emperor Snarling Jaguar. Since they weren't legitimate children—born outside the institution of mateship—they bore neither parent's name. Instead, the males had taken the surname of Puma and the females, Brook.

Among the seven siblings was Rearing Elk, the child Fawning Elk had borne at the caves of Leaping Elk. Seeking Sword knew him to be part of the bargain between Bubbling Water and Leaping Elk. Since the Southern bandit had had no inclination to use the child as pawn against the child's sire Snarling Jaguar, Leaping Elk had sent the child to the Southern Empire as soon as he was old enough to travel, where he'd taken the name Rearing Puma.

These seven siblings were all physically attractive and multiply talented. In addition, because of their shared parentage and nearly simultaneous births—within twenty-four hours of each other—they could communicate with each other across great distances, their similar signatures facilitating their contact.

For three years the Puma/Brook siblings had helped Seeking Sword, going where he couldn't, carrying messages, surveying potential farmland, building factories, founding cities, grading roads, and scouting for mines and quarries.

When the three years was over, they'd left behind the foundations of the Northern Empire, much of the work their own. Their departure had coincided with the flood that had inundated everything between Emparia City and Cove. For the next six months they'd helped the Eastern Empire dig itself from the mud, returning to the Southern Empire afterward.

The Puma/Brook siblings were welcome almost everywhere. Born of Southern sperm and Eastern ovum, and citizen of neither, the siblings seemed to be the best of both races, cultures and Empires, without their worst aspects. Having grown up in the Eastern Empire, the siblings were welcome there. Being Snarling Jaguar's progeny, the siblings traveled freely in the Southern Empire. Since Leaping Elk was their uncle and Fawning Elk their niece, Seeking Sword considered the siblings his relatives, and allowed them free access to the Northern Empire. Only in the Western Empire were the siblings forbidden, miscegenation illegal in that insular and xenophobic land.

Seeking Sword envisioned a time when the four Empires existed in relative amity, helping each other instead of fighting each other. He doubted he'd see it in his lifetime. He knew it was possible, the Puma/Brook siblings proof that it could happen.

"Leaping Elk always *was* resourceful, eh?" he said.

Fawning Elk nodded, smiling. "And imaginative. That was quite a show we saw on the psychic projector this afternoon."

The Bandit nodded. Leaping Elk had first conceived of the projector to enable the talentless Seeking Sword to view the psychic flow. This afternoon, it had proved its worth. Without it, Seeking Sword would've had to rely on someone's summary of the inquest at Emparia Castle. With it, he'd watched the inquest himself.

"I didn't understand everything that happened, Fawning Elk. Perhaps you could help, eh? Obviously, I didn't expect anyone to follow me from Cove. That helped exonerate the Heir, I think. Why was Flying Arrow so hostile, though? Did he want to indict his own son?"

Smiling, Fawning Elk eased herself to the grass, facing the setting sun. "Flaming Arrow's become a political embarrassment for him—or, rather, you've made him an embarrassment, eh?"

Grinning, Seeking Sword gingerly sat beside her.

"Are you still in pain?"

He nodded. The mysterious injuries that had afflicted him the morning after he'd assassinated Aged Oak still hadn't healed fully. "Why did they address the servants and the messenger by their patronyms only. Why no 'Lord'?"

"Only hereditary nobles, warriors, Wizards of each talent, and very rarely, a person of vast accomplishments receive the title 'Lord.' Did you notice that even Flaming Wolf didn't merit the title, despite being the brother of the Imperial Consort and the adopted son of the General Scratching Wolf?"

He nodded. "They're both nobles, and Flaming Wolf isn't. That puzzled me."

"First, Flying Arrow elevated Flowering Pine to noble, eh? One of her conditions of becoming the Emperor's consort. Scratching Wolf is one of those rare persons who received the title because of his accomplishments—like Guarding Bear. They both emerged from the Caven Hills rebellion."

Seeking Sword nodded, remembering his history, and how important the rebellion was in changing the Eastern Empire. "I also saw that Flying Arrow really wanted to prove Flaming Arrow guilty, which I don't fully understand."

Fawning Elk smiled at him. "The Emperor might have a thousand reasons. Flaming Arrow's a political embarrassment, as I've mentioned. Flying Arrow might truly want to disinherit him. Yes, I know—he *could* use the circuit-generated link between the Imperial and Heir Swords. Flying Arrow might have *acted* as if he wanted to prove his son's guilt as an expedient to bring the riots to an end. Infinite knows, Seeking Sword, he could've had ten completely different reasons for it. Of all Flying Arrow's reactions during the inquest, I think only one truly represented what he felt."

" 'Then my sister, the Lady Consort Flowering Pine, is a traitor's daughter,' " Seeking Sword quoted. He and everyone else in the Council hall had roared with laughter at Flaming Wolf's words. Flying Arrow had heartily deserved the insult.

"The Emperor wants his citizens above all to perceive him as a sagacious ruler," she said. "Why do you laugh?"

"Everyone knows he's not!"

"True, but that's what he *wants*. If he disinherits Flaming Arrow now, after the inquest exonerated him, Flying Arrow thinks the citizens will perceive him as a tyrant. I'll tell you again, Seeking Sword: With Easterners, face is more important than substance."

He nodded, smiling. "Which face?"

She laughed, throwing her head back with abandon, her hazel eyes bright.

"Is Flying Arrow so influenced by what everyone thinks?"

She nodded. "Why do you ask that?"

"Flaming Arrow, won't he be one of Aged Oak's pallbearers?"

"More than likely. The old General had more titles than a psychological Wizard has talents. What are you thinking? I see that gleam in your eye."

Seeking Sword smiled. "I'll have to speak with Slithering Snake. I expected the Emperor to disinherit the Heir for murdering Aged Oak. Since he didn't, well, I think I can turn Flying Arrow's high opinion of his own face against Flaming Arrow, if face is that important to him."

"Of course it's that important. Look at Flowering Pine, for instance. I remember when Flying Arrow was courting her. She was incredibly beautiful and incredibly stupid. Vacuous, as someone described her to me. Since she's incredibly beautiful, she graces the appearance of Flying Arrow, eh?"

"True, if anything *could* grace his appearance," Seeking Sword replied. "Of course, until I assassinated his reputation, Flaming Arrow very much improved his father's looks."

"Ah," she smiled, "but we all know Flying Arrow has an empty quiver. At the time the twins were born, all the Easterners carefully hid that little fact in some compartment and proclaimed that the Empire was safe from the strife of an interregnum. Again, face was more important than substance. Otherwise, the citizens would've long ago denounced their own Emperor."

Seeking Sword nodded. "Knowing you're a bastard must be terrible."

Fawning Elk put her hand on his arm and sighed. "I remember the day I first saw you. Twenty years ago your father came to the Elk Raider's cave with a newborn boy in his arms. He said that the mother of his child had died shortly after giving birth, in the earthquake that stopped the Empire's siege of the Tiger Fortress."

He saw she watched for his reaction. She's telling me my parentage is questionable also, he thought. "Did you believe him?"

"No," she said. "Before Guarding Bear led the Eastern Armed Forces against the Northern Empire, Lofty Lion was childless, the last of his line."

Frowning, he nodded. "Did you verify his story?"

"No, I didn't have any way of doing so. Of course, I was nursing you and Rearing Elk right then, and couldn't. Eventually, I forgot about it. What woman would whelp for him, much less fornicate with him, eh?"

Seeking Sword chuckled, nodding and remembering his father's terrible bathing habits. "Leaping Elk told me many times never to be happy at another's misfortune. The same would happen to me. Oh, Infinite knows I suspected Lofty Lion wasn't my father. I didn't want to know." He sighed. "Any suggestions on how I might find my parents?"

"If you had talent, you might just listen to the flow for a signature like yours," Fawning Elk replied. "Since you don't, I don't know if you can do anything."

The Bandit grunted, in this instance regretting his lack of talent, wishing he knew his parentage. He sighed, then shrugged.

"At the inquest, the eight-arrow Broken Arrow banner indicates they've split into two factions. Some of them support Flaming Arrow because he *is* a bastard. I'd like to meet this dark deity Breaking Arrow. I hear he's a psychological Wizard with overwhelming powers. I just wonder how someone that powerful could remain that obscure."

"Perhaps that's evidence of his or her talent, eh?"

"Her?" Seeking Sword laughed. His laughter died at the terrible look she gave him.

"Listen, you man," she said. "Just because women don't hold the visible positions of power doesn't mean they don't have any talent. What's unusual about Flowering Pine, for instance, is that she's impervious to other's talents. Not a single Wizard can probe or manipulate her—at all! So, Lord Man, put your 'her?' into your back passage."

"Yes, Mother," he said contritely.

"I'll wager you a thousand taels Breaking Arrow's a woman and highly visible among the most exalted women in the Eastern Empire."

"Oh? How visible?"

"She's either the mate of a Patriarch or a Matriarch in her own right."

"I'll take that wager, Fawning Elk. Not possible."

She grinned, shrugging. "Anyway, did you need me to clarify anything else about the inquest?"

Seeking Sword shook his head. "Shall we return to Seat?"

They stood and turned northward. As mother and son walked back, to their left was the castle plain, where Lofty Lion's castle had once stood, destroyed when the Eastern Empire had razed the Northern over thirty-five years before. A spider web of scaffolding now rose from the plain, the foundation of Seeking Sword's castle. In five years he hoped to have it completed.

"*That* is the most uplifting sight in all the northern lands."

Smiling, the Bandit nodded. "I hope my father sees and rejoices, wherever he is now."

"How couldn't he? It looks as if it'll be huge."

Two years ago, when famine had followed drought in the Western Empire, Seeking Sword had shipped the Northern Empire's surplus crop across the border, a hundred thousand taels worth of grain. In return, he'd asked the Emperor Condor for ten thousand laborers—ten thousand people that the Emperor Condor wouldn't have to feed. Six months later they'd arrived. Seeking Sword had put them to work building a castle where his father's had stood. For a year the Westerners had worked for him. The bargain had benefitted the Western Empire in two ways: They'd received the food they needed, and reduced the number of citizens they needed to feed. Some bandits had thought it ironic that, almost exclusively, Westerners had laid the foundation for the Northern Emperor's castle.

The Bandit looked northward. "I want to show you something. Perhaps you can explain a mystery to me. Ahead is a tree, a giant oak. Five years ago, I saw Healing Hand put his palms on it. The trunk split and into his hands leaped that sword he wore during the inquest."

"I wondered about that! Why would a medacor wear a sword? He got it from a tree?" Her voice was full of disbelief. "Are you sure that's what you saw?" she asked, peering at him dubiously.

Seeking Sword nodded gravely. "I'm sure. My eyes didn't deceive me, because I've seen it happen twice—the same tree."

"Are you Infinite-blessed?"

"No, not at all. Remember when I came to the Elk Raiders and asked someone to teach me to use this?" He indicated his sword at right hip.

She smiled. "You looked so amusing—five years old and holding a sword as big as you were! We all laughed and loved you even more."

The Bandit smiled. "That's where my father got it."

"Eh? What did you say?" She looked as if the sword had struck her with the flat of the blade.

"My father got this sword from this tree."

"Somehow, I believe you now." In her voice was wonder and awe.

"When I last saw the tree, it was burning. Guarding Bear and Healing Hand had come north with Aged Oak to help him besiege Seat. The night before the siege, they came to the tree. Guarding Bear—who seemed fully *compos mentis* at the time— told the Medacor what he'd learned about the Medacor Sword—"

"*That* old legend!"

"—and how he'd concluded that it was inside the tree. Healing Hand opened the tree by placing his palms on the trunk and out leapt the Medacor Sword. Then the tree began to burn. I'd guess the fire killed the tree, so I haven't been back since then. It's right through here, beyond this ridge of broken granite block."

"That's an incredible story, Seeking Sword," she said as they climbed the canted granite.

"That was the first time I impersonated the Heir," he added. "When I hugged Guarding Bear and he thought I was Flaming Arrow. Flashing Blade wanted to skewer me for letting them live. I convinced him we were much better off knowing exactly how much I resemble the Heir. Better *that* than dead, eh?"

"You don't think you could have beaten Guarding Bear?"

"No, not then. I was fifteen, by the Infinite! Only days before, I'd killed for the first time. I'd have been a fool to try to kill *the* General, eh? Undefeated in two major wars, countless battles and skirmishes, and Infinite knows how many duels. No, I was young, but not an idiot. I wanted to live a little long—"

Stopping, Seeking Sword put his hand on Fawning Elk's shoulder. "That's the tree."

"Is someone at the base?"

Seeking Sword nodded. A hooded figure knelt beneath the boughs.

"Who is it?" she asked. "Seeking Sword, something's amiss. I can't identify him from his signature." Then she explained more thoroughly. "His name's not part of his signature, and I don't recognize that signature, although it's familiar to me."

Nodding, Seeking Sword started to draw his sword. He winced and nearly dropped the weapon, shaking his head.

"I can use it, Lord."

He began to give it to her.

She recoiled in horror. "No," she whispered, her terror plain on her face, her hands raised as if to fend off an attack.

"Infinite blast it," he said. "Leaping Elk did the same!"

Smiling, she bit her lip, then looked toward the figure at the base of the tree.

Sighing, Seeking Sword stepped toward the person, gesturing Fawning Elk to remain where she was.

"Send the woman away!"

The Bandit stopped, surprised. "Melding Mind?"

Fawning Elk gasped in recognition.

When Seeking Sword had become steward of the empty northern lands five years ago, Melding Mind had just lost his daughter Thinking Quick. Ashamed that she'd helped the Heir Flaming Arrow by betraying her liege lord Scowling Tiger, the Wizard had wanted to fall on his knife. Seeking Sword had asked him to live for a year and to investigate the psychic storms. When the year was done, Melding Mind had disappeared. No one had seen him since.

"I'm not Melding Mind anymore, bandit! Melding Mind's dead."

"May I ask your name then, Lord?"

"Send the woman away!"

He glanced at her.

"I'll be all right. Seat's not far away."

The Bandit hugged her. "Infinite be with you, Mother."

She smiled, turned and walked away.

Thanking the Infinite for her, Seeking Sword sighed, then turned to look at the figure kneeling toward the tree in an attitude of prayer or obeisance. What was prayer but obeisance to the Infinite? He looked up into the dusk-darkened branches and saw not a sign of the fire five years ago. It looked as if it hadn't burned at all.

"Who are you?" Seeking Sword asked.

"I'm Changing Oak. I'm steward of this land." The voice had changed and softened, had become more feminine, but still emanated from the Wizard crouched at the base of tree. "You might be the Emperor and might rule the people, but I'm steward here, Lord Emperor Sword. Please remember that.

"I was a human being once, a morphological Wizard. My transgression was that I loved an Emperor. I turned his mate into a toad so he'd love only me. That's my talent, changing living beings. When I refused to change the gargantuan toad back into his mate, the Emperor gave me a choice: Remain imprisoned until I died, or assume the shape I have now. I chose to be an oak. After I morphed, the Emperor made a talisman to prevent me from changing back. My prison for a thousand years."

"Infinite be with you, Lady Oak. It's my pleasure to make your acquaintance."

"It's a political necessity, Lord Emperor Sword. You'll be steward over the people until you die. I'll outlive you, though, as I have your every predecessor. I've watched over this land for nearly a millennium. I've seen it ravaged three times, and the last time was the worst."

"How can I help you repair the land, Lady Oak?"

"Oh, my, an Emperor who cares! I don't believe it!"

Seeking Sword smiled. "A few days ago, a storm washed away the east-west road in ten places. Can you tell me why, Lady Oak?"

"Would you correct it, or would you just turn on me, like so many other Emperors? Know this, Seeking Sword: The wealth of your nation depends on your careful husbandry of the land. All else is superfluous."

"Yes, Lady Oak, I *do* know. I share your concern. I'm sorry to hear that other Emperors haven't dealt fairly with you. I'm not other Emperors. Please help me a little, and watch what I do with your help."

"Very well, since you seem assiduous in your other concerns. *I* appreciate what you've already done to heal the land's wounds. The Windy Mountains is only one upon this hurting land. When you've started there, come back. I'll tell you more."

"Yes, Lady Oak, I'll return. I appreciate your help. Will Melding Mind act as intermediary?"

"Who? Oh, you mean this human groveling at my roots. Yes, he'll be our intermediary. Now, about the Windy Mountains. Bandits have lived amidst the mountains for thirty years, stripping the hills without regard for the future. Now they lay bare, vulnerable to erosion from rain and wind. So, Lord Emperor Sword, plant trees."

"Eh? Uh, I mean, what did you say, Lady Oak?" Of course, Seeking Sword thought, why didn't I think of that!

"Infinite swab your ears, human! I said, 'Plant trees.'"

"Oh, plant trees. Yes, Lady, I understand."

"Trees, shrubs, grasses—plant! Lock up the soil in roots! Anchor the hills themselves so they don't wash or blow away."

"Yes, Lady Oak, of course. I'll plant—whatever I can find. Thank you for your help, Lady." Seeking Sword felt puzzled but curiously awed. Sensing she'd dismissed him, he felt obligated to make an obeisance. He knelt and bowed, then got to his feet. "Infinite be with you, Lady Oak."

Melding Mind didn't respond.

Seeking Sword walked away, bemused.

Chapter 8

O N TOP of cascading silks, dressed in high-collared robes of black, sat the personage mourned. In their last testaments, women usually specified a fashionable hair style and robes, and men their most-prized ceremonial battle helmet and armor. Standing on pilings three feet high, the bier stood ready. Around it milled the highest of nobles, also dressed in black, the dead noble having chosen these eight persons to bear the pall cast by his or her death. These eight people stood near the funeral bier between the two outermost battlements of the castle. Over the towering battlements seeped the noise of the crowd. Through this crowd these pallbearers would carry the deceased to the pyre grounds. Only nobles of high rank or members of the Imperial Family merited all the panoply and fanfare of such a grand ceremony.—*Social and Political Customs before the Fall*, by Shriveling Stalk.

* * *

Flaming Arrow sat on a battlement of Emparia Castle, awaiting the Emperor's return and knowing now what he needed to do. The castle bulk behind him hid the setting sun. Wondering why his father had fought so hard to indict him, the Heir stared toward the east.

Toward the coliseum where five years before he'd helped carry the remains of the Matriarch Bubbling Water.

Toward the Imperial pyre grounds.

Now, an Empire gathered there to burn the remains of the Matriarch Shading Oak and the Patriarch Aged Oak. Everyone of importance had gone to their pyre. Everyone except the Heir Flaming Arrow.

In his testament, Aged Oak had specified the ten people he wanted to bear his carcass to its burning, the Heir among them. A half-hour ago, however, the unthinkable had happened.

* * *

On signal, Flaming Arrow and the other nine male pallbearers lifted Aged Oak's litter and walked toward the castle gate. Propped in a sitting position on the litter, Aged Oak looked fierce, dressed in black-lacquer armor, winged shoulder mantles and a winged helmet. The insignias of his many positions were embroidered into the left breast of his outer robe.

The gate opened in front of them, and the crowd beyond suddenly hushed. Through the gate walked the bearers, onto the Cove road. The bier of Shading Oak, her pallbearers all prominent women, followed by a few paces, the small Matriarch similarly positioned and wearing flowing silk robes of black.

Ten miles away was the pyre grounds, the route lined with mourners. Flaming Arrow, bearing the rung at Aged Oak's knee, had no warning at a hundred paces beyond the gate.

An overripe tomato slathered his ear.

Subdued laughter rippled through the crowd.

Flaming Arrow tried to ignore it and pushed on.

A rotten peach caught him in the shoulder. A third fruit narrowly missed his face, splashing sticky red juice all over Aged Oak's knee.

The procession ground to a halt.

"What does it matter, Lord?" Probing Gaze said behind him.

"Then why did we stop?!" He felt so angry he wanted to plunge into the crowd, sword out and swinging. He was the Heir, though, and couldn't behave so irresponsibly.

"Go back to the castle, Lord," Probing Gaze said, his voice gentle.

Flaming Arrow knew he should. He didn't prolong the decision by agonizing over it; he just went, not wanting to endure all ten humiliating miles to the pyre grounds.

The miscreants in the crowd waited until he had passed the two biers, then deluged him with a rain of rotten fruits and vegetables. When he was fifty paces from the castle gate, they began to throw rocks. His face and shoulders already runny with rotten produce, he prayed none of the rocks hit him directly. Proudly, he walked toward the gate, neither lengthening his gait nor hurrying his step. One stone bounced harmlessly off his shoulder, but none struck a vital area directly. He stepped into the castle before a rock hurt him seriously.

* * *

He'd bathed immediately, then dressed in fresh clothes. Ascending to the battlement, he'd begun to contemplate his future.

I've never felt so humiliated in all my life! Soon, now, I'll be done with it. Then I won't have to endure another mortifying moment!

Sometime in the past three days, since waking at the sleeping hostelry, Flaming Arrow had come up with an idea. Rippling Water had given him a clue. Healing Hand, Spying Eagle, and Guarding Bear had all shown him. For three days, Flaming Arrow had held the idea in his mind, had weighed all the factors, and earlier this evening, while rotting fruit and then rocks had pelted him, had decided.

The riots across the Empire and the incident a half-hour ago were evidence that his decision was what the citizens of Empire wanted. The rioters and those trying to emigrate demanded the disinheriting of Flaming Arrow.

He sighed, numb.

Breaking wind caught his attention. Strolling mindlessly toward him, holding the bear's chain, was the insane General Guarding Bear.

Flaming Arrow watched him closely.

The eyes—they appeared to *see* him. Guarding Bear seemed to be staring at him, his face composed, his gaze focused, his mouth mirthful. The old General didn't look crazy at all!

The Heir stood as Guarding Bear stepped close.

"You've decided," the old General mumbled.

Flaming Arrow struggled to keep his composure. Pain and joy battled to usurp control of his features. "I have."

"Good, you kept your reaction off your face. Listen, Flaming Arrow, I know your reasons. They're similar to mine, despite the different circumstances. Will you seek revenge?"

"No, Lord Bear, only resolution." He looked into the General's eyes. "Have you returned to us? Will you stay?"

"I don't know," Guarding Bear said, compassion on his face. "I'm glad you don't want revenge. I made too many similar mistakes with Scowling Tiger. Listen, Lord, I want you to promise me something."

"How can I persuade you to stay?"

The General looked surprised. "Eh? You can't, not if I don't want to stay. Promise me something."

The Heir smiled. "Of course—anything for you, whether you stay or go. I want to throw my arms around you and hug you, you know."

A smile touched Guarding Bear's lips. Joy danced in his eyes. "Promise me you'll give the Bandit the Sword."

Flaming Arrow was suddenly furious. "Absolutely not!"

The old General cuffed him across the ear. "I'm Guarding Bear!" he protested, as if that meant something. "I'm no stinking noble who worries if I've face enough or if my nose is brown enough! Don't you let your stupid pride or fear or hatred interfere with what you know is better for the Empire!"

Flaming Arrow smiled. "Yes, Lord Emperor Bear."

The General loosed a raucous laugh. "Give me that hug now, eh?"

"Yes, Lord." He threw his arms around Guarding Bear. "I'll be in the audience hall, waiting for my father. I'd like you to be there."

Guarding Bear gave a brief nod, pointed at an empty patch of sky and roared with laughter again. Then, without an obeisance, he walked whence he'd come, singing a tuneless song.

Flaming Arrow remembered how, five years ago, he'd have given away the Heir Sword to have Guarding Bear's insanity somehow cured. He glanced down at the diamond on the pommel. The ways of the Infinite were inscrutable.

He turned toward the nearest stairwell, making for the audience hall, where yesterday the Emperor had held a formal inquest to determine if he should face charges of murder.

He sat on cold stone in exactly the same place. Looking around the now-empty hall, he remembered the jubilation he'd felt at his exoneration and how he'd expected the citizens of Empire to welcome him into their hearts once more.

Instead, the rioting had increased, especially in Cove. Today, in Emparia City, they'd thrown rotten fruits and vegetables at him, and then stones. Maybe everyone thinks the Emperor orchestrated the inquest findings for political purposes, even though he seemed determined to indict me, Flaming Arrow thought.

After the inquest, he'd embraced each of his friends, whose support had filled him with confidence and conviction.

Before the inquest had ended, his mother Flowering Pine had disappeared into her sanctuary high inside the castle, aloof and inaccessible once more. At Healing Hand's suggestion, they'd then hurried Flaming Wolf from the castle, knowing that Flying Arrow had recognized the son of Brazen Bear, knowing the Emperor's wrath. Flaming Arrow would have to find another place for Flaming Wolf, regretting that the man had had to expose himself to the Arrow sights.

What will Flying Arrow do about the Imperial Consort, now that he knows she's Brazen Bear's daughter? Flaming Arrow wondered.

Worry and anxiety crowded the Heir's mind. The uncertainty of his future was a palpable weight on his shoulders.

Flaming Arrow closed his eyes a moment, took three deep breaths, then looked at one of the obsidian statues at the forward corners of the dais. Focusing on the stone nose, he began to breathe deeply. Tension and stress flowed from him with each exhalation. He breathed inward the love and strength of the Infinite. Soon the nose was all he saw. A bright glint of light off the obsidian proboscis filled his sight. Nothing but that point of light and the spiritual strength of the Infinite.

He sensed a presence. The time had come to return to the living.

He bowed to the Emperor.

"Lord Heir," Flying Arrow said without delay.

Flaming Arrow settled back on his haunches. "Lord Emperor."

So, the delayed acknowledgement yesterday had been a bone thrown to the dogs howling for the Heir's disinheriting. His father's immediate acknowledgement today confirmed the suspicion.

Then, a woman with hair of flame and robes of emerald strode from the door behind the Emperor. Tall and regal, she stared straight at him as she walked around the dais and lowered herself slowly to the first step.

"Mother?" Flaming Arrow asked.

Something about her was different. She looked too … intelligent! "Infinite be with you, my son," Flowering Pine said. "You look well. How are my grandchildren? I'd really like to see them more often."

Flowering Pine had seen his and Rippling Water's two children only once, when each was born. He'd never seen this side of her! "Mother, what happened to you? Why are you so … so attentive?"

A layer of mask fell aside. "I'm getting old, Flaming Arrow. My time for enjoying what I most love slips past me ever faster. Too, I must atone for the negligence of my youth."

She even *speaks* differently, he thought, unable to grasp that the articulate, forthright woman right here right now was his insipid, brainless mother. How…? "Mother, can you love another human being?" he asked.

She chuckled amiably and nodded. "Yes, I can. I'm sorry if I've hurt you. I haven't always shown you how I really feel. I *do* love you."

Nodding, Flaming Arrow melted inside. The dull ache of her absence eased a little with her presence. "Thank you for telling me."

"I can guess why you're here, my son, so I'll let you and your father conduct your affairs. He loves you and supports you in your every decision, Flaming Arrow. He may howl and froth like a rabid dog, but he'll never act against you. Keep that wisdom beside your heart. Remember that he simply doesn't have the strength to show his love."

The Heir felt her words resonate with knowledge deep inside him. He knew she was right and knew he'd always known.

"Forgive me, my son, but I'm not much different from him." She looked away briefly, then raised her gaze to his face. "Forgiveness is only for yourself, not for other people, no matter whom you forgive. No one but you has to live with you throughout your life." Her sigh was deep and pained. "I was young and frightened once. I locked myself away because only then was I safe—or so I believed. I want you to forgive me. Don't do it because I've asked. Do it because you'll be more at peace, eh?"

Smiling, Flaming Arrow nodded, marveling at this wise, wise woman who'd given birth to him. "I will, Mother. I love you."

She stood, stepping toward him.

He rose to embrace her.

Then she let go of him and retreated through the door behind the dais.

Feeling as if he'd just witnessed a miracle, he eased himself to the floor of the audience hall.

"That was disgraceful behavior at the gate! Those contemptible—"

"I don't agree, Father," Flaming Arrow interrupted. "They did what they thought was right." The Heir looked carefully at his father, wondering why he'd said not a word about his mother's uncharacteristic behavior. He tried to recall Flying Arrow's reaction to Flowering Pine's interrupting their audience. The whole time she was present, Flaming Arrow had kept his attention on her. Not once had he glanced at the Emperor.

"They were wrong!" Flying Arrow spat.

Smiling, Flaming Arrow shrugged. "Even after yesterday's inquest, if some still choose to believe I killed the Lord Oak, what does it matter?"

"What matters is that they've all made a terrible mistake!"

"They have," Flaming Arrow said, shrugging. "What do *you* believe, Lord Emperor?"

Flying Arrow smiled. "I believe that the Bandit has thoroughly muddied your reputation. I *know* you didn't kill Aged Oak, or do any of those other despicable deeds. Yesterday, though, I had to act as if I wanted to indict you for murder. The Lord Hand proved too good an advocate. I had to exonerate you or appear unduly harsh. I thought to solve this political nightmare without sending the Eastern Armed Forces, but the inquest didn't work. We have to find some other way to quell the insurrection. If you have any suggestions, they're most welcome."

"Thank you, Lord, I appreciate your confidence in me," Flaming Arrow said, sensing a presence behind him.

Guarding Bear entered the hall, mindlessly examining the ceiling. The bear followed him in. The General dropped his gaze to Flaming Arrow, then examined the floor with equal vacuity. No one refused entrance anywhere to Guarding Bear, the deified insane retired peasant upstart usurper.

"I have only one suggestion, Lord Emperor," Flaming Arrow said. "But first I have a request: I want to you to leave Flaming Wolf alone."

Flying Arrow laughed coldly. "You're afraid I'll have him killed because he's the Traitor's son? I've known that for years. I wouldn't have made your mother my consort without a thorough background investigation, Lord Heir. If I'd wanted Flaming Wolf dead, I'd have killed him long ago."

Flaming Arrow sighed. "Thank you, Lord, I needed to ask. As to my suggestion: Since I have to settle this vendetta between myself and the Bandit anyway, I propose we give the citizens of Empire what they want."

"Eh? Those imbeciles? They're peasants. Who listens to them?"

"I do, Lord—they're citizens first and peasants second."

Flying Arrow looked exasperated. "Is that one of those backward ideas you learned from Guarding Bear? I knew I shouldn't have let him near you." Flying Arrow looked toward the General at the rear of the hall. "What other stupidities did you teach him, Lord Bear?"

Guarding Bear didn't reply. The bear broke wind.

"Thank the Infinite, he didn't teach you to usurp."

"No, he didn't, Lord," Flaming Arrow said. "He *did* teach me that a position of power is as constricting as one of subordination. Therefore, Lord Emperor Arrow, I humbly ask that you accept my resignation."

Blood drained from the Emperor's face. "What-did-you-say?!"

"I asked you to accept my resignation, Lord."

"*You can't resign!*" Blood rushed into the Emperor's face.

"May I explain something, please?" Flaming Arrow asked, his voice mild.

"That's treason!" The Emperor stood. "You Infinite-forsaken, banner besmirching, honorless imbecile! Where do you think you are—the Northern Empire? If you want to break every ancient custom in all four Empires, go live with all the other bandits! I ought to have you—"

Guarding Bear's loud raucous laughter interrupted the Emperor's tirade. Sitting on the floor, the retired General was examining the sole of his moccasin, and laughing insanely at whatever he'd found there.

Flaming Arrow took advantage of the break. "I can resign the Heirship and still want the position, Father."

Flying Arrow looked puzzled, a vein pulsing at his temple.

"While I'm settling my feud with the Bandit, Father, I can't be the Heir. If the Heir Flaming Arrow were to attack the Bandit, nearly everyone in all four Empires would condemn me—*and* the Eastern Empire—for trying to start a war. The Northern Empire has immense face right now. My attacking the Bandit would isolate the Eastern Empire—as the Bandit wants—and we'd lose the war that that act might provoke. Do you understand, Father?"

The Emperor frowned in thought. "You mean you're only resigning temporarily?"

"That's what I mean, Father."

Flying Arrow sighed and sat down. "Oh, well, if you insist. You've obviously given this problem some thought. Beside the path, some Broken Arrow intermediary approached me and asked me to disinherit you and invest Rolling Bear."

"Oh? What did you say, Lord Emperor?"

Flying Arrow shrugged. "What would *any* good father say?"

The Heir laughed, his father's duplicity immeasurable. "You said you'd think about it."

"Of course! Wouldn't you?"

"No, I wouldn't. I'm not in your position, either, thank the Infinite." Flaming Arrow sighed. "I won't need this, Lord Emperor." He loosened his sash and laid the Heir Sword on the floor.

Bowing, he wanted to say something, but he had nothing more to say. Rising, Flaming Arrow walked from the audience hall, a free man.

Somewhere inside him, a small voice whispered that he'd never return for the Eastern Heir Sword.

Chapter 9

F LAMING ARROW's resignation was the one political move that I hadn't expected. In retrospect, I simply didn't want to face what his resignation would mean to the plans I'd made. It was surely the most shrewd move he could have made, a move that opened many doors for him and slammed others shut for me.—*The Heir, the Enemy*, by Seeking Sword.

* * *

Purring Tiger embraced Fawning Elk, thinking the older woman stupid to mourn over a barbarian traitor like Leaping Elk. Keeping her contempt carefully shielded, she walked beside the grieving woman as they returned to Seat from the pyre grounds, the nobility of the Northern Empire strung ahead and behind them along the north-south road. Ahead, Seeking Sword was talking quietly with Raging River. Propped on his hip was their daughter Stalking Tiger, her head tucked into her father's shoulder.

Purring Tiger frowned.

Since mating five years ago, she and Seeking Sword had both worked long and hard to bring forth upon the empty lands a new Northern Empire. Along the way they'd both begun to understand the extent of their differences. He wanted a class-less Empire in which the citizens were relatively equal. She wanted a highly stratified society that rewarded obedience and ruthlessly punished dissension.

She rankled that he implemented his every idea and ignored most of hers. Outwardly, she betrayed no hint of her dissatisfaction. Inside her though, it grew like a weed. Furthermore, she hated his frequent, protracted absences—even though she knew he couldn't be home more often. The Empire needed him to be ten places at once, and his efforts to obtain the Northern Imperial Sword required him to travel extensively across the Eastern Empire.

Oh, how she wished she still had command of the Tiger Raiders!

Like all bands, the Bandit had dissolved them and compelled them to give their allegiance to the Northern Empire. As the Bandit's consolidation had progressed, Purring Tiger had found her power and influence ebbing. More and more, Northerners had looked to Seeking Sword to lead them, and less and less to her. While she still had a voice on his Council of *Duces* and his Council of Matriarchs, Northerners regarded her to an increasing degree as merely the Bandit's mate.

I'd hack every one of them apart if I thought it'd help!

Her face serene, she spoke words of condolence to Fawning Elk, hating her.

"Thank you, Lady Tiger," Fawning Elk said, wiping her face. "You're so kind. Infinite bless you. I'm so grateful you're Seeking Sword's mate. He deserves someone like you."

"You're very kind, Lady Elk. It is nothing. I'd do the same for any of my friends," she replied, disgusted with the woman. *I hope a polite amount of time has passed.* "I need to speak with my mate, Lady. If you'll excuse me?"

"Of course, Lady Tiger. Again, bless you and thank you."

The two women bowed to each other. Purring Tiger hurried ahead to catch up with the Bandit. Relieved to have gotten away from that bloodsucking viper, she fell into step beside her mate and offered to take Stalking Tiger from him.

"I'll carry her," the Bandit replied.

"I insist. You're obviously discussing matters of state," Purring Tiger replied, taking the four-year old girl from him.

Seeking Sword frowned at her, Raging River looking away.

She pretended not to notice his frown and arranged the collars of her daughter's robes. She was grateful for the children, because without them she'd have dissolved her mateship to her overly-absent mate and found someone to give her the attention and affection she deserved, Infinite blast him!

Oh, how she hated his friendship with that salacious slut Fawning Elk. He spent more time with her than with his own mate! If he hadn't promulgated a law making the Imperial courts responsible for redressing grievances, Purring Tiger would've sliced in two every strumpet who looked at him with even the slightest suggestion of desire.

She smiled at her mate, hating the way his gaze moistened her loins and made her forget that she saw him too little.

"Mommy," Stalking Tiger said.

"What, Salky?" When Burning Sword was three, he'd tried to say his sister's name and had inadvertently given her the diminutive.

"Why don't Dada be home no more offend?"

She frowned, wondering if Stalking Tiger had detected her thoughts. "Daddy is an important man. He is the Lord Emperor Sword. Would you like him to be home more often?" Purring Tiger enunciated clearly to help her daughter learn how to speak. Throughout her first three years, the girl had emitted not a sound except when hurt, retarding her speech development. Now she spoke only rarely, her sentences usually garbled.

"I want Dada to be home more often," Stalking Tiger said, speaking slowly and repeating her mother's words clearly.

"You said that very well, Salky," Seeking Sword said. "I'd like to be home more often."

"You surprised me. I didn't hear you approach," Purring Tiger said. "Are you finished with Imperial business, or are you merely resting?"

The Bandit looked around. "Lord River," he said, gesturing the old retainer over. Seeking Sword took his daughter and handed her to the gruff gristly grouch. "Would you take Salky home, Lord? Thank you, my friend." He nodded to dismiss Raging River, firmly took Purring Tiger's elbow and guided her off the road, onto a trail.

"Where are we going?" she asked. Thick trees overhead soon blotted out the little light left to the day.

Seeking Sword didn't reply. He increased his pace along the trail.

She tried to twist her arm from his grip. "Please let go. You're hurting my arm!" she complained, digging her heels into the rain-softened ground.

He tightened his hand on the joint until she winced. He didn't slow his gait.

She looked around to escape, beginning to panic.

Stopping, he let go, turned her to face him and spoke to her in a voice so devoid of emotion that she knew he was exerting his iron self-control. "You're an excellent mother and I thank the Infinite for that. I don't like the way you treat me or my friends—who happen to be *your* friends as well—and I wish I could say that all my absences weren't of my choosing but most *were* of my choosing because, to be blunt, my love, you're a terror to live with."

Involuntarily, she took a step backward, dumbfounded.

He looked at her with resignation and sadness.

She found she had to look away. Was she so transparent? She felt angry that he could see the hurt and fear that she always tried to hide. How could he know her innermost anguish? She always kept her mind carefully shielded—lest others tell him about her dark and terrible thoughts—and never let her behavior betray her feelings. How had he known? She frowned at him. "What did I do? I don't understand."

He looked relieved.

Did he expect some other reaction? she wondered. What did he think I'd do—gut him?

He glanced toward a pine tree, the lower boughs having long ago fallen away. "Let's sit over here, eh?" He pulled an electrical shield off his belt, set it and turned it on.

Nodding, she followed him to the bed of dry pine needles, wondering why he, the talentless Emperor, had activated a shield.

When they were both seated, he glanced toward the road, sighing. "When you were consoling Fawning Elk, I glanced at you as you looked away from her. Your disgust was all over your face." He looked at her and frowned. "No, I can't fault what you do or say, but your face mirrors your soul. Perhaps because I don't have a talent, I've learned to read faces instead. Your face can't conceal anything from me. I've seen your anger and dissatisfaction too many times to count."

A shaft of fear sank into her heart.

"What bothers me, first, is that you don't talk about it. You won't share your feelings with me. Second, if feeling the way you do makes you happy, I encourage you to continue it. *I'm* not happy living with a quiescent volcano, and I don't want my children to live in its shadow."

She looked up when he didn't continue. She didn't know what to say. She knew she was unhappy but felt powerless to correct it.

What would my father do? she wondered. Her father was dead and she wasn't him. Nothing could heal the terrible rent his death had torn in her soul.

What would my friend Thinking Quick do? she wondered. She too was dead and Purring Tiger missed her only friend and hated her for betraying her father and for betraying her by dying so young and...

The hole in her soul sewed itself shut over her wounds, covering the agony she didn't want to confront.

Purring Tiger didn't understand why she was crying. Seeking Sword's arms were around her. She knew she needed his comforting embrace more than anything. Pain and fear were anathema to every precept her father had taught her. She therefore shoved the two emotions so deep in the bowels of her mind she forgot they were there. Then forgot what she'd done with them.

"I'm sorry. I didn't mean to cry. It just ... happened."

"I'm glad you did," he said.

"What'd you say?"

"I said I'm glad you did."

"That's what I thought you said," she replied, puzzled but covering it with a smile. Sniffling, she wondered why the Infinite another's tears would please anyone. He mystified her sometimes. Since she'd met him in the forests of the empty northern lands six years ago, he'd puzzled and intrigued her. His tolerant freedom of thought scared her yet drew her. He seemed interested in everything and would listen to everyone, yet he took his direction from a voice only he could hear. She guessed she'd never understand him.

"Nothing has changed," he said.

"No. I don't know what to say. What do you want me to do?"

He merely looked at her.

She'd known he wouldn't tell her. She felt so frustrated that she wished she'd never met him at all! If they'd never met, she'd now command the Tiger Raiders, and her bandits would terrorize the sterile cripple across the border and his bastard whelp and …

* * *

"You've decided," he said, interrupting her reverie.

"Eh? What are you talking about?"

"Your soul was all over your face again. The soul that looks, smells, sounds, and acts like a volcano." *I'm so afraid for her*, he thought, watching her face reflect her emotions, all terrible to see, trebly terrible because he loved her more than he could ever tell her.

Seeking Sword knew how it'd happened. Her slow descent into her private dungeon had been agonizing for him to watch. His being helpless to help her had only exacerbated his agony. He knew that until she wanted help, any help he gave would prove instead a hindrance. Having waited as long as he could, he guessed he'd waited too long in the vain hope she'd awaken to the corrosive cancer consuming her.

He glanced down at the electrical shield. Fawning Elk had told him that Purring Tiger's thoughts often seeped through the cracks in her mindshields. His foster-mother had explained to him that shields didn't literally have cracks, but that moments of inattention caused a person's shields to slip sometimes. His mate was frequently inattentive.

Thank the Infinite we were happy that first year, he thought, treasuring the memories. She'd seemed to bloom then, both of them freely drinking the elixir of their love. The interruptions in their bliss had seemed minor and trivial, their disagreements quickly resolved and their separations brief. Seeking Sword had left the northern lands only five times that year.

Rarely was Purring Tiger detained by duty. Her peregrinations took her away more often than obligations.

He remembered the first time he'd seen her while she was away, four months after they'd mated.

* * *

Ascending to the mountain cap of the Tiger Fortress for a moment alone, Seeking Sword looked to the north, over lands hidden by the moon-less night. Stepping toward the low balustrade, he saw the figure reclining in the chair. "Forgive me, I hope I didn't disturb you," he said.

The figure didn't respond.

He stepped closer and saw ... Purring Tiger. "You said you'd be on a peregrination this evening," he said, surprised to see her here. "Did you decide not to go?"

She didn't answer.

Feeling apprehensive, he bent to peer into her face.

Wide, unblinking gray eyes stared at the stone under his feet.

"Are you all right?" he asked, alarmed. He gently shook her shoulder and couldn't rouse her. With both hands he shook her more roughly. Again, she wouldn't awaken.

His heart racing, Seeking Sword tried to gather his thoughts. Test for a pulse, he told himself. His middle and index fingers on her carotid artery, he felt a faint beat. Relieved, he put his cheek in front of her mouth and felt a soft puff of air strike his skin.

She was alive.

Breathing easier, he debated whether to carry her to the fortress infirmary or summon Easing Comfort here. He stepped over to the staircase leading down into the Lair. "Lord Breeze," he said.

"Yes, Lord Sword?" the guard at the base replied, looking up.

"Fetch the Lord Comfort here immediately, please. Immediately."

"Yes, Lord!" Rustling Breeze disappeared.

Sighing, Seeking Sword returned to watch his mate, not knowing her affliction and scared she'd never wake up.

A few minutes later Easing Comfort ascended, bowing to him. "Infinite be with you, Lord. A lovely evening, eh?" The blond, blue-eyed medacor glanced at Purring Tiger and looked not the least bit alarmed. "How may I serve you, Lord Emperor Sword?"

He disliked the title but knew it necessary to bring forth a new Northern Empire. "This doesn't bother you, Lord Comfort?" he asked, pointing at the recumbent figure in the chair.

"No, not at all, Lord Imp. She's on her peregrination."

Seeking Sword smiled at the medacor's variation but shook his head, mystified. "Her peregrination, Lord?"

"Your pronunciation's flawless, my lad," Easing Comfort said jovially. He looked like a proud teacher after a pupil's exemplary performance.

"She appears to be sleeping, Lord Comfort. Peregrination means a traveling from place to place. Am I not seeing something?"

"Yes, exactly. Oh, my, you're perceptive! Your definition could've come straight from a dictionary. You should be proud of yourself, young man." Easing Comfort grinned at him.

Seeking Sword laughed, knowing that the only imp present was the medacor. "All right, Lord Discomfort. I'm dying of curiosity."

"Oh? Should I revive you when you're dead of it?" The large-handed man guffawed. The medacor's bedside manner would make the terminally-ill think their malaise temporary. "Forgive me my impertinence, Lord."

"I'll forgive you the ertinence but not the imp."

They both laughed and Easing Comfort pointed northward. "Somewhere in the empty northern lands, Lord Sword, the tiger is running wild and free. Her mistress is with her. The top of this mountain is the perfect place for the Lady Tiger's peregrinations, because from west to north to east is an almost unobstructed view. She hasn't really left her body. She and the tiger are deep in a communion that rivals an identical-twin empathy link. All her senses have merged with those of the tiger. My guess is she's feeding now on a fresh kill, probably a tender young buck. *That*, Lord Sword, is her peregrination."

* * *

Sitting on pine needles in a descending gloom, Seeking Sword watched his mate struggle with herself, knowing no victors ever emerged from such a struggle—only the vanquished remained.

The first year of their mateship had been beautiful and fulfilling. Purring Tiger had dealt well with her grief for her father and her friend. Seeking Sword, whom no psychological Wizard could treat, had muddled through his grief for his father Lofty Lion. Their shared tragedies had, in some ways, brought them closer together.

Soon after Stalking Tiger was born, an earthquake had ripped through the Windy Mountains. One of the twin towers north of the fortress had collapsed, killing all the occupants. Inside had been the wizardly tiger from the Jaguar Menagerie, with whom Purring Tiger had had a near-symbiosis. She'd never really recovered from the animal's death and had begun her descent not long afterward.

Looking at the woman he loved, Seeking Sword said, "I can't stay mated in the present situation. I'm sorry, my love. I just can't. No, wait, please, don't go, not yet, eh? Would you hear me, please? I won't take long. Just give me one minute. I'd appreciated it. Thank you. I think you'll be glad you stayed. I want to compromise. I don't want to dissolve our mateship. I love you dearly and I think we can find a solution. I *do* want us to live apart for awhile, and—I don't *know* how long. For how ever long we need, all right? I'm sorry. I wish I hadn't raised my voice. I want you to do something. Please look at me. Thank you.

Purring Tiger, I want you to seek help. Psychological help. Yes, from a psychological Wizard. Don't say that! Take some time to *think* about your decision, eh? Please? Take the time you need. Whatever decision you make I'll abide by and support, eh? Yes, even if you decide not to. What will *I* do then? Infinite knows, my lovely kitten—I don't. I *won't* know until the time comes for me to decide. Yes, I want to stay very much. Do you want me to stay? Hearing you say that warms me in all the right places. I love you too, Purring Tiger. I? Handsome? You're joking, eh? No? Well *you're* the most beautiful creature ever to prowl this— yes, right there, oh that feels good, oh you do that so good, oh, that feels even better, oh, no no no, don't stop doing that, come closer, yes, yes, oh, my, uh! oh! yes, oh good good, faster, oh, huh? what? why'd you stop? Noise? I didn't hear anything. Do that again, you know how much I like ... Who's there?"

"Forgive me for disturbing you, Lord Emperor Sword," Slithering Snake said. "I thought you should know immediately. The news just reached us on the psychic flow. Flaming Arrow is no longer the Eastern Heir, Lord Sword."

Purring Tiger yelped ecstatically and laughed, leaning against him.

Seeking Sword said nothing. He saw the outline of her face in the nearly complete dark, but couldn't see Slithering Snake at all.

"Lord, I can't see you in the dark, so—"

"Yes, I realize," the Bandit said, interrupting him. "I have an important question to ask, Lord Snake."

"Eh? Has the Infinite addled your brains? Why aren't you celebrating like the rest of the Northern Empire?"

He ignored the questions. At the deepest levels of his being, he already knew what had happened. It was like a puzzle whose solution had just leaped into his mind. And of course, it meant disaster for his carefully orchestrated plan to impugn the reputation of the Heir Flaming Arrow.

"Tell me, Lord Snake, did the Emperor disinherit him, or did Flaming Arrow resign?"

"He resigned, Lord."

"Infinite blast it," the Bandit said calmly, guessing from Slithering Snake's inflection that the sectathon didn't understand the importance of his answer. "That's bad news, Lord Snake, very bad news. Call the *Duces* to council. Do it quietly, eh? Flaming Arrow's resignation destroys all our plans."

"Yes, Lord Emperor Sword," Slithering Snake said, moving off in the dark.

Seeking Sword began to dress.

"Blast," Purring Tiger muttered. "We never have any fun."

Chapter 10

A FTER LAYING aside the Heir Sword, I stumbled from the audience hall. Waiting for me in the corridor was the Colonel Probing Gaze, a newly-forged sword in his hand. "You should have a sword, Lord," the blond-haired sectathon said.

Numb, I took the sword and secured it to my side.

"I want you to come with me."

Nodding wordlessly, I obediently followed Probing Gaze. We left the castle and entered the southern quarter of Emparia City. A great emptiness inside me, I didn't question where the sectathon was taking me.—*The Bandit, the Enemy*, by Flaming Arrow.

* * *

Flaming Arrow looked around the room and smiled.

He knew this room well. Five years before, it'd been the central room of the Bear residence. After the Matriarch Bubbling Water had died, Rolling Bear, executor of all Bear properties outside the Caven Hills, had sold the mansion to Scratching Wolf, Prefect of Crag. After the Matriarch's death, the house had stood empty and forlorn. Neither Rippling Water nor Rolling Bear had wanted to occupy the ghost-infested mansion.

During his childhood, Flaming Arrow had come to regard the Bear residence as his second home, the Bear Family having all but adopted him. He couldn't count the number of times he'd been in the central room of what was now the Wolf residence.

Seated around the room now were his friends. He hadn't asked them to come. They'd gathered spontaneously upon learning that he'd resigned. Rippling Water had told him that the news had traveled across the continent like lightning. A half-hour after the Heir had resigned, the Emperor had placed the announcement on the psychic flow from the spire of Emparia Castle. Flying Arrow hadn't needed to; everyone had known of the Heir's resignation already.

When Flaming Arrow and Probing Gaze had arrived at the Wolf residence an hour ago, Rippling Water greeted them at the door. She led Flaming Arrow to a bedroom on the third floor, where they spent a precious hour without interruption.

* * *

She pushed him away, breaking their kiss. "We'll have time for that before you go north." She looked dismayed. "I want to hear what happened during the audience." Sitting on the bed, she bade him to sit beside her.

Smiling, he did so, feeling sad. He let his shoulders slump and looked at her, wondering where her sadness had gone.

She stared back at him, as though his last fifteen years of intense training and education meant nothing.

If it means I'm not happy with who I am, he thought, she's right.

"Giving up the Sword wasn't as difficult as I thought," he said, turning toward a window. "I just … set it on the floor and left. I don't know how many times I've considered resigning. Many times I've thought, 'I'd give away the Heir Sword to have Guarding Bear sane again.' I think Wizards call it bargaining, part of the grieving process or something." He felt a tug on his bound and coiled hair. He glanced over his shoulder, then sat meekly on the bed.

She pulled his hair free and flame fell to his waist.

As she began to brush his wealth of bronze, he continued, "I remember saying to myself after your mother died how I'd give away the Heir Sword to have from my mother the affection *your* mother always showed me. The ways of the Infinite are inscrutable, Rippling Water, truly inscrutable.

"On the day I give up the Heir Sword, what happens, eh?" Flaming Arrow snorted in disbelief. "I was on the battlements of the castle while you and all the other nobility were at the Lord Oak's pyre. Guarding Bear appeared. He looked right at me. I couldn't believe how whole his gaze was. Remember when he first lost his sanity? No one really knew if he was truly Infinite-blessed or simply playing the madman to fool us all. This evening, he was the same old Guarding Bear he'd always been. 'Promise me something,' he said. 'Promise me you'll give the Bandit the Sword.'"

"He said *that*?" she asked, the brush pausing momentarily.

Flaming Arrow nodded, shaking his head. "When I refused, he cuffed me and said, 'I'm Guarding Bear,' as though that meant something. I told him that I would, of course. I couldn't have refused him if he'd told me to give *him* the Sword. I love your father, I really do. I wish I saw him more often."

Flaming Arrow sighed. "He came to the audience hall later, after my father and I'd already begun to talk. You remember how the Emperor made me grovel yesterday? Today he acknowledged me instantly. I wish he could just be himself. I think he'd be a better Emperor. More important, he'd be happier. He's probably so lonely he can't help bend with every breeze that blows past him. I wish he weren't the Emperor. Perhaps then we could be friends. I guess you know how it feels to lose your father, to know that he's so close but unreachable even then. I should feel accustomed to it by now. I've had to live with it all my life. That's why I love your father so much. He's been the only father I've ever known." He looked at her. "Am I boring you?"

She shook her head, separating his hair into three equivalent tails. "Not at all, my love."

"You aren't saying much."

"I'm not the one who needs to talk."

Flaming Arrow smiled, his sadness deepening. "I wish I could just have a father who acts … like a father. If I had a mother, I wouldn't need a father so much, eh? She came to the audience hall, too, just before Guarding Bear arrived. You won't believe what she said to me. *I* don't! She asked about our children, said she'd like to see them more often."

"She said *that*?!" she asked, her hands pausing momentarily. Flowering Pine had seen each of their two children only once, when they were born.

"She said more than that. I've never heard her speak with such caring. She was a different person, Rippling Water. Remember during those insufferable Imperial Balls how she'd trap someone in a corner and talk nonsense until the person melted just from the heat of her breath?"

Rippling Water laughed, surprised and delighted by his observation, having endured exactly that.

"Probably because occasions like that made her so uncomfortable. I never thought I'd hear ten successive words from her on something other than how she was so happy to be a peasant and how all the rules of nobility were so far beyond her puny powers of thinking. 'I just don't understand all these rules of nobility I should know,' she pined all the time," Flaming Arrow said in a high-pitched voice.

Rippling Water bit her lip and frowned at him, three thick hanks of hair in her hands.

He sighed, sad. "This evening, she was a different person. Completely different. Her speech, her inflection, her pitch, her manner—if I didn't know my own mother, I'd say she wasn't Flowering Pine!"

She blinked as his inflection rose nearly to panic.

"I don't know why this upsets me," he said more calmly. "Are you almost done? I'll do yours when you're through. You have such beautiful hair. Nothing I like more than burying my face into your turquoise strands. Why'd you push me away? So? You like my face in your hair, don't you? Thought so. Yes, I know, we'll have time for that later." Flaming Arrow sighed, hurting inside and wanting some distraction.

"Have you ever talked with someone, and felt when you came away that he or she was the most incredible person you'd ever met? *That's* how I felt about my mother this evening. I don't know what happened to her, something she ate maybe?" He laughed at her expression. "You know what I asked her? I asked if she could love another human being. 'Yes, I can,' she said. 'I'm sorry if I've hurt you,' she said. 'I haven't always shown you how I really feel,' she said. 'I *do* love you,' she said.

"She said *that*?" she asked, finished braiding his hair.

"You're repeating yourself," he replied, gesturing her to turn around. He undid her hair and began to brush it with sure, practiced strokes. "Then she said, 'I can guess why you're here,' as if she knew—as Guarding Bear knew—that I'd be resigning! Am I that predictable? 'Your father loves you,' she said—in front of him! 'He loves you and supports you in your every decision, Flaming Arrow. He may howl and froth like a rabid dog, but he'll never act against you,' she said. 'Remember that he doesn't have the strength to show how much he loves you.' The insufferable wench! It surprises me that he didn't electrocute her on the spot! As if she has any strength herself!" Then he added in a grumble, "Takes her twenty years to decide to 'atone for the negligence' of her youth!

"Well, yes, she *did* tell me. Perhaps that took courage. You're right, of course. She did say she's little different from him. Then she began to talk about forgiveness. She's right. Somehow I need to find a way to forgive her. I *am* the person I'll have to live with the rest of my life. 'I was young and frightened once,' she said. 'I locked myself away because only then was I safe—or so I believed,' she said. Then she told me she wanted me to forgive her, but that I should do it not because she'd asked but because I'd be more at peace.

"I'm *at* peace, aren't I?!" he yelled. "If I'd been someplace else I'd have …" Flaming Arrow wiped his face. "I don't know why I'm crying. I haven't wanted her love for so long that I forget she's my mother. I guess I felt so shocked that I didn't have time to feel the pain. Don't say that please. You *can't* understand how I feel—you just can't! Oh, I know, there's an Infinite of caring around me and not a feather of it touches me. The caring I've always wanted and needed wasn't in the only person who *could* touch me. She wasn't capable of it. Please, no, just sit back down on the bed. I know you're trying to help. I appreciate that. It's more a hindrance. I'm sorry but it just is."

Weeping softly, Flaming Arrow dropped himself into a chair near the window and heard the voices of his friends and mentors, the two Wizards. "Let the pain flow through you, Lord," Spying Eagle had told him many times. "Your face is the best place for your pain," Healing Hand had often said. Flaming Arrow's pain roared through him like a sudden squall through a fishing fleet. His thoughts scattered like boats, swamped by his salty tears.

Beneath the maelstrom and underneath the waves, however, was a curious peace. Downward he reached, pulling toward the light that was deep in the dark. There, deep inside his heart, was the glowing warmth and love of the Infinite, the source of his spiritual strength. Establishing a connection with the all-powerful and all merciful, Flaming Arrow knew that he'd find peace. The storms would be no less tumultuous, but he knew they were temporary. That tiny fact gave him hope. He'd remain when the storms had gone.

Flaming Arrow opened his eyes, a curious contentment upon him. This, he thought, is how the other side of pain feels, the far side of pain. Here was where he wanted to be. He'd have to remember this, and remember too that when he was hurting, the better path to take was the one that led straight through the pain—not around it, not away from it.

"I'm sorry I spoke to you that way," he said. "I shouldn't have."

Smiling, she bit her lip. "I was more worried about you."

"Thank you, Rippling Water. For caring. For listening." He stepped to the bed, sat beside her and enfolded her in his arms.

"Thank you for talking. You'd been silent for so long I thought you'd forgotten how to speak." She ran her hand over his chest. "I feel closer to you now than I have in a long time."

He nodded, frowning. His ordeal had cost them both. "Let me finish your hair," he said, enjoying her presence, comforted by her.

She refused to let go of him. "I don't want you to finish my hair," she replied. "Do you want to know what I think? About your mother?"

"What do you think?" he asked, knowing he could, eventually, forgive her. How long that might take was unimportant.

"I think she's a wonderful person who regrets she hasn't always been herself. I also think she'd like to become better acquainted with her son and thus come to know herself. She took a terrible risk telling you all that. I'd like to see you respond with equal courage and strength. From what you told me, I think you already did—you asked for what you wanted and needed, eh? That can't have been easy. Finally, I think you two will become friends. I'm sure you will."

Smiling, Flaming Arrow nodded, guessing his mate was right.

Someone knocked on the door.

She rose to answer it.

A voice Flaming Arrow couldn't hear replied.

"Who's here?" she asked in response, looking puzzled.

The voice answered.

Rippling Water shut the door. "All your friends are here," she said to him.

"I don't have any friends," he mumbled, remembering how empty he'd felt on his way from the castle.

"You have more friends than you can count," Rippling Water said, pulling him to his feet. "Let's go, eh? Oh, and beside the path, Flaming Arrow, thank you for throwing away that blasted Heir Sword!"

Laughing, they descended the stairs, treasuring each other.

* * *

With few exceptions, everyone of considerable political or military position had come. Absent were the Emperor Flying Arrow and the new Prefect of Cove, Towering Oak.

Rippling Water led Flaming Arrow to a chair, and one by one his friends greeted him and expressed their regrets at his resignation.

For awhile, they talked amiably, aimlessly, as if waiting for someone to begin. Sighing, feeling melancholy, Flaming Arrow wished that this gathering had occurred under circumstances less momentous.

From across the room, Spying Eagle looked toward him. "What will you do now, Lord Arrow?"

Twenty different conversations ceased abruptly. All interlocutors looked toward him, now silent.

The absence of title felt like a hole in his soul. Fifteen years of being the Heir had deeply scored his mind with the expectation of the address. He sighed, lamenting the loss. "Become accustomed to others calling me 'Lord Arrow.' "

Some laughed nervously. Others winced.

A servant appeared from the antechamber and glanced at Scratching Wolf, who nodded. The servant announced, "The Lady Consort Flowering Pine."

She walked into the central room as if her presence were natural. Flaming Arrow had expected anyone but his mother to come.

He rose as she stepped toward him. Mother and son embraced.

"I hope I'm not intruding," she said, kissing him lightly on the forehead. "I know you have decisions to make."

Nodding, he smiled in awe and wonder. For the second time that day she'd acted in a way that defied his expectation. "Thank you for being here, and thank you for your love and support earlier."

"I want to see my son become who he wants to be. Forgive me for not coming immediately." She turned to Scratching Wolf and stepped toward him. "Infinite be with you, Father. You've a beautiful home. Forgive me for not visiting sooner, eh?" She took his calloused hands in her soft and supple ones. "Have I ever thanked you for being such a good father? I'm sorry. I've always meant to. Thank you for being such a good father." She kissed him lightly on his cheek.

His eyes glistening, Scratching Wolf vigorously scratched his hair. "I don't understand, Daughter. Are you the Flowering Pine I reared? If so, you took the time of the Infinite to bloom. I've never seen you so charming. Well, who cares? It pleases me you're here. That's what's important." He pulled her to him and embraced her, looking very happy.

She smiled, stepped to a chair and made herself comfortable. A servant brought her coffee and refilled the cups of those who wanted more.

Yes, she's here, Flaming Arrow thought, that *is* what's important.

Spying Eagle and Healing Hand exchanged a glance. Across the room beside his bear, standing near a window, Guarding Bear stared at Flowering Pine. Rippling Water quietly greeted her mate's mother and sat on the arm of her chair, as if the two women had always been friends. Amused, Flaming Arrow watched how his mother polarized the people in the room. Revered by the Empire as the mother of the Heir, Flowering Pine was nonetheless a mystery to all, her reclusiveness better known than her personality.

Flaming Arrow looked toward the Wizard, remembering the question. "First, Lord Eagle, I want to see how my resignation has affected the Empire. I hope I've satisfied the rioters' demands for my disinheriting—not that such scurrilous scum deserve to have their violence sanctioned, even implicitly. The hundreds who tried to leave the Empire must know that I've heard their voices. Incredible what expatriates say with their feet, eh?"

Spying Eagle frowned. "Even if they're wrong?"

"Yes," Flaming Arrow said, "even if they're wrong."

"Most the rioting *has* ceased," Probing Gaze said, "Many who were about to emigrate have turned back."

"That's a relief to hear," Flaming Arrow said. "Second, Lord Eagle, I want to settle my feud with the Bandit."

"Will you take his head?" Scratching Wolf asked.

While Guarding Bear chuckled, Flaming Arrow shook his head. "I hope to convince him that the scales balance between us. I don't know what I'll do if he disagrees."

"I'd have killed him long ago," Rippling Water said.

"Then the Bandit's friends would've sought to avenge his death," Flowering Pine said. "Guarding Bear and Scowling Tiger feuded for nearly forty-five years and passed their feud onto the next generation. Isn't the feud between Flaming Arrow and Seeking Sword an extension of theirs? What began as an attempt to address the problems of the Caven Hills is now a personal vendetta between the Heir of one Empire and the Emperor of another. I wouldn't want my grandchildren to become the third generation of victims in a conflict that appears to have no end."

It didn't surprise Flaming Arrow, somehow, that his vacuous mother understood his motivation. He wondered, as he had about Guarding Bear's madness, if she'd feigned stupidity most of her life. It seemed the only explanation.

"I disagree, Lady Consort," Healing Hand said. "When Flaming Arrow assassinated the bandit general, his only interest was ameliorating the bandit scourge. Scowling Tiger's being the bandit general was immaterial. Had he commanded a minor band, Flaming Arrow would've ignored him." The Wizardmedacor sipped at a glass of water. The priesthood of the Infinite proscribed even mild drugs, such as the stimulant in coffee.

"Perhaps, Lord Hand, perhaps not," Flowering Pine replied. "How often did Guarding Bear speak of the indignities he suffered because of Scowling Tiger? How many assassins died attempting to kill him?"

"Too many to count," Guarding Bear said. Sleeping soundly, the bear sat wedged into a corner of the room, its head brushing the ceiling.

"The bandit general's daughter certainly carried on her father's vendetta, eh?" the Consort said. "She was fourteen years old when she first conceived a plan to kill Guarding Bear. Fourteen!"

Flaming Arrow looked at her, puzzled. Everyone's attention focused on Flowering Pine.

"What did she do, Lady Consort?" Spying Eagle asked, sipping coffee.

Then she noticed they all were looking at her. "No one here knows?" she asked. She saw only shaking heads. "Perhaps, then, this isn't the time or place to tell."

"Every person here has proved his or her loyalty beyond doubt," Flaming Arrow said. "I think we'd all like to know."

Her reluctance obvious, Flowering Pine sighed. "Purring Tiger asked the Wizard Melding Mind to intercept Running Bear during one of his frequent carousals and implant him. That was seven years ago."

Across the room, Guarding Bear expelled a hoarse breath and stared at his niece, looking stunned.

Glancing toward him, she bit her lip and continued. "For two years, the Wizard gradually increased the strength of the implant. His parents disowned him after he killed all the courtesans in one of his brothels. That night, the Wizard implanted him to kill his own mother. Purring Tiger had hoped by killing Bubbling Water to kill Guarding Bear through their mate-empathy link."

"I'll gut the bitch," Rippling Water said softly, vehemently.

Guarding Bear stepped toward his daughter. "No, you won't."

She looked up, surprised. "What'd you say, Father?"

"I said, 'No, you won't.' The feud ends here." The implacable gaze of the General bore into Rippling Water.

"Why?" she lashed at him. "She stained my name, killed my mother and my brother, and took my father from me! Why *shouldn't* I kill her?"

"Haven't you heard a word of the conversation here, Daughter?"

"Some of us have the refuge of insanity, Father. Some of us have to face our pain."

"And instead of facing yours, you'd bring the wrath of the Northern Empire upon yourself and your children?" Guarding Bear shook his head and snorted. "If you've heard nothing to dissuade you, consider this: She's your sister."

"You put your sword in every woman's sheath, didn't you?" Rippling Water accused viciously, looking into his scarred and ugly face. "Blast you, Father. You don't know how difficult it is being your daughter." She looked ready to weep with rage.

"I've made your life terribly difficult, haven't I?" Guarding Bear looked ready to weep with remorse. He gathered her in his arms. The great big man with black and grey hair held the slender girl with turquoise hair. "Your life hasn't been easy. I just don't want you to make it more difficult. Leave your sister be, eh?"

Sighing, she looked at the floor. "Yes, Father." She looked up at him, her expression mutating rapidly through several emotions. Finally, her face settled on resignation and acceptance. "I'm sorry I spoke to you like that. Thank you for returning. I'm glad you're back."

"I am too, most of the time. Lady Consort, how do you know Purring Tiger tried to kill me that way?"

"Allow your niece a few secrets, eh?" Flowering Pine replied with aplomb. "Infinite knows women have little enough anyway."

Smiling, Flaming Arrow wondered what other secrets his mother knew. He guessed, because Emparia Castle stood at the center of power in the Eastern Empire, that she knew a great many. "Like the Lord Bear, I want the feud to end," Flaming Arrow said. "So I won't try to kill the Bandit. I only want to talk to him. How I'll accomplish that, I don't know yet."

Healing Hand stepped over to Spying Eagle and whispered into his ear. They then nodded at each other and looked toward their friend. "Lord Arrow," the medacor said, "perhaps my father can help with that."

"Or perhaps my daughter Fawning Elk," Rippling Water said.

"I haven't heard anything about Melding Mind recently, Lord Eagle. Has he joined the Infinite?" Flaming Arrow asked.

"No, I don't think so," the Wizard said. "We'd have heard, eh? It's true that he's no longer one of Seeking Sword's intimates." Then Spying Eagle frowned. "My father's attitude toward me might be an impediment to his helping you, but Fawning Elk and Easing Comfort are both members of the Bandit's Council of *Duces.* They should be able to help."

Fawning Elk, formerly Trickling Stream, was a member of the Water Matriarchy. "Rippling Water, have you contacted your daughter since Leaping Elk died?"

She shook her head. "Would you carry a message north for me?"

"Absolutely, Lady Water," he replied, grinning.

"Tell her that I instruct her to arrange a meeting between yourself and the Bandit. It surprises me she didn't immolate herself on Leaping Elk's pyre. She's wanted to die for a long time. Tell her too that for serving the Matriarch Water faithfully, I absolve her name of all dishonor, and that she may take her life if she so wishes."

Nodding, Flaming Arrow asked, "Shall I suggest she become unofficial ambassador between yourself and the Bandit?"

"Yes, do that. What about you, Lord Hand?" Rippling Water asked. "You've never met your father, eh?"

Shaking his head, Healing Hand looked at Flaming Arrow. "Lord, may I come with you?"

"Eh?" Startled, Flaming Arrow frowned at his friend. "You'd risk charges of treason for crossing the border?"

"He would if he were still the Medacor Apprentice," Guarding Bear said.

"I'm an insignificant priest," Healing Hand added, supinating his palms beside his shoulders in an elaborate shrug.

"Lord Eagle," Flowering Pine said, "you met your father once, eh—an encounter that wasn't very friendly."

The Wizard nodded at her, nearly everyone knowing that his father had implanted him to assassinate Flaming Arrow. "I'd like to go too, Lord," Spying Eagle said.

Flaming Arrow laughed. "Would anyone else like to join me?"

Chuckling, Guarding Bear said, "You'd have an army if you were serious. I wouldn't take more than the Lords Hand and Eagle."

"No one here but yourself, Lord Bear, has so low a station as not to threaten the Empire's security," Flowering Pine said, all of them knowing the swift justice that Flying Arrow meted out for treason.

"I don't agree, Lady," the retired General replied. "Easterners have deified me to such an extent that the Northern Empire could ransom me—if they could capture me."

"The Empire grovels at the feet of the Great God Bear," she said facetiously, smiling. Guarding Bear laughed.

A servant appeared and stepped toward Scratching Wolf.

"Hopefully, I can settle this senseless feud," Flaming Arrow said. "What I'll do then, I don't know." He didn't tell them of his tacit agreement with his father to take up the Heirship afterward. Public opinion would determine when he'd ask the Emperor to give him back the Eastern Heir Sword.

Scratching Wolf stopped beside his chair and whispered in his ear. "Two women have come to see you, Lord. One is Healing Hand's mother, Gentle Hand. They wish to speak with you."

Flaming Arrow nodded. Privately, he thought. "Can you have them taken unobtrusively to a private place, Lord Wolf?" he asked, whispering also.

"Yes, Lord." Straightening, the General stepped toward the antechamber.

"When will you be leaving, Lord?" Probing Gaze asked.

"A few days, I think. I'm not sure. I want to know that the rioting and emigration has stopped. I want to know what the citizens truly think about my decision. I also want to be visible enough to sow some doubt in the Bandit's mind. I'd guess right now he's discussing with his advisors what to do about my coming north to settle our feud, eh? If I leave immediately, he won't have a doubt about my plans."

Guarding Bear smiled. "Take the luck of the Infinite with you, Lord, because you'll need it all."

"Thank you, Lord Bear."

The others chorused their agreement.

"All of you," Flaming Arrow said, grateful for his friends, "thank you for supporting me, especially now. Infinite bless you all."

Chapter 11

CARRYING OFFICIAL announcements, news of importance, rumor and speculation, the psychic flow is the medium that Emperors often use to disseminate their opinions, sometimes in very subtle ways. The Imperial Swords enable Emperors to infuse the flow with the intensity and duration needed for each particular message. The Emperors Condor, for instance, generated feelings of racial superiority and xenophobia with the Western Imperial Sword. Always on the flow were the subliminal suggestions that pure Western heritage was better than mixed extraction, and that anyone without blue-black hair and epicanthic eyes was barbaric and untrustworthy. The Emperors Condor infused very little energy into this suggestion but never ceased broadcasting it. Hence, despite the suggestion's weakness, its very endurance and pervasiveness indoctrinated everyone within the borders of the Western Empire.—*The Great Universal Mind*, by the Sorcerer Flowing Mind.

* * *

"I hereby call this meeting of the Council of *Duces* to order." Looking around the room, Seeking Sword saw bewilderment in some faces, frustration and disappointment in others. "Thank you, all of you, for assembling on such short notice.

"The Heir Flaming Arrow has resigned from the Heirship, a move that leaves our long-range plan to obtain the Northern Imperial Sword in shreds. The basis of our plan was Flaming Arrow's disinheriting and Rolling Bear's investiture. With a disinheriting, Flying Arrow wouldn't have likely reinstated Flaming Arrow. With a resignation, Flying Arrow can and probably will reinstate him. Now that the problem is clear to all, I'd like to hear what each of you suggests that our course of action be." Looking around the room again, the Bandit eased himself into his chair.

No one spoke. Some, he saw, were still digesting the painful reality that their plan had failed. They simply hadn't expected Flaming Arrow to resign.

Upon the psychic projector a few minutes before, they'd watched the Eastern Emperor announce the Heir's resignation, then had retired to this conference room. While all debate in the Council of Swords was public, the other three councils usually held theirs in private. The silence lengthened.

After ordering the Council of *Duces* to gather, Seeking Sword and Purring Tiger had walked back toward Seat. A ponderous sadness had settled upon him, then he'd felt angry at his father and mother—whoever she was—and he'd begun to cry. None of the emotions seemed to have a reason. His mind had felt clear the whole time. His emotions had oscillated like waves during a storm out to sea, scattering his thoughts like boats. Underneath the waves he'd felt calm. Just before he'd entered the Council hall, his sadness had lifted. In its place had been a curious contentment. His causeless changes of mood alarmed him. He reminded himself to ask the Wizard-medacor about the phenomenon. Seeking Sword glanced toward Easing Comfort.

Seated three chairs from Seeking Sword, the Wizard-medacor grunted. "What we *don't* know, Lord Sword, is the veracity of Flying Arrow's announcement. We must remember that he's a master of deceit, eh? He might have forced Flaming Arrow to resign and feigned his sadness during the announcement."

"He *did* act as if he wanted his son to face charges of murder, yesterday," Raging River said. "Which would seem to conflict with his attitude a few minutes ago. We've got to decide whether Flying Arrow was dissembling today or yesterday."

"Why not both, Lord River?" Fawning Elk asked.

"He's certainly capable, Lady Elk." Raging River, like Fawning Elk, knew the Emperor's mercurial moods intimately. Both of them had suffered upon Flying Arrow's duplicitous barbs.

"What would motivate him to be truthful today and lie yesterday?" Screaming Gale asked. He was the younger brother of the Westerner Howling Gale, whom the Heir had assassinated. Five years ago, Screaming Gale had assumed command of the Gale Raiders. After the Bandit had first ordered the raids to stop, Screaming Gale's band had been the second to violate the new law. Seeking Sword had convinced the Westerner that stopping the raids was wise. The Westerner had been one of the first to commit to the Emperor Sword's law. Since then, he'd become a respected voice in the Bandit's councils.

"The riots!" Purring Tiger said. "Flying Arrow probably dissembled yesterday to stop the riots, so he didn't feign his sadness when he announced the Heir's resignation this evening, eh? Lord Snake, do you have any current information on the riots?"

"No, Lady Tiger, nothing really current. I'll need a day or so before I know if they've stopped, unless something comes across the border on the flow," Slithering Snake said. "I wouldn't trust the flow completely. Flying Arrow often uses it to circulate his opinion as if it were fact, eh?" The sectathon, the Emperor Sword's expert on foreign relations and his spy master, had researched the subject of how Emperors commonly employed the psychic flow. Seeking Sword himself would never use the flow, but he needed to know how his fellow Emperors used it.

Flying Arrow's use of the flow was usually blatant. Twenty years ago, just before the negotiations between himself and Snarling Jaguar, Flying Arrow had generated a rumor that the Southern Emperor had entered into an alliance with Scowling Tiger. More subtle and insidious usage was possible, as exemplified by the Emperors Condor. Fortunately for the Northern Empire, Flying Arrow seemed incapable of employing the Eastern Imperial Sword similarly. The Bandit's popularity and the former Heir's unpopularity among the people of the East were both manipulable. The Eastern Emperor could easily disseminate the subtle suggestion that the opposites were true. Slithering Snake suspected Flying Arrow simply had too little power.

Seeking Sword leaned forward. "The Lady Tiger is correct, since Flaming Arrow resigned, partly, to stop the riots."

"How do you know, Lord Emperor Sword?" Screaming Gale asked.

The Bandit smiled. "I *know* it as I do Flaming Arrow. I know now that I'd have resigned if I were he. The court of public opinion found him guilty of every action that I took to have him disinherited. The fact that he's innocent is superfluous. The citizens of Empire demanded his disinheriting, so he resigned. It's the perfect solution to an insoluble problem. He gave them what they most wanted—his removal from the succession—in a way that doesn't prevent his reinvestiture."

Those around the table nodded, having become accustomed to Seeking Sword's ability to predict the mind of Flaming Arrow.

"I'm not *always* right, eh?" Seeking Sword added. "I didn't predict that he'd resign. Somehow, the likelihood never occurred to me."

"You did what you could, Lord Emperor Sword," Easing Comfort said. "We must decide what to do now."

Again, silence settled around the table. Seeking Sword didn't know what to do either. He'd lived so long under the assumptions of his original plan that thinking beyond it was an unwelcome chore. He wondered how he'd become trapped like that. "Lord Snake," the Bandit asked, "have you received a reply from the Emperor Arrow through our intermediaries?"

At Seeking Sword's behest, Slithering Snake had suggested through the Eight Broken Arrows that Flying Arrow consider disinheriting Flaming Arrow and investing Rolling Bear. "The reply was noncommittal, Lord Emperor Sword. He'll 'think about it,' which we expected, eh?"

The Bandit nodded, smiling. Flying Arrow was renowned for inaction and duplicity. He sighed, frustrated. "Any ideas, *Duces*?" No one replied. "Let's consider the next question while we think about that one. Now that Flaming Arrow has resigned, what will *he* do?"

"He'll come north to kill you, Lord Sword," Flashing Blade said.

"Why *did* he resign?" Lumbering Elephant asked, the large man making the large table look puny. "He could've come north to kill the Lord Emperor Sword without resigning, eh?" The levithon had replaced Melding Mind on the Council of *Duces* when the latter had disappeared.

"He could have, yes, Lord Elephant," Fawning Elk replied. "That's what the Lord Sword wanted. The Eastern Heir's assassinating the Lord Emperor Sword—or even trying—would've incited the Southern and Western Empires to ally themselves with the Northern Empire against the Eastern Empire, perhaps even provoking a war. The people of the East would've denounced Flaming Arrow more vociferously than they're doing now. Flaming Arrow resigned so he'd have the freedom to act."

No one dissented.

"What should we do about him?"

No one answered.

Five years before, no one had been able to stop the Heir's inexorable decimation of the bandit population. Of the five major bands, not one had survived Flaming Arrow's scourge, not even the strongest band, the Tiger Raiders. Now, no one knew how to stop Flaming Arrow from coming north to end Seeking Sword's assassination of his character, probably by assassinating Seeking Sword himself. None of the *Duces* knew how to stop Flaming Arrow.

No one but Seeking Sword. "He'll come north, of that I haven't a doubt. He won't find me, though. I'll be elsewhere."

"Eh? Where *will* you be?" Raging River asked.

Smiling, the Bandit didn't answer.

"I know where you'll be!" Screaming Gale answered. A cunning strategist, the Westerner often knew Seeking Sword's actions before the Bandit himself did. "You'll cross the border, eh?"

Seeking Sword nodded, liking the man. "Flaming Arrow will come after me without the one object he and his Empire value most: The Heir Sword. I'll be at Emparia Castle for what I hope to be my final impersonation of Flaming Arrow. I'll ask the Emperor Flying Arrow to give me back the Heir Sword."

Raging River guffawed and pounded the table.

Most of the others weren't so enthusiastic.

"What if he discovers you're the Bandit?" Fawning Elk asked.

"Won't he try to capture you?" Purring Tiger asked.

"That's the most insane idea I've heard from you yet!" Slithering Snake said. "You'll find so many arrows impaling you that you'll be able to eat without swallowing."

Seeking Sword laughed softly. "What better merchandise can we trade for the Northern Imperial Sword than the Eastern Heir Sword? We *have* none. We now can get what we want. To do so we'll have to take a desperate risk.

"One, we'll have to create a cover, some legitimate reason for my absence. Two, our plan depends on Flaming Arrow's coming north clandestinely, eh? If the Empire knows he's here, he can't also be at Emparia Castle. Three, we need to plan for the contingency that they'll capture me. Four, we need to capture

Flaming Arrow, whom we can use as additional leverage, should we need it."

He saw that the possibilities overwhelmed them. Seeking Sword knew the plan could work, Infinite willing. They'd begun to discuss options telepathically. Having often asked them to keep the discussion verbal, the Bandit refrained from reminding them now. This time he needed their full expertise. If that meant they excluded him temporarily, he'd abide by that. He'd long since become accustomed to feeling like a bird yearning to fly amidst a flock not needing leg.

Purring Tiger looked at him and frowned. "I'm ... worried," she said, looking frightened. Her face was pale beneath winter-sallow skin.

The Bandit knew she'd never admit to fear. Scowling Tiger had believed fear infectious, a belief he'd bequeathed to his daughter. Seeking Sword smiled at her and spoke softly. "I'll survive. I love you, Purring Tiger." He placed a large calloused hand on her midnight wealth of hair and stroked her affectionately.

Sighing, she returned his smile. He saw her look toward the others. He turned his attention to the *Duces*.

"Lord Emperor Sword," Raging River said, "it appears that two Prefects in the far north need you to settle a border dispute between them and that you'll return in 'a few days.' We'll call up all inactive reserves and our armies will mobilize on the border in case they *do* capture you. You *don't* return to the Northern Empire for at least five days, with or without the Eastern Heir Sword. Finally, that when you *do* return, you recite to each *Duce* a codeword only we'll know. Two things we couldn't decide, Lord Emperor Sword, were the reason we're mobilizing and how we're going to capture Flaming Arrow."

Seeking Sword nodded, liking most their advice. "I think I have a pretext for having warriors near the border—reforestation. Lord Snake, the reason the east-west road washed out in ten places was erosion. You'll gather tree and bush seedlings and grass seed, and distribute them among the mobi-lized warriors. Plant as much as you can along the Windy Mountains. The main part of the force will gather north of Emparia Castle. Any questions, my friend?"

The Northern Empire was incapable of supporting a standing army. The only full-time military force was the elite cadre of warriors whose function was to protect Seeking Sword. Hand-picked, their loyalty given to no one but him, these warriors wore the purple and green robes embroidered with the Bandit's single-sword insignia. Although voluntary career service was an option, the military granted the higher ranks from Major to General, as in civil service, on the basis of tests and experience, their numbers few. Nearly all were elite-cadre warriors. To provide the Empire with an army, should they need it, Seeking Sword had enacted compulsory military service for everyone ages sixteen to forty for two months of every year. The innovation had blurred social distinctions even more in the class-less Northern Empire. The institution of part-time military service for everyone irrespective of station was anathema to the other Empires, where the nobility supported large armies from which Emperors levied troops. These nobles rigorously quashed peasantry who tried to rise above their station. In the Northern Empire, however, a peasant *had* to become a warrior for two months of the year. Even the lowly and reviled merchant suddenly found him or herself exalted to the station of warrior, if briefly. Composed mostly of peasant-farmers, the Northern Armed Forces was particularly well suited to carry out the reforestation of the Windy Mountains.

The sectathon frowned. "Why do I always get the odd tasks?"

The Bandit laughed. "You do them so well, Lord Snake." To the others he said, "Unfortunately, I don't have any suggestions for capturing Flaming Arrow. His capture may be necessary if they capture *me*, eh?"

"Lord Sword," Fawning Elk said, "perhaps I can help. Maybe I could receive a message from my Matriarch for the Lord Arrow, asking him to stay for a few days…?"

He frowned at her. "That would jeopardize your integrity as a potential ambassador to me, wouldn't it?"

"It might, Lord," she replied. "My loyalty to you and the Northern Empire takes precedence. If they capture you or until I know you've returned—with or without the Eastern Heir Sword—I'll do what's necessary to keep him here."

Seeking Sword nodded, glad she'd decided to remain with the living. "Very well then. Thank you, Fawning Elk. The code word, which I'll use in casual conversation, is 'reforestation.' I don't expect to be gone longer than five days, nor do I expect to return in fewer than three. Any questions? Good. For now, we'll put aside our previous plan to disinherit Flaming Arrow. If our current plan works, we won't need it. However, until the council meets again, I want you to formulate another plan to get the Northern Imperial Sword. Questions, comments, additional matters?" Seeking Sword asked.

No one answered.

"Very well, then. I'll leave tomorrow at sunset. Between now and when I leave, I'd like to set aside my duties. Lord River, I appoint you regent until I personally relieve you."

"Yes, Lord Emperor Sword," Raging River said. In any other situation the old retainer would've mouthed polite banalities and protested his unworthiness. Seeking Sword had long before asked them each to dispense with obligatory humility and flattery, especially during council.

"Thank you, all of you, for your help. Infinite be with you."

Standing, Seeking Sword stepped to the door. Outside stood a pair of purple-and-green garbed guards. As the *Duces* wandered out the door, the Bandit spoke briefly with each, asking about their personal lives and about the health of their mates and children. In addition to being curious about his most trusted advisors, Seeking Sword also knew that he needed to keep current on their personal lives, wanting them healthy, whole and happy.

When only he, Purring Tiger and Fawning Elk remained, the Eastern exmatriate said, "Lady Tiger, could I speak with your mate alone please?"

Seeking Sword saw that his mate wanted to refuse.

"I'll be in the corridor," Purring Tiger said to him coldly.

The Bandit frowned as he watched her leave, then turned to Fawning Elk. "What is it, Lady?"

"Lord Sword, I have to ask you to leave your sword behind."

He looked at her blankly. "Eh? Why? It's just a sword."

"No, Lord. It's more than that." Fawning Elk stepped to the door and looked into the corridor. Then she returned to his side and leaned close to him to whisper. "Lord Emperor, it's the Northern Heir Sword."

Chapter 12

THE DAY that I resigned, the woman, Star, told me such a strange tale that I felt inundated. After the day that I'd had, I simply couldn't believe Star's story. First, Guarding Bear shed his mask of mania. Then, my mother acted like the mother I'd always wanted. After that, my father acquiesced to my plan, and finally, I resigned. Of *course*, I didn't believe Star—who would, after having a day like that?—*The Bandit, the Enemy*, by Flaming Arrow.

* * *

Flaming Arrow watched Healing Hand stretch, the Wizard-medacor warrior priest preparing to duel him. The two of them had often dueled, the previous time many years before. Flaming Arrow wondered if Healing Hand's initiation into the mysteries of the Infinite would affect his swordsmanship.

Breathing roughly, Flaming Arrow knelt at the edge of the meadow in Bastion Valley, resting between practice bouts with the friends who'd come here with him. After spending the night at the Wolf residence in Emparia City, they'd traveled with him to Bastion to help him prepare for his excursion north.

Flaming Arrow still didn't want to believe what the woman had told him.

Flaming Arrow entered the library of the Wolf residence.

At the window, looking outside, was the medacor Gentle Hand, Healing Hand's mother, her short, dust-blond hair framing her face. She turned to regard him with chilling green eyes.

In a chair, looking frightened, was a woman unknown to him. She rose to bow to him, looking scared.

He nodded to acknowledge their obeisances. "Infinite be with you, Hand," he said to Healing Hand's mother. He asked the other woman her name.

"I'm Singing Star, Lord Heir," she said, her voice quavering.

"Infinite be with you, Star. Please, I'm not the Heir, anymore. You wish to speak with me?" He found himself a chair and faced Singing Star, intuiting that she'd be the focus of his attention.

The medacor stepped forward. "Yes, Lord." She bit her lip and began to pace nervously. "If you'll indulge me for a few minutes while I explain a little? Thank you, Lord.

"Just before you were born, a man approached me. He identified himself only as an intermediary to someone important and wouldn't divulge more than that, not even his name. He asked if I were treating a person or persons who'd gotten pregnant about eight months before with a male child. He specified several times that the fetus be male. At first I refused, Lord— doctor-patient confidentiality, eh? He insisted, implying that my unorthodox practice would incur bureaucratic intolerance if I denied his request. Do you know about my clinic, Lord? Yes, it's for the indigent. I accept whatever my patients can afford to pay me.

"Reluctantly, I referred the intermediary to several patients. One of those patients, Star, came for an appointment two weeks or so after you were born, Lord Arrow. She'd given birth to her son. I asked where her child was. She told me she'd sold it to this 'intermediary.' I usually don't inquire into the private lives of my patients, unless treating the ailment requires my asking. With Star, Lord Arrow, I was curious why she'd sell a child. At the time she couldn't or wouldn't answer me. A few days ago, she told me what happened." Gentle Hand turned to the woman in the chair. "Star, I want you to know that your coming here took courage and strength. Can you tell the Lord Arrow what you told me? If not, I can tell him for you."

Frowning, Singing Star nodded and looked down. "I'll tell him, Hand. I'll try." She glanced toward Flaming Arrow, then fixed her gaze on the floor. "The child was the son of a warrior whose name I never knew, Lord Arrow. That sounds impossible, I know. I had sex with him only once, while he kept his mindshields intact. I shouldn't have gotten pregnant. I was only fifteen at the time. I didn't know enough to abort the fetus. Anyway, I went to Hand's clinic late in my pregnancy, too late to abort it. I ... I wasn't very wise in my youth, Lord. I felt scared at first, not knowing what my parents would think, not sure if I wanted the child, ashamed that I had ... Oh, yes, well. This intermediary contacted me and reminded me how full of shame I should be for carrying a boy whose father I didn't know. That only made my anguish worse. Other than killing myself, I didn't know what else to do. So I agreed to sell him the child."

The woman sighed. "After I gave birth, Lord, moments before your mother the Lady Consort herself did, I decided I wanted to keep the child. He was the most beautiful boy I'd ever seen. The intermediary returned only six hours after I gave birth and demanded the child. I told him I'd think about it. He seemed satisfied with that. Two days later, at midnight, the intermediary returned with another man who had very bad breath. They forced me to give up my boy and threatened to kill me if I told anybody they forced me. I didn't tell anybody for a long time, not until a few days ago." The pitch of her voice began to rise. "I was so afraid! Even though he's dead, I'm still afraid! Please, Lord, you won't let anything happen, will you?"

"No, Star, of course not," Flaming Arrow replied calmly, seeing her terror, hearing it in her voice. "Can you tell me who 'he' is?"

"When they were trying to get me to give up my boy willingly, the intermediary addressed the other man by the name 'Lord Illusion.' I knew he was the Lord Sorcerer. I got so scared. I still feel frightened that he left orders with someone to kill me if I ever tell. Oh, Lord Arrow, please don't let them kill me! Please?!"

"He's been dead for five years now, Star. If his minions haven't found you and killed you in the twenty years since this happened, they probably never will. Go on please."

Singing Star bit her lip and looked as if she wanted to cry. "It was so terrible the next morning, when they told us your brother died in his crib. I felt so bad about my own baby that I almost didn't pay attention to the announcement on the flow. I saw the image of your dead brother, which frightened me even more. I knew if I ever told, they'd kill me somehow. I know they'll find me for telling you now. I just *know* it!"

She'd drawn her legs up into the chair and was hugging her knees to her chest. Gentle Hand knelt beside the chair and talked to Singing Star in a soothing voice.

Flaming Arrow knelt in front of the chair. He put a reassuring hand on the woman's arm and told her, "The past is past. Exploding Illusion's dead. I doubt he had any allies who'd serve him even now, five years beyond his death: Most of his associates disliked him. We all knew him to be my father's puppet, who corrupted him beyond redemption. Still, I want you to know I'll protect you in all the ways that I can. My mate the Matriarch Water can help you find a new home and a new identity, if you need them. You obviously have something important and dangerous to tell me. I'd be remiss in my duty if I allowed anything to happen to you. Please, Star, please find the courage to finish your story."

Her eyes closed, Star nodded, taking several deep breaths. "Yes, Lord. I … I'll finish. The image of the dead child on the flow might not … wasn't your brother, Lord. It was my son."

She's insane, he thought.

"I knew you wouldn't believe me, Lord. It was my son. I recognized him by his pinky. Even though I knew the Lord Sorcerer could've killed me instantly, I wanted my boy! I wanted to keep him so much!" She began to cry. "I tried to fight the intermediary and the Lord Sorcerer away. During the struggle they broke his pinky. The boy cried so loud I thought he'd surely wake the neighbors. The next day, in the image on the flow, I saw the bruised pinky, the right one. I knew they'd killed my son. I *knew*! Oh, Lord Arrow, I feel so scared! I don't want to die in the dungeons! Oh, please, Lord, don't let them take me there! I wouldn't be able to stand it in…"

* * *

"Flaming Arrow?"

In front of him stood Healing Hand. Flaming Arrow looked around, saw Bastion Valley. He remembered he'd traveled here earlier in the day, a day that had faded, night nigh.

He'd done all he could to calm Singing Star. She'd been hysterical with terror. He'd found Rippling Water and asked her to protect the woman with all her resources and to have a psychological Wizard examine Singing Star. He doubted she'd lied to him. He knew she believed what she told him, her terror real. The chance someone had implanted her was also real, a chance they had to eliminate.

"Seems as if she told you the truth, eh?" Rippling Water had said later that night, as he and his mate had crawled into bed.

Flaming Arrow had nodded, not wanting to believe the story.

She'd seen his anxiety and caressed him gently. "If you don't want to talk about it yet, I'll accept that."

He'd sighed, confused. "No, I don't. Thank you for under-standing."

She'd draw him close and cradled his head. "I can't always be understanding. You surprised me earlier, by telling my father you'll give the Bandit the Sword. I don't understand how you could give anything to the man who has ruined your life, espe-cially something so important as the Northern Imperial Sword."

"It's no use to me, or to him. He *has* asked for it—how many times? It's what's better for the Empire, Rippling Water. We both know he won't rest until he has the Imperial Sword."

"No. He won't," she'd said, sighing. "Flaming Arrow, what would you do if I kept something secret from you?"

He'd shrugged, the feel of her beside him pleasant, peaceful. "I trust that you have good reason for keeping it and that you'll tell me when you decide it's important enough—or no longer important. Why do you ask?"

"Well," she'd said, "if you're going north to meet with the Ban-dit, and plan to give him the Northern Imperial Sword someday, the time's come for you to know. The Bandit, my love, has the Heir Sword."

"Flaming Arrow?" Healing Hand said again.

"Eh? What is it, my friend?" Flaming Arrow asked, remem-bering again where he was. Thank the Infinite, I have my friends here to help me, he thought, knowing his absence of mind dan-gerous.

"Your state of mind concerns me, Lord. You haven't been the same since you talked with that woman last night."

"No," he replied. "No, I haven't. Are you ready to duel, Heal-ing Hand?" Standing, he hefted his new sword again, the feel of it strange in his hand. Probing Gaze had instructed the sword-smith to make it as close as possible to the Heir Sword in heft, weight and balance. It still felt different. It wasn't the Heir Sword, and never would be.

"We should stop for the day, Lord. Dusk is falling. If you feel distracted, you might get hurt."

"All right. Yes. You're right." Flaming Arrow looked around the valley, trying to orient himself. Where's the house? he wondered. Guarding Bear had constructed and landscaped his Bastion retreat so skillfully that it didn't mar the purity of the valley and was, hence, difficult to find. If Flaming Arrow had been more familiar with the retreat, he might know where it was. He didn't often come here. He'd insisted that Guarding Bear keep this house, knowing the General cherished it. He decided to let Healing Hand lead him there. "Let's go in, eh?"

Healing Hand gestured to the others. Probing Gaze, Spying Eagle and Guarding Bear began to walk toward them.

"What do you know about the Peregrine Twins, Healing Hand?"

The medacor regarded him with a curious expression. "The Eastern Emperor Climbing Peregrine fathered identical twin sons. The Northern Emperor Ripping Talon couldn't have children because of a congenital infection. The solution they devised is an example of great diplomacy. The negotiations lasted three years. Eventually, they agreed that Ripping Talon would invest Plummeting Peregrine with the Northern Heirship. Together, Plummeting and Screeching Peregrine respectively ruled the Northern and Eastern Empires from the structure that's now the Tiger Fortress. Why do you ask, Lord?"

How can I tell him? Flaming Arrow wondered, not knowing.

The others were waiting for them. He and Healing Hand began to walk toward the mansion. "Can I talk with you, Healing Hand?"

Walking beside him, the medacor looked at him and smiled. "Yes, Lord, about anything." He glanced toward Spying Eagle, who was talking quietly with Guarding Bear, the pair walking a few paces away. "Alone or with our friends?"

Flaming Arrow shrugged, glancing back. A few paces behind them was Probing Gaze, carrying the accoutrements they'd used that afternoon. "I'd prefer alone," he said quietly enough that the others didn't hear.

Nodding, Healing Hand loosened the binding on his hair, which fell about his shoulders like a sheaf of harvested wheat spilling open. "As you wish, Lord; in the library, perhaps?"

"Yes, the library ... yes." Flaming Arrow looked toward the mansion, seeing instead the library at the Wolf residence. Seeing Star's terror. Knowledge formed and dissipated in his mind like clouds in a turbulent, saturated sky, too insubstantial to grasp and too substantial to ignore. The wind presaged a storm within him. He didn't know what that storm would precipitate. I don't want to cry again, he thought, despite last night's release and the tranquility that followed. I know I'll remain after the storm has passed. I don't know in what condition, he thought, feeling inundated already by terrible truths.

Is my brother alive? he wondered.

Flaming Arrow didn't know.

Chapter 13

I T WAS just a sword. It didn't look important. Three feet long and slightly curved, the blade looked tarnished. The dark color of the metal suggested it was simply brass. The edge was sharp and without a nick. The haft was pewter-colored, contoured for the human hand, and unremarkable—other than the single ruby set in the pommel.

The skillful construction belied the sword's modest appearance. Thousands of microscopic sheets of a chromium-antimony alloy layered one atop the other composed the blade itself. The painstaking process provided an exceptional degree of flexibility, resilience and edge integrity. Even master swordsmiths found the alloy difficult to work, making reproduction improbable.

In addition to its meticulous construction, the sword was ancient. Forged more than nine thousand years before, the sword had withstood all manner of use and misuse. The number of warriors who'd wielded the sword was a figure lost in antiquity. The number of warriors who'd died on the blade was many times that. The number of warriors mortally wounded while wielding this sword, however, was fewer than a hundred.

Called the Heir Sword, it prepared the mind of an Heir for the Imperial Sword, which looked no different, other than its slightly larger ruby. The Imperial Sword extended the range of an Emperor's psychic talents to the farthest corners of the Empire and protected the Emperor from all forms of psychic assault. In addition, the Imperial Sword electrocuted anyone inadequately prepared by the Heir Sword, killing the unfortunate (or treacherous) soul. The Imperial Sword gave the Emperor full control of the Heir Sword. Thus, the Imperial Sword was the figurative and literal source of an Emperor's authority.

Each of the four Empires had its own pair of Swords, each pair adorned with a different gem. The four Imperial Swords all served the same function: To confer upon the current Emperor complete and total dominion over his or her Empire. The four Heir Swords all shared their own function: To prepare the mind of the Heir to wield the corresponding Imperial Sword.

Despite this similarity of function, the most valuable of the four Heir Swords was the one adorned with a ruby, the Northern Heir Sword.

Flying Arrow had exterminated the people of the Northern Empire because of this Heir Sword. The Tiger and Bear Patriarchies had fought a civil war because of this Heir Sword. The Eastern Empire teetered toward the abyss of collapse, bandits proliferating along its northern border, because of this Heir Sword. Although the political system shared by the four Empires had existed in relative stability for more than nine thousand years, this Heir Sword revealed that system to be just a veil of illusion. Ironically, the purpose of the eight Swords was the preservation of this political system. That system was faltering because of this Heir Sword.

Despite everything about it, a single fact made the Northern Heir Sword the most important object in the world:

The Sword had been missing.—*The Fall of the Swords*, by Keeping Track.

* * *

Seeking Sword stared at it, disbelieving.

Gently, reverently, he caressed the ruby set in the pommel, thinking his possession of it ironic. His lack of talent made its awesome electrical circuits superfluous. Similarly, the Northern Imperial Sword was equally useless, except that it symbolized and legitimized his sovereignty.

Absurd, Seeking Sword thought for the thousandth time, to invest so much into a silly piece of metal.

Yet, all his life, he and those around him had lived with the specter that the empty northern lands, the land of bandits, could never truly be an Empire. Without the Northern Imperial Sword, any government that exercised dominion over the northern lands was illegitimate.

Before Fawning Elk had revealed the nature of his sword, the Bandit had wanted the Northern Imperial Sword only for its symbolic value. His possession of it had been necessary only to legitimize his government in the minds of the other three Empires. He and his progeny would never have been able to wield it. Thus, the succession in the Northern Empire would've always been an issue under contention.

Now, however, all that had changed.

Since he wielded the Heir Sword, the Bandit could pass his regency to his progeny with the same smooth succession that the other three Empires experienced. His children, unlike him, possessed abundant talent. His heirs would exercise dominion over the Northern Empire with all the symbolic *and* literal power granted by the Imperial Sword. If he, the Bandit, obtained it from Flying Arrow.

If.

Seeking Sword sighed, caressing the silly piece of metal.

After telling him that he wielded the Heir Sword, Fawning Elk had recounted what Leaping Elk had told her shortly before his death—about the Sword's ability to repel unwanted wielders.

Seeking Sword had always wondered why he had never lost it, especially when he'd been a boy. As boys will, he'd played with abandon, often leaving clothes, toys and other articles wherever he happened to set them down. His sword had been no exception. Somehow, no one had ever found the sword, not even when he left it where he knew others couldn't have missed it. Icy Wind had beaten him countless times for returning home without the sword, especially during the first few years after he'd given it to the boy. When young, Seeking Sword had hated hauling the heavy object around. Not really able to use it, he'd often simply left it behind, unconsciously wanting to rid himself of it. Somehow, even when Icy Wind had pulverized him with the staff and sent him into the dark with the ultimatum not to return without the Sword, Seeking Sword had always known where it was and found it again.

He'd always wondered why no one had ever taken it from him. A boy with a sword, no matter what his age, was easy prey for the unscrupulous. A sword with a ruby on the pommel attracted many an avaricious eye. At the time, the Bandit Council hadn't been able to unite all bandits, except very loosely. The council intervened between bandits only when the larger bands threatened to war on each other. The actions of individuals were beneath the council's notice. Thus, when Seeking Sword met some stranger, he always felt wary, knowing the sword valuable. Many times, members of the Elk Raiders killed these strangers and told him afterward that the miscreants had planned to take his sword from him. Not one stranger had ever laid a hand on the Sword—or on Seeking Sword.

He'd always wondered why he'd received only one injury during ten years of almost daily sword practice. Slithering Snake, his weapons instructor, had told him a hundred times that that was impossible.

Furthermore, when inquiring into their capabilities years before, Seeking Sword had learned that the Swords only increased the powers of their wielders—and didn't supply any talent the wielder lacked. If true, then Seeking Sword's paucity of injury, protection from strangers, and inability to lose the Sword were all caused by some strange, powerful talent that Seeking Sword himself exhibited.

I don't *have* a talent, he thought.

Then he remembered the two psychic storms that five years ago had swept through the empty northern lands, storms that had involved psychic exchanges with Flaming Arrow. His touching his father's talisman staff, despite its having killed everyone else. His uncanny ability to predict most the Heir's actions. Prescients' inability to see his past, present and future. All the maleficent talents that didn't affect him.

Perhaps I *do* have a talent, he thought. He felt he didn't. Having believed he had not a single talent for so long, he couldn't reconcile himself to the possibility that he did. All he could say now was that he didn't know.

I just don't know, he thought.

Sighing, Seeking Sword looked around the room, the central room of his house in Seat. The time was near noon. He'd scheduled his departure for dusk. He yawned, knowing he needed sleep.

Slithering Snake, his spy-handler, had told him earlier in the day that spies had reported that the Heir had traveled to Bastion with his four closest associates. The Heir had a new sword, forged by a swordsmith in Emparia City to Probing Gaze's specifications. The sectathon had told Seeking Sword that he knew the name of the swordsmith and that he'd have one of his intermediaries ask the swordsmith to make a duplicate sword by the morrow.

That Flaming Arrow hadn't immediately come north didn't surprise Seeking Sword. Such an action was too predictable. He guessed that his adversary would wait a few days, perhaps even a week, before crossing the border. The Bandit didn't begrudge the time. His strange injuries, the ones he'd received during his lapse of consciousness between the River Placid and the Tiger Fortress, hadn't yet fully healed. His oblique muscles still hurt. His bruises—so like those Aged Oak had given Flaming Arrow— were now yellow patches blotching his abdomen.

Slithering Snake had also received a report that on the morning after Aged Oak's assassination, Flaming Arrow had awakened in a hostelry whose occupants had all been asleep—all but Healing Hand. Flaming Arrow's waking had corresponded almost exactly to Seeking Sword's suddenly finding himself near the northern entrance of the Tiger Fortress. The Bandit had told Slithering Snake and Easing Comfort about his lapse of consciousness. Neither man had been able to explain it.

He wished the Infinite would cease with the mysteries.

"The Infinite giveth and the Infinite taketh away," said the Book of the Infinite. The Infinite had given Seeking Sword inestimable gifts—a fine mate (if now suffering), two beautiful children, a thousand friends, over a hundred thousand followers, a sharp mind, a sharp sword that only looked tarnished, a healthy body, an Empire to govern. The Infinite had taken relatively little—his friend and mentor Leaping Elk, his mate's mental health, his talents. He decided he could accept what the Infinite had given him and live without what it had taken away. "Thank you, Lord Infinite," he said softly. "For everything you've given me, for all that you've taken away, and especially for what you've left in my keeping." In his keeping was the fate of the empty northern lands, a fledgling Empire about to try its wings. In his keeping was the Sword forged to help assure that Empire's future.

The Northern Heir Sword.

Seeking Sword realized now that he needed to change his strategy. Asking the Emperor Flying Arrow to reinvest him with the Heirship was distasteful to Seeking Sword. His obtaining the Eastern Heir Sword by impersonating Flaming Arrow was spiritually corrupting. Silently, the Bandit blessed his mentor Leaping Elk, remembering his admonition to strive for inner congruence. Knowing the corrosive effects of assassinating the Heir's reputation, Seeking Sword wanted to regain his personal integrity, something he couldn't easily do if he impersonated Flaming Arrow again.

Now, he didn't have to. Since he wielded the Northern Heir Sword, the corresponding Imperial Sword *belonged* to him, which even Flying Arrow couldn't deny. Furthermore, Seeking Sword could compel the Southern and Western Empires to join the Northern in obtaining the Sword. After he told them that he had the Heir Sword, law and custom would compel them to commit all their political and military influence to wresting the Northern Imperial Sword from Flying Arrow. The other two Empires would only need proof.

So, what *is* my new strategy? he wondered, his thoughts flying like a peregrine riding thermal updrafts ever upward into an infinite expanse of possibility.

Why don't I simply ask Flying Arrow for the Imperial Sword? he wondered, trying to think of a reason he shouldn't. Flying Arrow might try to kill him, Seeking Sword knew. Flaming Arrow's capture, then, was far more important. Only if the bandits captured the Eastern Heir would the Eastern Emperor refrain from killing the Northern Emperor. Perhaps. Flying Arrow was so lacking in scruples and integrity, however, that the Bandit didn't know what he'd do. Seeking Sword looked deep inside, and saw that asking for the Imperial Sword openly, without pretense or subterfuge, was what he should do. It felt right.

The Bandit caressed a silly piece of metal, contemplating another just like it. He wondered briefly if Fawning Elk were wrong, if the Sword that he held were just a sword. He couldn't doubt Fawning Elk, the only person he'd ever called mother. Leaping Elk had convinced her that his sword was the Northern Heir Sword, because if she'd doubted for a moment what she'd told him, she'd have expressed those doubts. Fawning Elk believed.

Seeking Sword did too, but for a hundred different reasons. Thinking Quick, the Prescient Wizard whom he'd called friend, had told him of terrible purposes, of their inexorable progress, of their insatiable demands. She'd never said what his terrible purpose was, only that one day he'd know it with full conviction. Most people never knew theirs, she'd said, so he was fortunate.

Seeking Sword had often questioned the incongruities in his life. Until five years ago, he'd never dreamed he might be anything more than a simple bandit, living on the fringes of society, parasitic upon the honest sweat of another's brow. Leaping Elk had seemed to know he was destined for greatness. So had Scowling Tiger. So had a thousand other bandits who'd guided and nurtured him during his youth.

From the beginnings he didn't remember when he was a foundling baby whom Fawning Elk had given suckle, through a strife-filled childhood in a moldering cave from which his only escape was the Elk Raiders on the other side of the mountain, to his leap in elevation within the Tiger Raiders on the basis of his curiously coincidental similarity to the Heir Flaming Arrow, Seeking Sword had hurtled through life replete with purpose, as if each moment had been a rehearsal for one great moment, the ultimate moment when all the grandeur and terror of time would come together with all its awesome momentum and sweep away the prison of the past and unlock the doors of freedom for the future of humanity.

"Seeking Sword?"

He woke suddenly, not realizing he'd been sleeping. He looked around. Near the central room window stood his mate. "Yes, Love?"

"You're leaving soon. Don't you want to sleep?"

"I *was* asleep," he protested.

"Go to bed, love," she said, chuckling. "You'll have to be up in four hours anyway. Might as well sleep in comfort."

"What time is it?"

"Two hours after noon."

He wanted to leave at dusk. Nodding, he looked at the Sword again. "I have to talk with Slithering Snake before I leave. Has he left for the border yet?"

Purring Tiger consulted the psychic flow, her eyes traveling across the ceiling as if searching the skies. "No, not yet. He's still in Seat, says he'll be here in a few minutes."

"Thank you, love," Seeking Sword said, standing to hug her. "When I return—if everything goes well—I want to relinquish my duties to someone for a week, find someone to care for our children, and take you north to a very private place. What do you think?"

Smiling, she snuggled into his embrace. "I think I'll enjoy that. Very, very much. Will you ... make love with me before you go south?"

He smiled. "I'll do without sleep for awhile."

Laughing, she caressed him. "What did Fawning Elk say after the council meeting yesterday?"

He glanced at the Sword, which he'd left beside the chair. "She told me ... what my purpose is."

"Eh? I don't understand."

"You will, and soon," Seeking Sword said. "Everyone will soon know what my purpose is—everyone."

Yes, he knew what it was. He knew it could easily consume him. He didn't doubt any longer and never again would he be unsure of his path, of his direction.

He would be the Northern Emperor.

Chapter 14

ORN OF a sterile father? Not possible without divine intervention.

We know too well, however, that the divine is an invention that we employ to help us cope with the chaos inherent to the universe, a chaos that would otherwise overwhelm us. Hence, Flaming Arrow *does* have a father. Only the Infinite knows the identity of the father and the manner of the fathering.—*The Private, Unpublished Archives of Snarling Jaguar*, by Slumbering Jaguar.

* * *

Healing Hand saw immediately that Guarding Bear's presence inhibited Flaming Arrow. Whatever his friend had wanted to say to him would now remain unsaid. The former Heir loved the old silver-haired General too much to ask him to leave. The medacor guessed, in addition, that the unsaid was so important that Flaming Arrow couldn't risk Guarding Bear's knowing.

The Wizard-medacor knew that Flaming Arrow thought it important. Since his private conversation with his mother Gentle Hand and the other woman, Flaming Arrow had acted out of character.

Frequently looking into the distance as if in deep thought, he seemed to forget where he was. He often asked others to repeat themselves as if he hadn't heard what they'd said the first time. Each of Flaming Arrow's companions worried about him. Probing Gaze, Spying Eagle, and even Guarding Bear had all commented on Flaming Arrow's absence of mind, the former Heir usually exhibiting a presence of mind.

Obviously, the unsaid haunted him.

Watching the two men from across the library, Healing Hand felt pleased, the friendship between them undiminished despite a five-year respite. Smiling, the Wizard knew Guarding Bear hadn't been truly insane throughout his long hibernation. The General had simply retreated from the world, unable or unwilling to face the terrible tragedy of his son's murder of his mate, of Running Bear's murder of his own mother Bubbling Water. Flowering Pine's revelation at the Wolf residence that Purring Tiger and Melding Mind had arranged the killing was surcease to Guarding Bear's soul. The father had finally learned two nights ago that he wasn't responsible, directly or indirectly, for Bubbling Water's death. The knowledge had hastened the bear's awakening.

Trying to sleep, the menagerie bear sprawled in the middle of the room, the furniture pushed against the shelves. The bear now snored loudly, each inhalation a rumble of thunder, vibrating the floor. Healing Hand watched the two men from across the bear, the animal at the blond man's feet.

"Look at this old work, Flaming Arrow," Guarding Bear said, turning to take a book off a shelf, Flaming Arrow facing the same direction. "It's in its umpteenth translation. No one knows if it even resembles the original. *Subjugating the Shrew*, by Shaking Spear."

Flaming Arrow looked at the book from over Guarding Bear's shoulder.

The medacor Healing Hand saw their profiles within inches of each other.

* * *

"What happened to him?" a familiar voice asked from a distance.

Remembering the first terrible secret that he'd had to keep—Lurking Hawk's manipulation of Rippling Water's mind—Healing Hand felt again the power that it had over him. While the Matriarch Bubbling Water had meant well, the Wizard still struggled with the inhibitions inculcated by that terrible secret. What Healing Hand confronted now was Lurking Hawk's motivation for implanting Rippling Water. Twenty years ago, at Flying Arrow's behest, Lurking Hawk had delved into the child's mind to lure Guarding Bear to Emparia Castle. Why Flying Arrow had wanted Guarding Bear at the castle had been a mystery, one that nothing had ever fully unravelled.

Until now.

"I don't know. Looked as if he fell on my bear," said another voice, also sounding distant, also familiar.

Despite being a psychological Wizard, and the best to have walked the continent in a century, Healing Hand struggled to reestablish control over his own mind. He'd never thought this could happen. Having trained in the psychic arts from the age of seven, the Wizard knew nearly every mental gymnastic in the repertoire of humanity, and how to apply them. Yet he struggled now to compartmentalize the knowledge facing him. That a single fact could render his every mental trick useless stunned him.

"I only caught a glimpse in my peripheral vision. Did you see what happened?" asked the first voice.

The knowledge itself was less important than its result. His quiver known to be empty, Flying Arrow's dishonesty of necessity twenty years ago had deceived an Empire unwilling to endure the anarchy of an interregnum. The personal cost to the individuals involved was an account unsettled, a balance outstanding. Twenty years of compound interest had accrued, payable in pain, a debt that even uninvolved individuals would shoulder. Those who shared the burden would, rather than lighten the load, only magnify the weight borne by the principal debtors.

"No, not really—I was talking. You know how I get when I talk, eh? Don't see or hear much. He looks all right, if a little pale. His pulse is good and his breathing steady. He's so limp—watch."

A sensation, like motion, but removed, traveled along his arm.

So knotted was the tangle of relationships within any Imperial family that they often consulted genetic Wizards to insure that the offspring of such closely-related mates would have a reasonable chance of living full, healthy lives. Some Imperial families employed the genetic Wizards to sift sperm and ova for a compatible combination when the chances were great that inbreeding would produce genetically inviable progeny.

"No voluntary muscle control—and look at him sweat!" said the first voice. "Let's carry him over to the couch, eh? You get the legs. There, like that. Ready? Lift." Motion again, but different, more like gentle swaying.

Healing Hand remembered the day he'd met the retired General Guarding Bear on the streets of Emparia City. Guarding Bear had been going to Emparia Castle. He remembered the morrow afternoon, when the Captain Silent Whisper had found Guarding Bear in a brothel, heavily intoxicated and unable to remember getting drunk or going to the brothel. Healing Hand had found a gap several hours long in Guarding Bear's memory. Hours during which he might have been at Emparia Castle, hours that Lurking Hawk had removed from his memory.

"I'm glad his involuntary muscles still work. If they didn't, he'd have blasted everywhere," the second voice said. "I wonder if he sees anything? Set him down now, gently. Good. Look. The eyes don't follow my hand at all." Far away, he saw something move.

The reason Flying Arrow had lured Guarding Bear to Emparia Castle stood before Healing Hand now. He saw some differences. The similarities were many more. The shape of the cheekbones, the same. The profiles, the same, except where the scar across Guarding Bear's nose marred the original form. The spacing between the eyes, the same. The set of shoulders, the same. The pattern of hairline, the same. The hair on chest and abdomen, which he recalled from their afternoon of swordplay, the same.

"What do we do now?" the first voice asked.

He couldn't recall if Lurking Hawk had had the skills to sift sperm and ova. Healing Hand guessed that Lurking Hawk, his power more smoke than fire, had been more facile at engendering the fear of his talents than he'd been with any particular talent. No, Lurking Hawk hadn't sifted Guarding Bear's sperm.

"Let's get Spying Eagle, eh?" the second voice suggested.

Then, like an arrow hurtling into a target, his mind snapped into place.

"What a strange sensation," Healing Hand said suddenly, looking from Guarding Bear to Flaming Arrow and back. "Spying Eagle won't be necessary."

"He speaks!" Flaming Arrow said. "Are you all right?"

Healing Hand sat up and wiped sweat off his face. He was once more in command of his own mind, the terrible knowledge safely compartmentalized. "Forgive me my behavior, my friends. I feel … odd, but I don't feel hurt. I heard you speak, but from a long way away. I felt motion when you lifted me, but as if you lifted someone else." He sat up on the couch and looked around. The bear had propped itself in a corner, its head near the ceiling and its gaze on him. "I must have I frightened the bear."

The other two men glanced toward the animal. Guarding Bear laughed in sympathy. "You scared *everyone*, Lord Hand. What the Infinite happened to you?"

"I, uh, had a revelation," Healing Hand said.

The two men waited for him to continue. "Well?" Guarding Bear asked impatiently.

"I want you to trust, Lord Bear, that I'll tell you when I think the appropriate moment has come."

Flaming Arrow looked at Guarding Bear. "He's not telling, Lord Bear."

Guarding Bear looked at Flaming Arrow. "He's not. Let's gut him."

Flaming Arrow frowned. "Then he'll *never* tell us."

"True, Lord," Guarding Bear said. "Listen, Lord Hand, that was the strangest behavior I've ever seen. Now, I *do* trust that you'll tell me and the Lord Arrow when you think it's appropriate. Infinite blast it, though, every time I see you, I'm going to think that you're hiding some terrible secret. I'll have to work to remember that you're my friend, and always have been."

Healing Hand nodded, as if understanding completely. "Deep inside you is a force that can grant you the strength to do anything. I wouldn't want to corrupt your spiritual growth, Lord Bear."

The old, silver-haired General regarded him silently a moment. Then he guffawed, lowering himself to a chair. "I'll never understand priests. You're the most baffling and incomprehensible man I've ever met, Lord Hand. I've had to understand the motivations of thousands of people, a few so diseased of mind that their thinking no longer represented anything we regard as sane, mine included. Yes, Lord Hand, I do trust you. I know you have good reason. I'll live with that."

"Good, Lord Bear," Healing hand said. He pulled his sweat-sopped robes away from his body. "I need a bath, Lords. I'll wager I lost ten pounds, eh? Forgive me my abrupt departure.

Infinite grace your dreams." He stood unsteadily, shaking, and bowed to the two men. Then he left the library and walked toward his room, two floors up.

Robust children could still result without such sifting, however, so Flaming Arrow's health wasn't a mystery. Since Flying Arrow had used Guarding Bear to inseminate Flowering Pine, Flaming Arrow had mated his half-sister Rippling Water.

The half of them not related through their sire Guarding Bear had common ancestry in other ways. First, Frothing Water was Rippling Water's grandmother and Flaming Arrow's great-grandmother through the Empress Steaming Water. Second, Crazy Bear was Rippling Water's grandfather and Flaming Arrow's great-grandfather through the Traitor Brazen Bear. Knots inextricably tangled their consanguinity.

Healing Hand sighed as he entered his room in the Bear mansion at Bastion Valley. Miles away, their presence haunting him, were the two children Trickling Water and Burning Arrow, three and four years old respectively. On every occasion he'd met them, Healing Hand had felt pleased that the Infinite had blessed his two friends with such talented offspring.

How did such closely-related siblings parent such perfect children? Healing Hand wondered.

Chapter 15

SEEKING ANSWER experimented to test the effects of interrupting an identical-twin empathy link, placing both twins inside electrical shields. After six months, each twin reported experiencing extreme anxiety and a strong desire to see the other twin. At eight months, both twins began to exhibit paranoid personality disorders. At ten months, because of the severity of the symptoms, Seeking Answer halted the experiment and reunited the twins.

In a later experiment, this same researcher separated the same twins by a distance of one hundred miles and closely watched the flow between them. Again, after six months, each twin reported similar anxieties and desires. At eight months, however, the psychic field monitors began to register pulses of energy along frequencies corresponding roughly to the twins' signature. These pulses occurred while both twins were deep in dream-stage sleep. The experiment spanned a total of a year, but at no time during the later months did either twin exhibit the expected personality disorders. The researcher speculated— but didn't prove—that the twins restored their contact during dream-stage sleep and hence avoided developing severe symptoms.—*One Mind, Two Bodies: Identical Twin Contact*, by Copy Cat.

* * *

Wincing, Seeking Sword slowed to another stop on the Nest-Bastion road, his breathing rough from exertion and his whole body aching. Before leaving the Northern Empire, he had freckled his face, shoulders, arms, back and chest, and had dyed his hair black. His hood pulled far forward, he stepped off the road, wondering where he was.

The road was nearly empty of traveler and muddy from rain, the footing treacherous. Seeking Sword felt so tired, and hurt so much, that he wanted to curl up in his cloak beside the road and sleep forever. When he'd left Emparia City at noon with the new sword, identical to the one Flaming Arrow wielded now, he'd expected to arrive in Bastion at dawn. Now, he doubted he'd arrive before noon.

Seeking Sword had been awake for nearly forty-eight hours, having left Seat more than a full day before. He peered ahead through the dark, the time an hour or so after sunset.

Grimacing, he stepped back onto the road and continued east through the miserable drizzle, silently cursing Flaming Arrow for living so far from the northern border of the Eastern Empire.

Somewhere between Seat and Emparia City, he'd decided to travel to Bastion, where he'd learned Flaming Arrow had gone. He couldn't have said why, knowing the risk for him there, where the Broken Arrows supported Flaming Arrow. The ancient resistance movement to Arrow Sovereignty was now two distinct factions: Those who supported Flaming Arrow, and those who opposed *anyone* named Arrow, the legendary Breaking Arrow having lost half of his adherents by supporting the former Heir. Few of the Eight Broken Arrows, as they now called themselves, could operate in the Caven Hills without incurring the displeasure of the Seven Broken Arrows, Breaking Arrow's faction. The danger for Seeking Sword was that any Broken Arrow whom he contacted might secretly be Flaming Arrow's adherent and might betray him. Thus, he'd refrain from contacting them.

As he ascended the steep hill on the Nest-Bastion road, he doubted he'd need to, planning only to watch Flaming Arrow. Curiosity, more than anything, took him to Bastion.

Cresting a hill, Seeking Sword winced and slowed, seeing the crossroads ahead through the rain. He was making better time than he'd thought. Crossing the Nest-Bastion road ahead was the Burrow-Eyry road. Set back from the crossroads was a small stone structure. A combination refectory and hostelry, the main part of the structure was underground, the weather torrid during summer.

He considered stopping at the hostelry.

Remembering he hadn't eaten since noon, he pulled sword and sheath from his right side and secured it to his left, then pulled his hood far forward. He walked to the door. Putting his right palm over the pommel, Seeking Sword pushed open the door and stepped into the building. Opposite a circular stairwell was a counter, behind it a man who looked nonchalantly toward him.

"A room, please, with a private bath."

Standing, the man tried discreetly to peer at his face. "Will you be needing servants to help with the bath, Lord?"

"No," he said too sharply, regretting it immediately. "No, I won't need servants. A meal, however, if you have it."

"We do, Lord. Any other victuals for your pleasure, Lord?"

Courtesans, he thought. "No, I don't have energy for your victuals."

"Very well, then, Lord...?"

"Chameleon. Have the meal delivered to my room, please." He remembered that the Heir had used the name before assassinating Scowling Tiger.

"Yes, Lord Chameleon. Glad to have you back. Five taels please, Lord."

The price was usurious. He didn't complain. With his left hand—his right remained on the pommel—he dug into the purse attached to his belt, pulled out a ten-tael coin and tossed it on the counter. "First I'll bathe. How long until the water's hot?" he asked, wondering if he'd been here before. The clerk seemed to recognize him.

The man snatched the coin off the counter and replaced it with a five-tael piece. "It's already hot, Lord. You probably forgot. We keep a cistern hot. Filling the bath will require a few minutes though. While you're waiting, Lord Chameleon, would you like to visit our den of iniquity?"

"No, thank you." With his left hand he pursed the five-tael coin.

The man turned to issue orders to subordinates. Seeking Sword turned toward the stairwell, hearing sounds of revelry from below. More than likely, the "den of iniquity" probably served alcoholic beverages and presented other entertainments. He hoped, if he chose to sleep, that the revelry wouldn't be so raucous as to keep him awake.

"Your bath's almost full, Lord. Three floors down, last door on the left. Thank you for your continued patronage, Lord Chameleon."

Seeking Sword nodded to the man's obeisance and descended, thinking him mistaken, having never patronized the place.

The first level below ground was the source of revelry. From a dimly-lit, smoke-filled room, vague faces peered at him as he descended past. The next level was more quiet and contained what looked like private rooms. A young woman stepped from a room, adjusted her robes, touched up her coiffure, saw him and gave him an enticing smile. The makeup caking her face defeated any allure it might have added. "A pittance for my pleasures, Lord," she said, striking a pose.

Shaking his head, he descended to the third level. He counted three more levels below his and entered the corridor. At the end was a stout oaken door. Entering, he bolted it behind him.

Through a doorway opposite the entrance came the sounds of flowing water. Investigating, he saw that a pipe jutting from the wall poured steaming water into a deep bath. An excretory stood against another wall. Gratefully, he used it, then stepped to the sink to wash.

After pulling off his sodden clothes and carefully hanging his nondescript, poor-quality robe, Seeking Sword began to lather himself. The bath almost full, the water stopped by itself. Just then he heard a knock. Picking up his sword, he went to the door, unbolted and opened it. A servant stood there with his meal. He took it and flipped the boy a tael, regretting the extravagance.

In the excretory, after scrubbing himself, he dipped a bucket into the bath and poured water over his head. The canted tile floor shunted soapy water toward a drain.

Gratefully, he climbed into the bath, placing his food and sword within easy reach. Roast pheasant, baked potato, cranberry sauce, spinach. He felt as if he'd eaten the meal before. Hungrily the Bandit began to wolf down the food.

When it was gone, he burped and sighed. Feeling suddenly weary, he climbed from the bath. At the doorway between rooms, he fell to a knee, almost losing consciousness. Through bleary eyes, he saw the bed and stumbled toward it, then crawled underneath the blankets, not caring that he hadn't dried himself off.

* * *

I talked at length with Healing Hand in the library. Shelves and shelves of rare and contraband books filled the room, some of the books centuries old. One whole wall was exclusively books on talismans, their design, construction and use. More interesting to me were the treatises on sociological phenomena, such as government policy. I didn't have much use for knowledge about talismans, not having a talent.

"I want to know whatever you can tell me about my birth," I said casually, perusing titles while the blond man stood nearby. I felt haunted by Singing Star's story, not wanting to believe it.

"The Medacor said your birth was unusual because of your mother's unconscious talent. If she'd had complications, he wouldn't have been able to help her much. Fortunately, everything went well. Why, Lord?"

"What about after I was born—shortly afterward?"

"I wasn't there when you were born, Lord. A few days afterward and a few weeks before, yes. I was in Burrow when you were born, helping those injured in the collapse of the garrison."

"You know more about the extant political conditions than most people. Weren't you there when my brother died?"

Briefly, my friend looked sad. "No, Lord. I arrived at the castle less than an hour after the wet nurses discovered his body. The Lord Medacor was doing an autopsy when I got there. Why do you ask, Lord?"

"The woman I talked with two nights ago, she told me something odd." I recounted what she'd said.

"That's *it*!" the medacor said jubilantly, spreading his large hands beside his face as if to grasp something there. "I *knew* we'd all made a bad assumption! I *knew* it! Lord, you don't know what this means! That's the key that unlocks us all from this whole deadly prison we've struggled to escape! That explains everything!"

The woman's revelation last night had rekindled the tiny, nearly extinguished spark of hope that had glimmered within me for as long as I could remember. I never knew my brother. Always haunting me was the ghost of what might've been. As a child, because I had few playmates other than the woman who was now my mate, I created an imaginary friend, a brother who'd *not* died at three days old. The memory of that treasured companion mixed with the woman's extraordinary story fanned my spark of hope into a smoldering coal, a lump of heat in my breast. I frowned, guessing that my blond-haired friend had drawn the same conclusion as I. Having wanted my friend to refute it, I felt disappointed. Mixed with the spark of hope. I was an emotional mess. "What assumption?" I asked.

"Five years ago, I was talking with the Emperor Jaguar about it all—the Heir swords, the psychic storms, the similarities between yourself and him, and that your healthy twin brother died a crib death. I said, 'Somehow, I feel I've made a bad assumption somewhere.' Lord Arrow, the bad assumption I made—that we *all* made—was in thinking that your brother's dead. The Sorcerer always *was* incompetent. He should've killed Singing Star. Thank the Infinite, he didn't, eh? Lord, with your permission, I'd like to tell Spying Eagle."

"Yes, of course, but only him, eh?" I sighed, wishing briefly that the Sorcerer Exploding Illusion had been more competent.

"Speaking of Sorcerers, Lord, I did an autopsy on Lurking Hawk, who died the same night as your brother supposedly did."

"I thought he died the next day."

"No, Lord. That was the official version publicized by your father. Lurking Hawk didn't die peacefully in his sleep, either: He died abusing his talents, an aneurism rupturing in each of his prefrontal lobes. The Emperor—the ever-consummate actor—let me think that Lurking Hawk had murdered your brother. We couldn't publicize the 'fact,' or the Eastern Empire would've lost face, eh? If true—and I've *always* wondered—why didn't he kill you both? Obviously, he didn't murder your brother. He was in the nursery at about the time your brother 'suffocated.' What *did* he do there, Flaming Arrow, if he didn't kill your brother?"

Healing Hand's stare was intense. My own thoughts flew like falcons riding thermal updrafts into an infinite expanse of possibility.

"He buried your talents! What better vengeance upon the man who'd murdered his people? He wouldn't kill you because Flying Arrow would've merely arranged another insemination, eh?" The medacor looked upset about something, then he quickly recovered. "No! Lurking Hawk did the most damage he could to your talents. Since he probably knew Flying Arrow would give your brother to Lofty Lion, the Northern Sorcerer needed to insure that your identical twin contact would keep you apart. Now it all makes sense, even the psychic storms. Over here, Lord, look at this book: *One Mind, Two Bodies: Identical Twin Contact.* I remember reading it twenty years ago. What particularly struck me was the incredible distances that identical twins' minds will reach across—merely to maintain contact with each other." Healing Hand found the volume and pointed out passage after relevant passage to me.

For the next hour, I read about psychological experiments on identical twins, occasionally commenting on what I read but mostly too engrossed in—and shaken by—the ways that the information supported my conclusion. "Listen to this, Lord: 'Studies of identical twins separated at birth nearly all show that each twin developed similar interests and lived similar lifestyles. Furthermore, unless separated by insurmountable obstacles, such as extreme distance, all twins reported having an awareness of his brother or her sister, mostly through dreams. In addition, many reported experiencing the sensations of inexplicable physical or emotional trauma at the same moment the other twin experienced those sensations. In the case history of twins alpha and beta, for example, when twin alpha broke her left leg in a fall, twin beta screamed aloud, grabbed for an object as if she'd fallen, then rolled on the floor as if in great pain, despite the lack of injury to her left leg. Furthermore, one hundred fifty miles separated twins alpha and beta at the time.

" 'It must be borne in mind that at the time of the studies nearly all the separated identical twin pairs had reunited. Thus the phenomena they report are scientifically subjective. Despite this qualification, and despite the difficulty of finding *un*-reunited pairs to study, the number of separated pairs who *do* reunite is significant enough to warrant speculation on the rate of reunification. Being genetically identical, twins have identical psychic signatures and identical talents. Hence, one must conclude that little but extreme distance can keep them separated for long. Their predisposition to being in contact must eventually bring them together, no matter how adverse the conditions of their separation.' Would that still be true for me and him, Lord, even though the swords have changed our minds?" I asked.

"I don't know, Lord. I wouldn't think so, because the Peregrine Twins—who each wielded a sword—found that their signatures began to diverge. If that were true, then why the psychic storms? Your dream at the hostelry was also contact between you, although he was almost a hundred miles away, across the River Placid, eh? How did that happen if the swords changed your frequencies?"

The story of the Peregrine Twins, familiar to most people and to all who studied government, held a promise of something unnamed, a dream of impossible proportions, a template that my father, sire of identical twins, might have used as a guideline. The pieces fit too well. Lofty Lion had been childless. His death would've thrown the Northern Empire into civil war upon his death, if Guarding Bear hadn't conquered it, and if Flying Arrow hadn't exterminated the people. For nearly thirty-years, everyone in all four Empires had thought Lofty Lion dead—until five years ago, when he'd come within a feather's thickness of assassinating my father. Then the rumor circulated that he left behind a son, exactly my age and resembling me so much physically *and* psychically that we might've been identical twins. He seemed gifted with an Infinite amount of luck and charisma. He mated the bandit general's daughter and took command of the fortress. Eventually, of the empty lands themselves. Somehow, Seeking Sword had also obtained the Northern Heir Sword, missing for thirty five years.

"*I* can't explain it," I said helplessly. "*You're* the Wizard."

Laughing, Healing Hand shook his head. "You two have been a mystery for such a long time we might never know the cause of all your quirks and anomalies. What do you think? About the identical twin studies. About your impersonator?"

I'd hoped, in talking with him, to hear something that would contradict my conclusion. Sighing, I frowned, ran my hand through my waist-length bronze hair and looked at Healing Hand. "I think he's my brother, Infinite blast it."

He looked cowed, as if surprised by my reaction. "Better to have a brother who's an enemy than no brother at all, eh Lord?" he said tentatively.

I snorted in disgust. "Better not to have a brother."

I recognized an important distinction between Flying Arrow and the Emperor Climbing Peregrine. It bothered me: My father's faking of my brother's death.

I remembered that my father had let Lofty Lion live so he might lead him to the Heir sword. The plan had failed, the reasons obscure. By the time the old Emperor had died, his son had already wielded the Sword for a long time. In my discussion with my mate, she said she didn't know how long Seeking Sword had had the sword.

I knew that he wasn't really Lofty Lion's son. If he had been, the deposed Emperor would've sired a child long before. Singing Star's and my mate's revelations two nights ago indicated the shape of the final pieces in the whole puzzle. I thought only one conclusion reasonable:

My brother hadn't died. Instead, Flying Arrow gave the infant to Lofty Lion. The infant twin, my brother. My enemy.

I began to weep.

* * *

Sweating profusely, Seeking Sword woke from the dream, disoriented. Where are all the books? he wondered. Then he knew where he was: At the hostelry near the crossroads. Somehow, that frightened him even more. He subdued his terror long enough to look around the room. No, Seeking Sword hadn't stayed here before under the name Chameleon. Flaming Arrow had. The Bandit recognized the room in a memory not his own.

He began to weep.

Through most the night, he wept. When, exhausted, he slept again, Seeking Sword thanked the Infinite that his dreams were incoherent.

Chapter 16

"LORD BEAR, what happened a moment ago?"

When Flaming Arrow asked me that question, I didn't answer. I remember the moment vividly, though: As Flaming Arrow lifted his right foot, so did the stranger, Threatening Nightmare. As the unknown warrior looked left to measure the length of day left, Flaming Arrow looked left toward the warrior. As Flaming Arrow scratched his cheek with his empty right hand, so did Threatening Nightmare.

Behind me, my bear gave off a disconsolate howl. I didn't tell Flaming Arrow that my bear's disturbance was my own.—*The Lectures of Guarding Bear, 9323 to 9335.*

* * *

Flaming Arrow pivoted, caught the warrior's blade on the hilt-guard of his sword and ripped it out of his hands.

The warrior looked at his empty palms, surprised, then bowed to Flaming Arrow and went to retrieve his sword.

Wiping the sweat from his eyes, Flaming Arrow looked toward the group of warriors at the edge of meadow to see who would step forward to duel him next.

For three days he'd practiced his swordsmanship against the best warriors in Bastion. None had been able to disarm him. After dueling his four companions a second day, Flaming Arrow had sought others to practice against, none of the four able to master him, not even the undefeated Guarding Bear.

The retired General, miffed that his pupil dominated him time and again, had muttered something about the resilience of youth.

Flaming Arrow had smiled.

Early that day, at the former Heir's request, Probing Gaze had gone into Bastion and had returned with twenty warriors of superior swordsmanship. Against them, Flaming Arrow had practiced all day, and each of them, he'd dominated at least twice.

Two hours ago, another warrior had joined the group. The man was black-haired and freckled, his robes poor but his weapons the best. Thus far he hadn't volunteered to duel, had only been content to watch.

Looking for a fresh fighter, Flaming Arrow tried to find the new man amidst the group. He didn't see him.

When he'd go north, he didn't know. Spies reported that the Bandit was in the north, settling a dispute between two Prefects. If he didn't return soon, Flaming Arrow would go anyway, wanting to meet Seeking Sword at or near Seat, the center of the Bandit's government.

In the northern foothills of the Windy Mountains had gathered a large number of bandits. Reportedly, they were planting what appeared to be indigenous flora. Has the Bandit ordered the foothills reforested or is all the planting simply a cover for mobilization? he wondered, having received conflicting reports from his spies. Whatever they were doing, he doubted they'd intercept him as he crossed the border.

Do I tell him I think he's my brother? Flaming Arrow wondered, his conversation with Healing Hand last night haunting him.

"Lord Prefect Arrow," said a voice so familiar it disconcerted him.

He turned.

Standing a few paces away was the black-haired warrior who'd belatedly joined the group on the south edge of the meadow. "Would you like to try your blade against mine, Lord Prefect? I'm Threatening Nightmare."

"I'm Flaming Arrow. The honor is all mine, Lord Nightmare," Flaming Arrow said genially. The two men bowed to each other.

Guarding Bear, subdued panic on his face, strode toward them. "Lord Arrow, if I may speak with you a moment?"

Nodding, he followed the General a few paces away.

"No, Lord, not him," Guarding Bear said quietly, fervently.

"Eh? Your brains addled again?"

"Something about this man disturbs me," Guarding Bear said. "I don't want you to duel him."

"Don't be such an old woman, Guarding Bear. I've never met a warrior I can't disarm."

" 'Old woman,' my balls! The Infinite will take your hubris and strangle you with it! Listen to me, boy: He's invisible to all my trace talents. Furthermore, I've watched him since he came over the valley rim. I can pick out where a warrior trained just by the way he walks, but I haven't been able to discern where he trained or who taught him. He's a strange one and therefore dangerous."

Flaming Arrow nodded, listening to the General and watching the newcomer.

Near the group of warriors, Threatening Nightmare was divesting himself of accoutrements—pack, bow, quiver, knives, and weapons belt. The man was a walking armory. His robes of poor-quality silk were dusty and sweat stained, as if he'd traveled most of the day. He took them off, revealing a freckled, well-developed body with excellent musculature. His shoulders straight and his hips level, he had good carriage, upright and even, and appeared to favor neither left side nor right. He used both hands equally, as if ambidextrous. He looked as if he'd learned from the best and had trained with the best.

"Should I tell him to return tomorrow?" he suggested.

"You tell him what you like, pup. I don't want you to fight him." Guarding Bear frowned at him. "You'll do what you'll do. No one can turn you aside from that, probably not even the Infinite."

Ten paces away, the bear stood on its hind legs and loosed a melancholy roar, then dropped to all fours.

Flaming Arrow smiled. "I'll be careful, Guarding Bear. Thank you for the warning. Explain the rules to him, would you?"

Guarding Bear glanced toward the sky, then shrugged and led his protégé toward the stranger. "Lord Nightmare, we aren't here to kill, only to disarm. At first blood the match ends, whether intentional or accidental, serious or negligible. The luck of the Infinite to you both, Lords." Bowing, the General stepped away.

Again the bear reared and roared.

The two men bowed to each other with motions identical.

"You fight with rules, Lord Arrow?" the man asked, looking amused.

"Only when I don't intend to kill, Lord Nightmare," Flaming Arrow replied amiably.

Swords sang from scabbards and the two men squared off, Flaming Arrow switching his to his right hand, like the other man. Both feinted and neither succumbed to deception. Flaming Arrow felt the challenge of this unknown quantity and watched the gray-blue eyes that looked so like his own. The two men circled each other. He sensed a danger beyond any he'd encountered and, strangely, felt a kinship, a common basis, a brotherhood whose nature eluded him.

They fell to fighting right-handed.

For fifteen seconds, metal rang against metal, neither man finding an advantage. They broke and circled, the black-haired warrior in a cat like crouch. Suddenly, he feinted with an empty hand. Flaming Arrow ducked the left-handed slash, hacked upward expecting to cut into groin, surprised as the other man leaped nimbly away. He used the respite to switch hands, then parried, slashed, and locked hilts with his opponent. For five long seconds, each man tried to throw the other.

Both relented right then. For the next five minutes, they slashed and parried. Dissecting Threatening Nightmare's style, Flaming Arrow knew it could tell him who'd taught the man. All teachers inadvertently taught their flaws as well as their skills. The pupil subconsciously adopted characteristics such as stance, bearing, angle of sword, and motions of the unarmed hand. Guarding Bear was the most flawless swordsman he knew, but wasn't completely without flaw, relying sometimes on his unpredictable talent. Knowing his mentor's flaws, Flaming Arrow knew how to compensate when using the General's techniques. By analyzing Threatening Nightmare's style, Flaming Arrow hoped to discover the man's teachers. By extension, his weaknesses.

What he saw alarmed him: The man imitated Flaming Arrow's style. The former Heir had made a practice of imitating whomever he fought. To his chagrin someone had done the same to him. Not even Guarding Bear displayed the mutability he saw in Threatening Nightmare.

As if by agreement, both men then retreated a step. "You're good, Lord," both men said. Flaming Arrow didn't find their doing so strange.

Again they fell on each other, fighting left-handed again. Flaming Arrow tried every move, every gambit he knew. The other man always countered reflexively. The former Heir saw not a single opening or weakness in Threatening Nightmare's manner of fighting, his style reminding the former Heir of no one but him.

Onward they fought. Flaming Arrow eased up in his offense, wanting to see if the other man would display a few tricks not in his repertoire. For a minute or so—an eternity during a swordfight—Threatening Nightmare attacked only haphazardly, wary of his opponent's diminished intensity, deliberately leaving his guard down for that extra fraction of a second, his eyes studying his opponent, a tactic Flaming Arrow sometimes used. Then, left-handed, Threatening Nightmare attacked with such speed and ferocity that Guarding Bear cried out. Flaming Arrow defended himself with agility, but still suffered a scrape that removed the hair from his right forearm. As the black-haired man relented in his attack, Flaming Arrow pressed his own, sweat stinging his eyes, fatigue shrieking through his muscles.

"Hold!" yelled the General.

The two men backed away from each other but didn't avert their gazes.

"The Lord Nightmare wins," Guarding Bear said, pointing at Flaming Arrow's right forearm, where blood beaded along the stitches of a scratch.

Flaming Arrow began to protest, the scratch ridiculously minor.

Before he spoke, the other man bowed to him. "Thank you, Lord Arrow. It's an honor and a pleasure to have this opportunity." Sheathing his sword, he turned as if to go north.

"Lord Nightmare," Flaming Arrow said. "A man with your skill is valuable. I want your blade beside me."

"Forgive me, Lord. I have other obligations." Again he turned.

"Who's your Patriarch, Lord Nightmare?" I can have him reassigned, Flaming Arrow thought.

The man stopped again, facing north, but didn't turn toward Flaming Arrow, hesitant.

"Lord Nightmare," Healing Hand said from the watching group, "your weapons are over here."

The man nodded mutely and went to retrieve his accoutrements.

Flaming Arrow saw the bow and quiver amidst the possessions. "Lord Bear, set up the targets. Will you pull beside me, Lord Nightmare?"

Smiling, Threatening Nightmare put his weapons belt back down. Slinging his quiver onto his back and grabbing his bow, he stepped toward Flaming Arrow.

Cub brought Flaming Arrow his bow and quiver. He slipped the quiver onto his back and gestured toward the targets fifty paces away, each a round cross-section of large tree trunk mounted on a tripod. Guarding Bear planted a wind vane a pace to the side of the targets and retreated. "Is that too far, Lord?" Flaming Arrow asked.

Laughing, Threatening Nightmare walked away from the targets. At two hundred paces from them, he stopped. "Is this too far, Lord?"

Flaming Arrow smiled, knowing he was a superior swordsman but only an adequate archer. Even so, he stepped toward the other man and took up a position to his right.

They were both still breathing roughly from their duel.

Threatening Nightmare knelt on one knee, the bow in his right hand, the first sign that the man favored his left hand. "How many can you launch before the first one strikes, Lord?"

"At this distance? I don't know, Lord." He sighted along the bow in his right hand, his left arm relaxed at his side. The targets looked impossibly small. Then his left hand came up, reached over his shoulder, extracted an arrow and fitted it. On the pull, he automatically calculated wind strength. His perception suddenly shifted. The target on the right rushed at him. He loosed the first and followed with a rapid succession while the man beside him did the same.

The first arrow struck, and Flaming Arrow froze mid-motion. Time stopped. The peace of the Infinite filled him with a connection to the universe.

Then the moment passed and he was simply a human being again.

He couldn't see from this distance how well he'd pulled. He knew he'd never shot better. "Thank you, Lord, I've never felt such transcendence."

Threatening Nightmare sighed. "Thank *you*." He saw that the former Heir was looking toward the targets. "How many arrows we launched and how accurate they were is beside the point. More important is the form we displayed and how we transcended this world of pain. Thank you, Lord Arrow. I'll be going now."

The two men walked to where the man's accoutrements lay. He put on his robe and picked up his weapons while Flaming Arrow watched, oddly saddened by the other's departure.

"I can't convince you to stay awhile?"

Threatening Nightmare smiled. "No, Lord, but thank you. This humble warrior is grateful for the honor you've shown him."

"Well, then, Lord Nightmare, walk with the Infinite, eh?" Flaming Arrow said, slapping the man on the shoulder companionably.

He stood in front of the targets and tried to remember walking the fifty or so paces to get there. He didn't find the memory.

Sticking in each target was a cluster of eight arrows in a space the size of his palm, a degree of accuracy he'd never hoped to achieve in all his years of practice. He looked from one target to the other, astounded that they both had pulled so well.

"Did you hear me, Lord Arrow?" Guarding Bear asked.

"Eh? What'd you say?" He didn't remember the General's speaking.

"I said, 'He shoots like Scowling Tiger,'" Guarding Bear repeated. "Where the Infinite is your mind, Flaming Arrow?"

"Look at the patterns, Lord Bear."

Guarding Bear glanced from one target to the other. "Unbelievable."

Flaming Arrow nodded.

The arrangements of arrows in each target were identical to each other.

"Like Scowling Tiger, eh?" Flaming Arrow said. "He shoots better than Scowling Tiger, eh?" he said, wondering how he knew. An image came to mind: Fifteen arrows in two different clusters stuck in a tree, its bark split, the upper cluster widely dispersed, the lower tight and compact. Scowling Tiger had launched the upper cluster, he knew. He thought for a moment that he, Flaming Arrow, had shot the lower. How could I? he wondered, shaking his head in disbelief and confusion, having never seen the bandit general pull.

"When I was young," Guarding Bear said, "I paid an old woman a thousand taels to tell Scowling Tiger that the man who pulled a bow better than he would inherit his domains. He killed her to still her lies and practiced until his hands bled. Brazen Bear and I laughed so hard we pissed all over ourselves."

Chuckling, Flaming Arrow regarded the wily General affectionately. "Do you think he taught Threatening Nightmare to shoot?" The former Heir looked to the north. Threatening Nightmare was ascending the steep path that led toward the Bastion-Eyry road, still carrying his accoutrements.

Guarding Bear shrugged. "I couldn't tell. In fact, whoever taught that warrior was a master. I didn't see any flaws in his fighting or shooting. It's almost dark, Lord. Time we put our weapons aside, eh?"

The former Heir nodded. "Incredible shooting, wasn't it?"

"I've never seen better. How you shot that well only the Infinite knows. You're not an archer, despite being an arrow."

The two of them shared a laugh. "Lord Bear, what happened a moment ago? I was over there, watching him dress, then I slapped him on the shoulder and found myself over here."

One of Guarding Bear's bushy gray eyebrows rose. Concern filled his eyes. "As he walked north, his weapons in hand, you walked over here."

The bear roared with displeasure.

"Does your animal have gas?" Flaming Arrow asked.

"Infinite curse the day. I warned you not to lock swords with that man. Do you listen to your mentor anymore? No, not you, not the former Heir Flaming Arrow, who hasn't a single obligation to anyone but himself! Mindless, arrogant rascal, you!"

"What's scared you, Lord Bear?" Flaming Arrow asked calmly.

"Disrespectful puppy! I ought to skewer you and your boundless pride! You'd better walk with care, 'cause the Infinite's looking over your shoulder for the first opportunity to shove it back in your face!"

"Whatever's bothering you, Lord, I hope it passes. It can't be too serious. We're here. We're alive. Let's go, eh?"

* * *

Sighing, deeply troubled, Guarding Bear psychically ordered the Captain Silent Whisper to take a contingent to capture the warrior, intuiting that Threatening Nightmare was more than he seemed. I won't have him haunting *my* sleep, the General thought.

"Spying Eagle," Flaming Arrow said, calling the Wizard over and taking him aside to whisper something. Spying Eagle nodded, bowed and loped in the direction Threatening Nightmare had gone.

"What did you tell him?" Guarding Bear asked, looking suspiciously at Flaming Arrow. The rascal has probably sent the

Wizard to countermand Silent Whisper's order, the General thought.

"Oh, nothing, Lord Bear. How did I fight today? How was my posture? Did you like the way I switched hands?"

Flaming Arrow's endless questions distracted Guarding Bear. He soon forgot what had upset him so much. He began to dissect his pupil's skill and style, as he had a thousand times before.

Chapter 17

THE NIGHT I spoke with him, I felt my whole being opening up, as though my soul had had closed places inside it throughout my life. Something gathered in me, along with the conviction that we were on the edge of a fundamental change. What I didn't recognize until later was that he had helped free me from the bondage of my own past, and so had helped in my personal Gathering of Power.—*The Gathering of Power*, by the Wizard Spying Eagle.

* * *

The Bandit stepped onto the muddy trail that led from Bastion-Valley to the Bastion-Eyry road, his accoutrements in his left hand. An inexplicable sadness settled upon him as he pushed up the hill, the trail little more than a seam between trees and bushes.

Sighing, Seeking Sword tried to remember walking the fifty or so paces between the dueling ring and the trail-head.

The memory wouldn't emerge.

The Bandit reviewed again what had just happened.

* * *

Bandit and Heir walked to where the accoutrements lay. Putting on his robe, Seeking Sword picked up his weapons.

Flaming Arrow watched, looking sad. "I can't convince you to stay awhile?"

The Bandit smiled. "No, Lord, but thank you. This humble warrior is grateful for the honor you've shown him."

"Well, then, Lord Nightmare, walk with the Infinite, eh?" Flaming Arrow said, slapping him on the shoulder companionably.

Then the Bandit stepped onto the trail.

* * *

Seeking Sword couldn't remember anything in the gap between Flaming Arrow's slapping him on the shoulder and his stepping onto the trail.

A profound disquietude spread through the Bandit like morning fog over quiet meadow. The abrupt shift was like the gap of consciousness during dreamless sleep, in which memory reported that nothing had occurred and no time had passed. Unlike such a gap, Seeking Sword had moved a considerable distance without a recollection of doing so.

It had suddenly, inexplicably happened.

Like his lapse between the River Placid and the Tiger Fortress days ago, during which he'd somehow gotten injured, possibly by his father's talisman staff. Like his journey toward the fortress, five years ago, while Imperial warriors pursued him.

Both of those lapses reminded him of his two dreams, the one in which he'd dreamt of fighting his way *from* the fortress, and the one last night at the hostelry near the crossroads.

Early that morning, the sky beginning to brighten in the east, he'd risen at the hostelry and stretched to see how his mysterious injuries felt. They'd seemed completely healed, which he'd thought odd. All the other patrons of the hostelry were asleep, some sprawled wherever they lay, as if in drunken stupors.

Seeking Sword wished he knew what it all meant.

Having slept fitfully last night and having traveled most of the day to get to Bastion- Seeking Sword felt tired. Defending himself against the Heir had nearly sapped his physical reserves.

He'd come to Bastion Valley to see Flaming Arrow himself, having never met the man. None of the descriptions he'd heard of the former Heir had accurately depicted his natural self-assurance nor his trusting openness. Expecting the self-assurance, Seeking Sword also had expected Flaming Arrow to be haughty, arrogant and disdainful of subordinates.

He was none of those. He was simply a nice man.

That bothered the Bandit. Flaming Arrow hadn't deserved the terrible acts he'd committed to assassinate the Heir's character. The former Heir had deserved neither the treatment nor its consequences. Seeking Sword felt as if he'd lost his own self respect. He felt disgusted with the necessities of his office.

Breathing deeply as he gained the crest, the Bandit glanced back. The meadow in Bastion Valley looked empty. To the west, a dusky, cloudy sky darkened slowly. The eastern sky was black with impending rain. To the north the lights of Bastion glowed softly. At the base of the hill on which he stood was the Bastion-Eyry road, meandering to the north and south. Segments of the road were visible through gaps in the trees.

Seeking Sword sensed someone behind him. He spun, sword out.

"Infinite be with you, Lord Nightmare," the other man said. Brown of hair, of eye, of skin, he looked familiar to Seeking Sword.

"Who're you?" he asked rudely.

"I'm Spying Eagle, Lord Nightmare."

Of course, the Bandit thought—the former Sorcerer, Melding Mind's son, Thinking Quick's brother.

Then Seeking Sword remembered the last time he'd seen the girl. Five years ago, outside conference room number one high inside the Tiger Fortress, Thinking Quick had interrupted him and Purring Tiger to give him a knife whose haft was a single chunk of emerald. "Here, I want you to have this. Take it—it's a gift," she'd said.

Seeking Sword sheathed his sword but remained ready to pull it. He wondered whether to present the emerald-hafted knife to Spying Eagle, to whom, he felt, it rightly belonged. "What do you want, Lord Eagle?"

"Simply to speak with you, Lord."

"What about, Lord Eagle?" Seeking Sword watched him warily.

"Flaming Arrow sent me to escort you, Lord Nightmare. You're in danger. He thinks Guarding Bear has ordered you detained. Flaming Arrow doesn't want that to happen."

"Eh?"

"Didn't I speak clearly, Lord?"

"I don't understand why Flaming Arrow would do that."

"The Lord Bear sometimes orders an end without specifying the means. His subordinates use whatever's expedient, even if unconscionable. Flaming Arrow doesn't want anything to happen that might hinder your serving him later."

Grinning, Seeking Sword laughed. "I'm sorry to say that nothing can *ever* remove the hindrances to my serving him. His consideration is unusual for a man in his position."

"Oh? Why is that, if I may ask, Lord?"

"Positions of power have a special allure to them. Sometimes they become the primary source of identity and self-esteem. When that happens, people in such positions may come to rely more on that external source than on internal sources."

"Indeed, Lord." Spying Eagle smiled. "It *is*, of course, far easier to lose external esteem. I watched you when you arrived, Lord Nightmare. You have an unusual amount of self-confidence."

"Are you lacking? I have extra," he said.

Grinning, Spying Eagle laughed. "I also saw that you often looked toward my friend—the priest Healing Hand."

Nodding, Seeking Sword had wanted to ask the medacor what he'd discussed last night with Flaming Arrow. He'd wanted to confirm that his dream last night was a reality. The Bandit had stopped himself several times from asking, still shaken by the clarity and content, and still feeling the loss of something unnamed, unsaid.

Suddenly feeling that he must, knowing that the action would reveal his identity, Seeking Sword pulled the emerald-hafted knife from a belt sheath. "Your sister gave me this. I think it's yours, Percipient Mind."

In the fading light, the Bandit knew he'd never see the Wizard more vulnerable.

The man didn't cry. Tears poured down his face, yes, but with no commensurate change of expression, no sobs, no sniffles, no change of posture, no averting of gaze, no wiping away of water, no attempt to hide the pain, no attempt to suppress it. Just tears.

Seeking Sword wondered what immense inner strength that required, what deep spiritual faith.

"My father, Melding Mind, in his loyalty to Scowling Tiger and his hatred of Flying Arrow, implanted me to assassinate Flaming Arrow when the boy was only five years old. Thankfully, I didn't succeed. This knife was my father's before me, and his father's before him, and his father's before him. He denied it to me after I failed. She ... Thinking Quick said that the man who bore this knife was my friend and hers. You were her friend?"

"I was. I miss her still," Seeking Sword replied.

Spying Eagle nodded, holding the haft close to his heart with both hands, as if treasuring it. "I heard she had no friends, that she'd forsaken them by betraying the bandit general."

Seeking Sword shrugged. "Better him than the whole human race."

"That's what Flaming Arrow told me. Odd, isn't it, that she had so much talent, yet so much torment? I hope she found peace with the Infinite."

"I think she did." Seeking Sword looked toward the Bastion-Eyry road, the path leading down to the road now too dark to see. "Warriors are coming up the path." He'd been aware of their approach for the past few minutes, hearing them in the wet brush.

"Yes, Lord, I know. Guarding Bear sent them." Spying Eagle put away the knife and wiped the tears off his face, sighing. "I'll handle them, Lord."

Smiling, Seeking Sword gestured Spying Eagle to step past him.

"You!" the Wizard said, pointing down the hill. "What are you doing?"

A man emerged from the brush beside the path. "Who wants to know?"

"The Wizard Spying Eagle!"

"Infinite be with you, Lord Wizard, I didn't recognize you."

"And with you, Lord Whisper. You're no longer needed. You and your men may go now."

"Not without the man behind you, Lord Eagle."

"Without the man behind me, Lord Whisper," Spying Eagle replied, his voice calm. "Here's the Lord Nightmare's pass of safe conduct, signed by the Lord Prefect Flaming Arrow." He pulled a roll of parchment from his sleeve.

Silent Whisper hesitated. "All right, Lord—as you wish. I don't need to see it. Answer a question, though, would you?"

"Gladly, Lord."

"Who is he?"

"His name's Threatening Nightmare, Lord."

Silent Whisper didn't answer for a full minute. "Very well, Lord Eagle. My report to the Lord General will conceal nothing."

"Nor will mine to the Lord Prefect. Infinite be with you, Lord Whisper."

"And with you, Lord Eagle." The two men bowed to each other. The Captain turned, barked a single order, then went whence he'd come. Others emerged onto the trail and followed Silent Whisper down the hill.

Spying Eagle sighed loudly. "Where are you going now, Lord Sword?"

Seeking Sword gestured vaguely north.

"May I accompany you?"

"Your company would be a pleasure, Lord Eagle. What's on the parchment?"

"Notes I took earlier while Flaming Arrow practiced—not a pass, I assure you."

Laughing, the two men started down the trail, the Wizard leading the way.

"He was once Scowling Tiger's spy."

"Who? Silent Whisper? I don't believe it!" Spying Eagle glanced over his shoulder at Seeking Sword.

"More than twenty years ago, Thinking Quick told me, Scowling Tiger sent an assassin after Guarding Bear—or so it appeared. In reality, the assassin's target was the Captain of the General's guard. The Captain died, and the mayor of Nest brought Silent Whisper to Guarding Bear's attention. He recruited the Captain, as Scowling Tiger intended him to do. Silent Whisper spied for a week, then said he couldn't continue. During that week, he asked you, Percipient Mind, to treat the Lord Bear. Eventually that led to your becoming Sorcerer Apprentice."

"So Scowling Tiger arranged all that, eh?" Spying Eagle chuckled. "Those two warred on each other for such a long time I'll bet neither remembered the original reason for their feud."

Seeking Sword smiled, concentrating on the dark, wet path, the footing treacherous. "Too bad it cost so many lives, eh?"

The Wizard grunted. "Such a waste, all of it. Lord, have you heard anything about … my father?"

The Bandit had wondered when Spying Eagle would ask. "I didn't see him for four years, until just last week. I didn't actually speak with him either, but he's alive. He was nearly inconsolable after Thinking Quick died. His life hasn't been easy."

"Do you know where I can … find him, Lord?"

"Near the castle plain is a large oak tree, where I saw him last. You'd find him there, if anywhere."

They reached the base of the hill and stepped onto the Bastion-Eyry road, turning toward the glowing city a few miles distant. They broke into an easy lope.

"I'm sorry he used you so cruelly, Lord Eagle."

"He … did what he thought was right. Looks as if you'll have my company for awhile, Lord."

"Oh?" the Bandit asked.

"Silent Whisper and his men are just ahead, watching us."

"If you'd like to return to the valley, I don't think I'll have any trouble with them."

"I doubt you would—the way you fight. The Lord Arrow asked me to see that you got away safely, though. In truth, I'd like to speak with you awhile longer. Are you staying in Bastion?"

Seeking Sword shook his head, not wanting to betray that his destination was Emparia City. "Lord Eagle, how would you get the Sword from Flaming Arrow?"

The Wizard laughed. "Ask him for it. Actually, you needn't even ask. When he becomes Emperor, he'll give it to you."

"Why?" he asked, astounded. "I've caused him nothing but trouble!"

"Perhaps because you've caused him nothing but trouble, Lord, and will continue to do so, as will your progeny, until you have it." Spying Eagle shrugged. "He'll do what's better for the Empire. What's better is eliminating the source of the trouble."

In the pause, Seeking Sword considered telling the Wizard that he'd cause Flaming Arrow no more trouble.

"Besides, the Sword's useless to him—*not* to you."

Does he know I have the Northern Heir Sword? the Bandit wondered, disturbed that the Wizard might know, when he, Seeking Sword, had only found out days ago. Unless the dream *were* true. "In what way?"

Spying Eagle glanced down at Seeking Sword's hip, at the sword sheathed there. "I've seen the Northern Imperial Sword. Supposedly the Heir Sword looks no different, except for the size of the ruby. You're not wearing it."

"Eh? I don't have the Heir Sword! Has the Infinite addled your brains? It's been missing for thirty-five years!" He hoped his voice was without vehemence.

Spying Eagle laughed softly. "Well, if you didn't know, someone should tell you. Several people think you've wielded the Heir Sword for fifteen years."

"That's dog dung! Who thinks that, eh?"

"Lofty Lion, Leaping Elk, Snarling Jaguar, Bubbling Water—"

"They're all dead, Lord Eagle."

"Indeed they are. Rippling Water and Healing Hand have both known for five years. I wouldn't expect you to trust them. However, I think Fawning Elk would know. Ask her, Lord, when you see her."

His spirit hurting, Seeking Sword said, "I'm sorry, Lord Eagle. I lied to you. Fawning Elk told me a few days ago. Forgive me for not being forthright. I, uh, had to confirm something."

In the glow from Bastion, the city gates ahead, the Bandit saw a smile on the Wizard's face.

To the left, skirting Bastion, a segment of road connected the Bastion-Eyry road and the Nest-Bastion road. Seeking Sword wondered whether to take it. He could always intimate that his destination was the border. Then he recognized the lie for what it was.

"Let's go toward Emparia City, eh?" he said, pointing to the left. "Listen, Lord Eagle, I want you to tell Flaming Arrow something for me. Oh, I know you'll probably report every word of our conversation, but that's not the same."

"No, Lord, it's not."

"Tell him I'm sorry. About killing Aged Oak and the rapes and the other ignominies I've perpetrated in his name. I wish they hadn't been necessary—no, wait, that's not true. I only *thought* they were necessary. I wish I hadn't done all those things. I'm sorry he suffered."

"Yes, Lord. I'll tell him exactly as you've told me," the Wizard said, chuckling. Spying Eagle glanced backward, the Bastion lights on their right. "Silent Whisper and his companions have stopped following us. Your peculiar psychic signature conceals you from them now. My staying near you gives them a marker to track. You're safe if you go on by yourself, now."

Seeking Sword chuckled. "You mean my peculiar *lack* of signature?"

"Exactly, Lord."

"Don't go, Lord Eagle. Talk with me awhile, eh? Didn't you compile a report on the psychic storms five years ago? What did you conclude?"

"Probably what my father concluded. Listen, Lord Sword, something I think you should know. Remember how Flaming Arrow's twin brother died at three days old? Flying Arrow may have faked his death. Three days ago a woman came forward and told him how Exploding Illusion had forcefully taken her baby, and how the publicized image of the dead twin resembled her child. The story rang of truth. We can't confirm it except by asking the Lord Emperor himself, who'll probably never tell. I thought you should know, because if the story's true, then perhaps, somewhere, Flaming Arrow's twin brother is alive."

Seeking Sword frowned. "Know this, Spying Eagle, my spirit grows heavy with every lie I tell, every truth I withhold. You, who've been a pawn in this struggle between North and East, between bandit and Empire, between me and the Heir, have suffered enough. I'll not inflict further suffering if I can avoid it."

"Thank you, Lord. You're very kind. Why'd you tell me that?"

"I know about the woman, Lord Eagle. Last night I dreamt I talked with Healing Hand about her. Singing Star's her name."

Stopping, the Wizard looked at him in disbelief. "Is that true, Lord? You dreamt?"

The Bandit stopped as well. "Yes, Lord," he said wearily. "Last night, an hour or two after sunset, I stopped at the hostelry near the crossroads, where Flaming Arrow stopped the night I killed Aged Oak. I nearly fell asleep *in* the bath, but managed to crawl into bed. I didn't even dry myself. Did you hear what happened at the hostelry this morning?"

"Yes, Lord. I was present when the messenger told Flaming Arrow. Shields short-circuited, patrons asleep where they lay— a repeat of the night Flaming Arrow stayed there. You know he dreamt about you that night?"

"I know. The content of *my* dream seemed to be the thoughts and perceptions of … Flaming Arrow. Healing Hand and he discussed Singing Star and the Peregrine Twins. He read to the medacor from a book called *One Mind, Two Bodies: Identical Twin Contact.* Flaming Arrow said, 'I think he's my brother, Infinite blast it.' He was thinking, 'The infant twin, my brother, my enemy.' Then I awoke and cried half the night." He noticed he was crying now.

Softly, the rain began to fall.

Spying Eagle looked too dumbfounded to respond.

"Don't suggest that I return to the valley, Lord," Seeking Sword said. "Flaming Arrow and I still have an Imperial Sword that's throwing the scales off balance between us."

"No, Lord … Arrow," the Wizard whispered.

The Bandit nodded. "Do you need more proof?"

"No, Lord Arrow, I don't."

"Don't call me that. I'm no more Arrow than *Flaming* Arrow, eh? Let's walk, Lord Eagle." Seeking Sword guided him along, both of them struggling with the truth. "We know the Imperial Sword is the least of the injustices, only a symbol, the only tangible imbalance. Flaming Arrow isn't the perpetrator. He's merely another victim, like myself. Didn't he create an imaginary friend, a brother who *didn't* died at three days old, to help him through the loneliness of his childhood? The injustice is that he needn't have."

"How do you know that?"

Seeking Sword shrugged. "I need your help, Lord Eagle."

"What can I do, Lord?"

The Wizard's willingness surprised him. "Why such an eager Eagle, eh?" the Bandit asked.

"Infinite help me, Seeking Sword, I like you. More important, though, is that we can't resolve this situation without accurate information or open communication."

"Exactly my thought. I like you too, Spying Eagle. We'll need courage, as well as information and communication. Flying Arrow's without morals, and more than politically astute to remain the largest block between us, eh? He'll do whatever he must. Infinite blast it, I won't hide anymore or run anymore! I'm a human being, not a stinking bandit!"

"You sound angry," the Wizard said.

"Wouldn't you be angry? Of course you would. Listen, Spying Eagle, I think I know how to balance the scales *and* make Flying Arrow pay for the injustices he perpetrates upon the northern lands. I need Flaming Arrow's help. I don't want revenge. That would be useless. I simply want to settle the future of the Northern Empire. Here's what I want you to tell Flaming Arrow."

Chapter 18

W HEN SPYING Eagle told me what the Bandit had said, I felt the burden lift from my shoulders. The crushing weight of his persecution was gone—and he'd also given me what sounded like a genuine apology. I knew I wasn't ready to forgive him, but I had few doubts about believing him. From what the Wizard told me, he sounded like the honorable and gentle man that rumor said he was. All that contradicted my impression were his acts to assassinate my character.

Those, he had said, would cease.

Even better was the plan to get from my father the Northern Imperial Sword. When we'd accomplished that, then I could rest, assured that the Bandit was no longer the enemy.—*The Bandit, the Enemy*, by Flaming Arrow.

* * *

Flaming Arrow looked among his friends for their reaction to Seeking Sword's requests. The bear snored peacefully in the corner.

He was becoming very familiar with this room, the library in the Bear mansion at Bastion Valley. Last night he'd told Healing Hand about the woman Singing Star's revelation. They'd both concluded that the Bandit was his identical twin brother. Then, today, Flaming Arrow had dueled the stranger, Threatening Nightmare. Knowing Guarding Bear, he'd sent Spying Eagle to insure that the man escaped the retired General's minions, not knowing what would eventually happen, not knowing that the man was actually Seeking Sword in disguise.

When Spying Eagle had returned from the errand, he'd said, "Lord Arrow, I have a message from the Bandit, Seeking Sword." In addition to the message, he'd recounted the entire conversation.

Afterward, his hopes soaring, Flaming Arrow had called this conference of his friends, knowing he needed their help. He had too little information to act on Seeking Sword's proposal.

When they'd all assembled in the library—Guarding Bear, Healing Hand, Probing Gaze, and Spying Eagle—Flaming Arrow had asked the Wizard tell them the substance of the Bandit's plan.

Guarding Bear was the first to speak after Spying Eagle had finished. "How do you know the Bandit won't try to have you killed?" Guarding Bear asked. "He's a bandit, blast it! You can't trust him!"

"Spying Eagle, tell Guarding Bear about the earlier part of the conversation, eh?" Flaming Arrow felt that he *could* trust the Bandit.

After the Wizard repeated it, Guarding Bear growled, "You still can't trust him, Lord Arrow! Remember his background, eh? Oh, he may act like a civilized human being. He grew up a bandit, though, and he'll always *be* a bandit!"

"I want you to put aside your reservations, Guarding Bear," Flaming Arrow said patiently. "I think we *can* trust him. Healing Hand, tell Guarding Bear and Probing Gaze what we concluded last night."

The medacor winced. "I draw strength from your example, Flaming Arrow. Few people have the fortitude to ask what you're asking. As you wish, Lord. Last night, Lords Gaze and Bear, Flaming Arrow told me he has evidence that the Lord Emperor Arrow staged his twin brother's death."

Guarding Bear turned white. The bear in the corner started from its nap.

"Furthermore, because of the peculiar similarities between them, we think that the twin whose death Flying Arrow faked is now the Bandit, Seeking Sword."

The bear moaned.

"Spying Eagle," Flaming Arrow said, "tell them what the Lord Emperor Sword said about his dream."

"Yes, Lord," the Wizard said, grinning. "The Bandit slept last night at the hostelry near the crossroads, where this morning, as we already know, all the patrons appeared to have fallen asleep—as on the night Flaming Arrow stayed there. The Bandit claims that he dreamt the entire conversation between Healing Hand and Flaming Arrow. He repeated enough of it to me to dispel any doubt. Furthermore, he agrees with their conclusion."

"Now, Lord Bear, Lord Gaze," Flaming Arrow said, "you know the basis of my indecision. The question I need to answer isn't whether I do what the Lord Emperor Sword has requested, but to what extent. Spying Eagle, did the Lord Sword arrange a contingency, a safeguard against my not adhering to his plan?"

"No, Lord. He did say that you'd do what's better for the Empire, as if he trusts you implicitly."

"Thank you. I'd say he does. Listen, Lords, in the past I've often asked that in my presence you talk verbally rather than psychically. On this occasion I withdraw that request. I need your full expertise. I need your help."

"Lord Arrow," Probing Gaze said, "if Leaping Elk taught Seeking Sword, as my spies have often reported, I'd say he's highly honorable. During my tour as an Imperial spy fifteen years ago, I spoke with Leaping Elk several times and found him to be forthright. I'd advise you do as the Bandit suggests, despite the dangers."

Guarding Bear looked unhappy. "I'm not sure I agree. The weight of my opinion looks insignificant here. All of you seem to think the Bandit's plan a good one. Perhaps it is. How will his fellow Northerners know? Will he really contact them and tell them what to expect, as he indicated he would? Will he allow Flaming Arrow to walk into certain death? How much influence does he wield, especially when he won't even be there? What's to stop the Northerners from disobeying the Bandit and killing Flaming Arrow? Most of the people in his administration I'd trust, knowing where their loyalties lie. Two of them are more dangerous than the rest, however. I worry that they'll act against the Bandit's orders. I'd suggest you stay away from them, Lord Arrow. Purring Tiger and Raging River both have overwhelming reason to kill you. You assassinated Scowling Tiger, remember? In their minds, you still have the Infinite to pay, eh?"

Flaming Arrow nodded gravely, knowing his mentor right.

"What about this reforestation in the Windy Mountains, Lord?" Probing Gaze asked. "Isn't it simply a cover for mobilization? Did the Bandit say anything about that, Lord Eagle?"

"No, Lord Gaze, he didn't," the Wizard replied.

"If he *has* ordered his armies to mobilize, Lord Arrow, I must ask for what purpose? To what end?"

"I don't know. Your question's relevant. I'd guess mobilizing was a contingency against his capture. An incursion to rescue him from Emparia Castle is much easier if the armies have already prepared. Spying Eagle, how long has the Lord Emperor Sword been here? Did he say?"

"No, Lord, he didn't."

"If he's like me, he plans quickly, and sometimes extemporaneously. Because of what's happened since he left the Northern Empire, he may have changed his plans. He couldn't have known that he'd have my help, eh? For the moment then, we'll assume that the Lord Emperor Sword has ordered his generals to wait a day or two after his capture before launching the incursion. How long they'll wait, we don't know."

"That's a dangerous assumption," Guarding Bear said.

"I know it," Flaming Arrow said. "What else can we do?"

"Ask our new Commanding General to mobilize on the northern border," the retired Commanding General said.

"I can't do that, Lord Bear," Flaming Arrow replied. "I'm not the Heir."

"You don't have to. Someone has surely told the Lord Emperor that bandits have collected along the border, eh? While they might be peacefully planting trees, you've heard rumors that they plan an armed invasion, haven't you?"

"I have, but I don't want to aggravate an already unstable situation. If we've got other options, I don't want the Eastern Armed Forces mobilized. What else can we do?"

"The Bandit said he'll wait until you've gone north before he implements his part of the plan," Spying Eagle said. "Since you'll now be going clandestinely, we'll have to inform Seeking Sword somehow that you've crossed the border. I, uh, told him how to contact your mate the Lady Water in Emparia City. You can send a message to the Bandit through her. In my opinion we should inform her of his arrival."

Flaming Arrow smiled. "Thank you, Lord Eagle. That will help immensely. I appreciate your suggestion. We'll send him a message requesting that he de-mobilize. Obviously, Rippling Water needs to know what's happened during the last few days. What else should be in that message?"

"What resources will the Bandit have in Emparia City?" Probing Gaze asked. "If you adhere to his plan, Lord, I'd suggest you help him as much as you can. The success of it all depends on you both, not on just one of you."

"Infinite help us now," Guarding Bear muttered. "Standing aside while the Bandit commits espionage is one thing, Lord Arrow. Helping him is treason."

"By whose definition, Lord Bear?" Flaming Arrow asked. "Is it treason to prevent the collapse of the Eastern Empire? Is it treason to keep humanity from plunging itself into ten thousand years of darkness?"

"Eh? You're talking nonsense!"

"He's not, Lord Bear," Spying Eagle replied. "Remember that Prescient Wizard whom the Lord Emperor sent me to find five years ago? Her name was Thinking Quick. She knew."

"How do you know she knew?"

"She was my sister, Lord Bear. She told me." Spying Eagle reached for his belt and drew a knife whose haft was a single chunk of emerald. "The Bandit gave this to me this evening, said she'd given it to him. You know whose this is, eh?" He put the knife away. "Like my forebears, I'm brown of hair, of eye, of skin. You know my name, Lord Bear."

Guarding Bear nodded, looking older. "I do, Percipient Mind, and have for a long time. I still say helping the Bandit is treason."

"Please forgive me, Lord General," Probing Gaze said. "*I* don't."

The Peasant Upstart Usurper wilted. "You, Lord Colonel Probing Gaze, of all people." He shook his head in disbelief. "Lord Arrow, Lord Eagle, Lord Gaze, Lord Hand, I ask your forgiveness and your leave. I can't listen to treason. Please forget that I was ever here, and I'll forget what I've heard. Infinite be with you, Lords." Guarding Bear rose, strode to the door, turned, and bowed to them all. For a moment he looked imploringly at Flaming Arrow.

"I love you, Guarding Bear."

"I know, Flaming Arrow," he replied.

Then he was gone.

Belatedly, the menagerie animal shambled after him.

The silence between them thickened. Flaming Arrow wondered if Guarding Bear would betray them to Flying Arrow.

Staring into the distance, Healing Hand rose. "I'll talk with him," the Wizard-medacor said. "You can brief me later." Without obeisance, oblivious to them, Healing Hand left the room.

Flaming Arrow closed his eyes and sighed. "I never thought I'd have to choose between my best friend and my brother. Infinite blast it!"

Chapter 19

WHEN RIPPLING Water told me what the Heir had said, I felt the burden lift from my shoulders. The crushing weight of his opposition was gone—and he'd also given me what sounded like a genuine promise. I knew I wasn't ready to trust him, but I had few doubts about believing him. From what the Matriarch told me, he sounded like the honorable and gentle man that rumor said he was. All that contradicted my impression were his acts to annihilate the bandits.

Those, he had said, would cease.

Even better was his agreeing to my plan for getting from his father the Northern Imperial Sword. When we'd accomplished that, then I could rest, assured that the Heir was no longer the enemy.—*The Heir, the Enemy*, by Seeking Sword.

* * *

Seeking Sword bowed to Rippling Water, liking what he saw. She nodded to his obeisance.

She's beautiful, he thought, pleased that his possible brother had mated so well. Looking carefully at her, he saw her resemblance to his own mate. They were exactly the same height and build, and very similar of feature. Other than hair and eye color, they could have been sisters.

He looked at the two children standing behind her. The boy, especially, reminded him of his own son Burning Tiger, and reminded him he'd been away from home longer than he liked. Yearning for home, he wanted to resolve the contention between Empires more than ever.

"Lady Matriarch Water," he said, "Infinite be with you."

"And with you, Lord Nightmare," she said, looking at him closely. "Have a seat over here, Lord. Would you like something to drink?" She led him toward a pair of cushions fives pace apart in the gardens behind the Wolf residence.

"I would, Lady, thank you. I'd like coffee, if you have it. It's beautiful here. This was your home once, wasn't it?" He knew already that it was, but he needed to take her measure before revealing the purpose of his visit. Spying Eagle had told him that he could contact her. He didn't know if the Wizard had informed her to expect him. If she were as quick with her sword as he'd heard, she might try to kill him when he told her who he was and why he was here.

"Yes, it was. I grew up here. The Lord Wolf has graciously allowed me to stay for a short time. Flaming Arrow insists he's always welcome in the castle and refuses to buy a home in Emparia City." She glanced in the direction of the castle, towering over the city to the northeast. "Now that he's … not the Heir, I wouldn't ask to stay there." She stopped beside the far cushion, her children peering at him from behind her. "Please take a seat, Lord. Star?"

A woman appeared from the rear door of the house.

"Coffee for me and my guest, Star."

"Yes, Lady." Bowing, the woman retreated.

Singing Star? Seeking Sword wondered, resisting the urge to look. Patience, he told himself. Lowering himself to the cushion, he looked at the complex fountain nearby. Water flowed from one small pool to another, the soft gurgle and scintillating sparkle pleasing to his senses. "Pleasing design to that fountain," he said, knowing already who had designed it.

"Thank you, Lord. My mother built it more than thirty years ago. The Lord Wolf liked it so much he kept it."

"I would've too," he replied, watching water spill. He turned his attention to the children, who now sat behind their mother. "You have such enchanting children, Lady Water. How old are they?"

"Thank you, Lord," she said, glancing at them, her face softening. "You may greet the Lord Nightmare."

"I'm Trickling Water," the girl said, "and I'm three." She held up four fingers. Her hair a deep auburn color, she smiled briefly at him and bowed properly. "Infinite be with you, Lord Nightmare."

Seeking Sword smiled.

The boy grinned at him. "I see you under that disguise, Daddy! You don't fool—"

"Burning Arrow!" Rippling Water interrupted, her face going pale.

The boy asked, "That's not Daddy?"

"No, my son, it's not. Forgive him, Lord Nightmare, his imagination, eh? You know how children can be."

"I do, Lady. No offense taken. I have a son about a year older. He's very mischievous. Infinite be with you both, Little Lord, Little Lady." Seeking Sword bowed to them, amused. "You both speak very well at your ages. My daughter, who's nearly a year older than you, Little Lady, doesn't speak that well."

If the menagerie tiger hadn't died days after Purring Tiger had given birth to their daughter, Salky would speak much better than she did. The animal's death had nearly severed the mother-child empathy link, vital to a child's early development.

"Thank you, Lord," Trickling Water said with a half-bow.

He smiled and turned to the boy. "No, Little Lord Arrow, I'm not your father, although he and I are very similar. You're very perceptive."

The boy glanced at his mother, looking apprehensive.

Rippling Water stroked the boy's auburn hair. "Thank you, Lord."

The servant, Star, appeared from the rear door with a tray. On it were two cups of fine ceramic, a pot of coffee over a candle warmer, three varieties of fruit and two small loaves of bread. She placed the low tray between them. "Does the Lady want this humble servant to serve?"

"No, thank you, Star, the Lord and I will serve ourselves. Trickling Water, Burning Arrow, go with Star into the house please."

"Yes, Mommy," they both said, rising and bowing.

Returning their bow, Seeking Sword watched them enter the Wolf residence.

"May I serve you coffee, Lord?"

"I'm not worthy of service from an eminent noble such as yourself, Lady. Please, let me serve."

"I wouldn't think of it, Lord. You're my guest, and I insist."

"Please, I must refuse, Lady. I don't deserve such an honor. I'm only a humble warrior."

"It would be an honor to serve such a humble warrior," she replied.

"It would be more than an honor if you'd let me serve you. I couldn't do any less, Lady. Already I'm indebted to you for the honor of your permitting me to meet you."

"Very well, if you insist, Lord Emperor Sword."

His smile slipped a little. He hadn't expected her to know. Shrugging to himself, he rose onto his knees to pour them both a cup of coffee. "How would the Lady Matriarch like her coffee?"

"Without condiment, thank you."

He handed her a cup and took his own, settling himself on his haunches. Cradling the warm cup, he sipped and looked at her through steam, waiting.

"Nothing like hot coffee to take the chill off the day, eh Lord?"

"Nothing, Lady—it's a gift of the Infinite."

They smiled at each other.

Seeking Sword found himself liking her.

"May I inquire, Lord, about my daughter Trickling Stream?"

Seeking Sword nodded. "She's doing well, considering the recent death of her mate the Lord Elk. I've asked her to act as liaison between us, Lady, if that would please you."

"Thank you, Lord, yes. I'd have suggested the same. Would you give her my condolences, please?" Rippling Water sipped her coffee.

"I'd be happy to, Lady, and any other message you might want to send her." He smiled at her, steam shrouding his face.

"Thank you, Lord. You're nothing like what I expected."

"Oh, and what was that, Lady?"

"An uncultured, uncouth bandit, please forgive me."

"What is there to forgive, Lady? My being a bandit doesn't mean I act like a rogue. Being the Lord Emperor Sword, I find the arts of war easier to master than the arts of peace. Hence, I've studied peace more intently than war—specifically, how to bring peace to my land."

"Some would say that to bring peace, one must war. Don't you agree?"

"No, Lady, please forgive me, I don't."

"Then, please excuse me, Lord, why has your army mobilized along the border?"

Seeking Sword laughed gently, his liking increasing. "I ordered them to mobilize because I thought I might need them, Lady. I know now that I don't."

"Then the Lord Flaming Arrow humbly asks that you demobilize, Lord."

"I'll consider it, Lady."

"Please excuse me, Lord, what is there to consider?" she asked blankly.

"Your bargaining skills are as sharp as I've been told, Lady. I'll think about demobilizing," he said, equally ingenuous.

She chuckled softly. "Come with me, Lord." Abruptly, she set down her cup, stood and stepped away from the house.

He followed, wondering what this signified. Has she reached a decision about me? he wondered, strolling beside her, a mere pace separating them.

The manicured lawn and trimmed hedges beneath a canopy of tree looked as if they extended far into the distance. An illusion? he wondered, noting that the placement of tree and shrub limited what he could see to fifty or so paces. Birds sang in the trees and butterflies bounced from flower to flower. He felt the presence of the Infinite in this peaceful place.

"My mate the Lord Arrow sent a message to me, explaining who you were and why you've come. Forgive me, Lord. I need to ask you several questions to confirm that you are, indeed, the Lord Emperor Sword. Your disguise is very good. It doesn't hide your lack of psychic signature or your voice, as Burning Arrow already noticed. However, the content of my mate's message is, well, simply not credible. I … don't know if I believe most of it …" Rippling Water sighed. "I don't know what to think. I just don't know."

Seeking Sword nodded, sympathizing. "I find it difficult to believe too, Lady. You may ask me anything you wish—even if it's impolite."

"Thank you. Star, my servant, what does she know, Lord?"

"Singing Star thinks that her infant son died in place of Flaming Arrow's twin brother twenty years ago. A bruised, broken pinky is the basis of her information. Odd, isn't it, that the fate of Empires may rest on so little?"

"Indeed, Lord. What's Spying Eagle's real name?"

"Percipient Mind, Lady."

"What is the name of the book?"

He smiled, knowing she didn't refer to the Book of the Infinite. "*One Mind, Two Bodies: Identical Twin Contact.* The passage that the Lord Arrow read aloud really shook me. '… unless separated by insurmountable obstacles, such as extreme distance, all twins reported having an awareness of his brother or her sister, mostly through dreams,' " he quoted.

She sighed. "Thank you for being so cooperative, Lord Sword." She turned to look at him directly. "Do you think you're Flaming Arrow's brother?"

"It's a strong possibility, Lady, yes," he said simply.

"Infinite take that whelp of a dog and reincarnate him as a tapeworm!" She looked furious.

He guessed she referred to Flying Arrow. "The Lord Emperor did what he had to do, Lady. Even so, in some ways I wish I'd grown up in Emparia Castle."

She frowned at him. "You're not angry, Lord?"

"Of course, I am, Lady. More than angry, though, I feel sad. I lost more than I'll ever know because he condemned me to life as a bandit. I've gained in some ways too, though, eh? I've heard Flaming Arrow's life at the castle wasn't the epitome of happiness." He laughed. "Remember what your mother said in predicting Flowering Pine's pregnancy during the negotiations?"

Rippling Water chuckled. " 'One would be too few.' Everyone thought it meant that one twin would die."

"They did. No one thought that perhaps it meant that one son would be too few to rule two Empires, eh?"

Nodding, she looked at him. "Infinite help me, I like you, Lord Sword. You remind me very much of my mate. I wish … I knew you better. I hope, when all of this is past, that we can become friends."

"I hope so, too, Lady Water. You honor me that you think so well of me."

They smiled at each other and walked companionably beside each other, both silent and both lost in thoughts of their own.

"I want to hate you, you know," she said.

"I certainly deserve it," he replied. "I'm sorry you suffered. I wish I hadn't thought that all those reprehensible acts were necessary. I was wrong. I ask your forgiveness."

Rippling Water looked at him, as if to see if his sentiment was genuine.

He heard sounds behind them and looked.

The servant, Star, came toward them. "Forgive me my disturbing you, Lady. Someone is here to see you."

"Who is it, please?"

"The Lady Consort Flowering Pine. She asked me to tell you that she's sorry she came unannounced, Lady, and said she'd understand if you're not available." She kept her gaze nervously on the ground.

"Would you tell the Lady Consort that if she'll wait, I'll be happy to see her? Please extend my apologies for the unconscionable delay. Other matters occupy my attention."

"Yes, Lady," Star said, bowing and quailing under Seeking Sword's stare. She turned toward the house.

"Star," Seeking Sword said.

She stopped, visibly frightened. She wouldn't look at him.

"I'm sorry your son died," he said. "I feel a great remorse that he died in another's place."

Only then did she look at him, struggling to control her features. "Thank you, Lord …?"

"Soon, you will know, Star. For now, be at peace, if you can."

"Thank you," she whispered. With a glance at Rippling Water, she bowed and retreated, looking relieved but a bit bewildered.

"I guess I scared her. I didn't intend to. Her son died in my place. Could I, uh, talk with her later, Lady?"

"I'd prefer that you didn't. She's frightened that those who killed her son will kill her for telling Flaming Arrow what she knows."

"All right, then. I guess on some level I'm still struggling to believe her." Seeking Sword shrugged.

"It'd be easier not to, wouldn't it?" She looked at him again as they resumed their stroll. "The Lady Consort Flowering Pine claims that your mate Purring Tiger had Melding Mind implant my brother."

The Bandit nodded. "She's ... not a nice person, sometimes. Terrible, all that we do to each other, eh?"

Nodding, Rippling Water frowned. "She's my sister."

"Eh?" Seeking Sword stared at her, surprised. "What'd you say?"

"Another of those terrible acts. My father went north nine months before I was born. He'd planned to end the feud between himself and Scowling Tiger. Fleeting Snow intercepted him and convinced him to fornicate with her. Nine months later, Purring Tiger was born."

"Who told you *that*?" he asked.

"My father." She shook her head, frowning. "We have an endless legacy to put behind us, don't we? All those killings and betrayals, the plots and counter-plots, the spies and assassins."

Sighing, Seeking Sword contemplated a cloudy sky. A drop of rain spotted his cheek. "We *will* move beyond it all, eh? I want the feuds to end. I want peace between our Empires. We have a chance at peace now, with my brother and I ruling our respective realms. We won't convince everyone, and we won't bring peace tomorrow, but we'll have it. Eventually, we'll have peace."

"You're very confident, Lord Sword."

"Am I? I don't *feel* confident."

Smiling, she sighed deeply, as if preparing.

"Lord Emperor Sword, my mate says that he'll adhere to your plan as you outlined it to Spying Eagle. He has asked me to help you, which I do at his behest despite the risk of treason."

"Eh?" he interrupted. "Treason?"

She stopped and looked at him. "Treason," she repeated. She then resumed strolling. "Were you going to rely on your Broken Arrow contacts?"

Seeking Sword nodded.

"That's what he thought," Rippling Water continued. "He'd prefer that you didn't, because they're splitting apart. You'll never know who supports whom, at least not for awhile. I'll get you whatever you need—weapons, uniforms, information, anything.

"Furthermore, I've asked the Lord Wolf for the use of a room with its own entrance. There's one in the basement that my father often used for his couriers. It has a secret entrance so you can come and go unobserved. You're welcome to stay there if that's what you want.

"Flaming Arrow would like you to order your armies to retreat, because the Lord Emperor Arrow might decide to mobilize. Flaming Arrow is sure someone will tell his father that your 'reforestation' is simply a ruse. He wants to avoid hostilities if at all possible.

"In two days, at dawn, Flaming Arrow will cross the border alone. Spying Eagle and Healing Hand will also cross the border, but elsewhere. They both want to see their fathers. Flaming Arrow hopes that they'll be able to do so without interference. Flaming Arrow wants you to inform Trickling Stream and Slithering Snake that he'll be coming. He asks that you don't inform your mate Purring Tiger or the General Raging River, who both have compelling reason to kill him, eh?

"Furthermore, Flaming Arrow says he'll pursue the outline of the plan for as long as he can, even if the result isn't what you expected. He says he's not impatient and has no reason to hurry.

"Finally, Seeking Sword, Flaming Arrow says that he's looking forward to meeting you. He asks that you walk with the strength and guidance of Infinite."

Smiling, the Bandit felt his hope soar. He looked up into the soft drizzle, enjoying the feel of the rain, the exhilaration of the moment. He'd gotten far more than he'd expected. He knew without doubt that his brother was his ally. If Flaming Arrow was his brother. "Thank you, Lady Water. Shall we walk back to the house?"

Nodding, she turned around, watching him.

He turned with her, oblivious to her and at peace with himself. "Beautiful day, isn't it?" he said as the rain grew stronger.

"Yes, it is," she said, as if understanding he was elsewhere.

"The room would be perfect, Lady. When you have a free moment, we can discuss what I need. Right now, I think I want to ..." He chuckled. "I don't want to do anything right now. Would you mind if I wandered here in the gardens for awhile?"

"No, Lord Sword, not at all. I'll instruct Star to take you to your room when you decide to come in." She looked up. "From the rain."

He smiled. "Thank you, Rippling Water."

"Thank you, Seeking Sword. Infinite be with you."

"And with you," He said, bowing to her, and watched her walk away.

Then he forgot about her, turned, and walked away from the house, his face to the sky. The rain of release and renewal washed the salt from his eyes.

Chapter 20

VENDETTA IS a cruel gauntlet, enslaving both the agent and recipient under the scourge of strike and counterstrike, flogging both onto more severe retaliation with the whip of hatred and intolerance, each lash laid upon wounds barely healed, further fomenting the spiraling cycle of reprisal, until the original transgression is a forgotten blur and the requiters resemble raw masses of flayed flesh, the gauntlet rarely killing early.—*Lex Talionis: The Unlawful Law*, by the Sectathon Wizard Probing Gaze.

* * *

Rippling Water hurried toward the house, liking Seeking Sword, wishing she could talk with him more, knowing she would later.

Flowering Pine awaited her.

Dread stirred in her bowels. Walking briskly toward the house, Rippling Water passed the fountain. Many years before, her mother had built the fountain for her spiritual contemplation. The Prefect Wolf had thought it so beautiful he'd kept it.

The sight of the fountain resonated with the memories her mother had bequeathed her. Rippling Water had assumed the management of the Matriarchy during the last years of her mother's life, preparing for the day she'd become the Matriarch herself. That day had come sooner than anyone expected.

Remembering the Consort's revelation four days before, Rippling Water sighed. She'd tortured and killed her brother for his murder of their mother. No one had known at the time that an implant had driven Running Bear's behavior. No one had known that Purring Tiger and Melding Mind had arranged Bubbling Water's death to kill Guarding Bear.

Stopping briefly by the fountain and closing her eyes, the Matriarch Water prayed for forgiveness from the Infinite, knowing she'd acted on what she'd known at the time. Oh, Lord Infinite, give me the strength! she thought in anguish, not wanting to hate her own sister, not wanting to hate her father, not wanting to hate herself.

"I wouldn't want my grandchildren to become the third generation of victims in a conflict that appears to have no end," Flowering Pine had said that night.

I don't either, Rippling Water told herself. Throughout her childhood, her father had been the target of so many assassins that he'd lost count, Scowling Tiger having sent most of them. I want my children to grow up without having to look over their shoulders for the enemy's next minion, she thought.

Her resolve gathered inside her. She let her eyes slide closed, feeling the strength of the Infinite flow into her from the fountain inside her heart. She could do it. She could and would forgive her sister, forgive her father, forgive herself. She could forgive her mate's mother, for revealing that she, Rippling Water, had killed her innocent brother Running Bear. His only fault had been letting the bandit Wizard implant him.

Rippling Water entered the rear door of the house, where Star met her. When talking with the woman about finding her a place to live, she discovered that Singing Star was a servant by occupation. Rippling Water had asked her to serve her for now, until she could arrange another position under a different identity.

"When the Lord Nightmare comes in from the rain," Rippling Water instructed, "show him to that room we prepared in the basement. Is the Lady Consort still waiting?"

"Yes, Lady, in the central room. The children have kept her entertained."

She frowned. "Tell her I'll be there in a few minutes. Please convey my apologies. I need to change." Her wet clothes clung to her. "Thank you, Star."

"My pleasure is to serve, Lady," Singing Star said, bowing.

What else does Flowering Pine know? Rippling Water wondered.

Bubbling Water's memories inside her protested that the woman whom she and Flaming Arrow had come to know in less than a week wasn't the Imperial Consort. Bubbling Water had known a vacuous, loquacious Flowering Pine who regretted she became a noble, who kept herself shut away in her private suite high in Emparia Castle, who seemed not to care about her only son.

Could she have changed so much? When had she become so intelligence, so caring?

A memory emerged from the thousands Bubbling Water had bequeathed her. The twins were only minutes old, in the infirmary of Emparia Castle where one twin would die—or seem to die—three days later. Shading Oak told Bubbling Water what she'd learned from other servants in the House of Oak about the former servant Flowering Pine.

As she entered her rooms, Rippling Water shivered, an idea gathering force like a tornado off the winds of her thoughts. Think carefully now, she admonished herself, stripping off wet clothes.

Flowering Pine was subject to neurological disorders, claiming only a mild epilepsy but receiving treatment for those disorders from a psychological Wizard throughout her early childhood. Brazen Bear's daughter, himself a subversive and perhaps, once, the leader of the Broken Arrows. The sister of Flaming Wolf, Flaming Arrow's Broken Arrow contact. Her presence in Cove coinciding with an increase in Broken Arrow activity. Seen ordering a shipment of arrows ambushed on its way from Cove to Burrow. Overheard having whispered conversations with an unknown entity in the middle of the night. Garnering the attentions of a man far above her own station. Charmed from that man a suite of twenty rooms in Emparia Castle, a servant staff of a hundred, elevation to noble status, and exclusive rights to his attentions. Coaxing a pair of arrows from Flying Arrow's quiver, proven empty many times. Protected by a talent curiously strong, impenetrably strong. Displaying the same charisma that had gotten her father killed, a charisma engendered by talent. Changing after the delivery, bestowing half her psychic reserve on each child despite claiming to have no control over her talent. Acquiring characteristics no one would ever expect from her.

Coming here to see her grandchildren.

As she finished drying her hair, Rippling Water struggled to tame the tornado of thought howling through her, the winds of conclusion uprooting the trees of her soul.

I don't believe I'm thinking this! she thought, shocked, but cinching her sword to her side with a fresh sash, as if she might need the weapon.

Walking into the central room, she felt dismayed. Each of her children sat on the floor on either side of Flowering Pine, the three of them talking and laughing.

"Trickling Water, Burning Arrow," she said. The two children looked toward her, their laughter dying. "Come sit behind me please."

The girl, only four years old, asked, "Why are you scared, Mommy?"

She'd never been able to hide anything from them, their psychic receptors able to scan nearly the entire bandwidth. Mindshields were diaphanous veils to them. Only electrical shields could keep them out of a person's mind. They were too young yet to have learned discretion.

"I ... Can I tell you later?" she asked, gesturing them over.

The children both obeyed.

Rippling Water bowed to Flowering Pine, stopping the flame-haired woman's approach. The Matriarch guessed that the Consort, who appeared flustered, had wanted to embrace her.

"Infinite be with you, Lady Consort," Rippling Water said, emphasizing the older woman's position deliberately, wanting the distance. "Forgive me, Lady, for not seeing you immediately. An indisposition afflicted me when you arrived."

"Infinite be with you, Lady ... Matriarch." Flowering Pine wore fine silk robes with grass-green and wheat-gold stripes. She didn't looked armed, but probably had some weapon secreted on her person. "No apology necessary, Lady Matriarch. I'm sorry to have come without asking first. I pray I haven't inconvenienced you."

"Not at all, Lady Consort. It's an honor that you'd visit."

"Grandma," Trickling Water said, "can I tell Mommy 'bout you?"

"No, child," Flowering Pine said gently. "Please, let me tell your mother, eh? Thank you, that's very considerate." She turned her attention back to Rippling Water. "I meant what I said when I told my son I wished to see my grandchildren more often. Although I rejoice that the Infinite has blessed you with a pair of wonderful children, their talents have kept me from seeing them. I see that that puzzles you. Perhaps I should explain."

Confused, Rippling Water frowned.

"Forgive me if I'm blunt, Lady. I don't have the patience for ritual today. I feel ... hurried for some reason. Trickling Water? Sit beside me, child."

"No!" Rippling Water said before she could stop herself.

The Consort looked sadly at the Matriarch, then at the girl. "Do as your mother says, child. Yes, I know. It saddens me, but we'll put that aside soon."

Rippling Water hadn't detected a whisper of energy between them. Furthermore, Flowering Pine didn't have conscious control of her talents—or so she'd always said. She stared at the Imperial Consort, frightened now.

"My child, my child," Flowering Pine said compassionately. "I don't mean to scare you. I'm sorry. I'd wager you know already, but I'll tell you openly. I've hidden for too long and don't want to hide anymore. Rippling Water, my name is Breaking Arrow."

Her terror consuming her, she drew her sword and began to lunge—but found herself sheathing her sword and sitting back down. She struggled against the Consort's awesome power in vain. "How ... did you do that?"

"I'm Breaking Arrow," she replied, shrugging.

The power of the legendary Breaking Arrow is real, she thought.

Rippling Water submitted, knowing her own talents useless. Her primary talent amplification, she could only increase someone else's expenditure. Unlike her father, she had no control over the direction and composition of ambient psychic energy, merely over its intensity. She couldn't diminish that intensity, only intensify it.

"Ah, you've concluded that your talent can only work against you. Please believe, my child, that I won't harm you if I can possibly do otherwise. Truly, I want only to help you."

"Help me? I don't understand, Lady. You're Breaking Arrow. You've committed your life to end Arrow Sovereignty. You can't possibly want—"

"You truly don't understand, do you?" Flowering Pine interrupted. "The Lord Emperor Arrow has an empty quiver. He *always* has shot pointless arrows and always will. Your mate isn't and never was his son. Yes, I'm Breaking Arrow. Yes, I've committed my life to ending Arrow Sovereignty. When Flying Arrow dies, I'll have accomplished my goal. Unfortunately, I regret the methods I've chosen to reach that goal. I'm ashamed of what I've done in the name of resistance to Arrow Sovereignty. If I thought slitting my belly would atone for it all, I'd have disemboweled myself long ago. That would've only added to my dishonor, though." The Consort sighed, looking sad as if lamenting her past.

Rippling Water struggled to understand. "Flaming Arrow said after talking with you in the audience hall that you were the most incredible person he'd ever met." Looking down into her lap, Rippling Water frowned, confused. "He ... I'm so angry that you've never treated him like a son!" She looked up at the woman, knowing now what she needed to say. "How could you ignore him all these years!?" She knew her voice was beginning to get loud. "You don't know, you *can't* know how hurt he was when he came away every week from your blasted sanctuary without the simple affection he so desperately needed from you! I dreaded those 'visits,' because when they were over, my mother or I'd have to console him and lie to him and tell him again and again that you did love him but just couldn't show it!" She knew she was yelling now, and she couldn't stop herself. "You were never there to see how he wanted to believe us so badly that it tore me apart inside and all I could do was hate you silently because he never wanted to hear a harsh word against you. Oh, dear Lord Infinite, help me still my tongue!"

She put her hands over her mouth, the fire in her eyes saying what she wouldn't let escape from her lips.

Flowering Pine simply nodded, looking old. "You're right," she said, her voice quiet. "I've struggled with my decision to tell you and my son for a long time. I ... don't blame you for being angry. I would too. I'm sorry that you are. I'm more sorry that I haven't been the mother my son needed. I decided to tell you first because I thought you'd be more understanding—and because telling my son will be much more difficult. I didn't mean to upset you. Forgive me if you can, Lady Water." Flowering Pine bit her lip, her eyes glistening. "Please excuse me for disrupting your day. I'll go now." She bowed more deeply than her station merited, then stood and stepped toward the antechamber.

Struggling with herself, Rippling Water said, "Lady Pine?"

The Consort stopped, but didn't turn.

"It's … raining, Lady. Would … would you … like a … cup of coffee … before you go?"

Chapter 21

A TRENCH GOUGED the meadow beside the road. The long line of bodies carried by the levithons split into several segments, each segment as long as the trench. Without much ceremony, the levithons lowered each segment into it, parallel to each other. Bodies filled a trench just deep and wide enough to hold them all.

From one end I watched the levithons move tons of earth over the bodies, piling it up high above the level of the road. Burial isn't our custom. We simply couldn't have burned so many bodies. Corpses would've rotted before we could've burned half of them. Burial was our only alternative.

Tears poured anew from my eyes as they covered the mass grave over. Stone masons were erecting a monument nearby, a simple arch over the road, on it a simple inscription: "Here lie 3214 bandits, killed by Empire in the Year of the Infinite, 9303."

How could I know that fifteen years later, fully ten times that number of bandits would die, also killed by Empire?—*Personal Accounts of Events before the Fall*, by Keeping Track.

* * *

Breathing roughly, Flaming Arrow slowed, approaching the twin towers of the Tiger Fortress. They looked no different from the way they had looked in his dream at the hostelry, and no different from the first time he'd seen them, five years before. He knew one of them had collapsed in an earthquake four years ago, killing the menagerie tiger. They must have replaced it, he thought.

Between them emerged a large man in purple and green, a single-sword insignia at the left breast. Entwined around the sword was a snake.

This is the man whom Seeking Sword instructed me to find, Flaming Arrow thought. Peering through the rain, he bowed. "Lord Snake, Infinite be with you." He threw back his hood. Flaming Arrow wore no disguise.

Bowing deeply, Slithering Snake looked at him carefully. "And with you, Lord Arrow," the sectathon said. Slithering Snake examined Flaming Arrow's face closely, disbelief on his own. "Incredible," he said, slowly shaking his head. Behind him, another man emerged from the ravine.

"The Lord Emperor Sword sends his greetings," Slithering Snake said. "Although he instructed me to extend to you all the hospitality we usually accord to a visiting dignitary, we don't have time for amenities. We need to go to Seat immediately. The Lord Sword asks that you remain armed and on guard until we've resolved everything. The Lord Flashing Blade and I will stay near you for the entire time you're here. We'll accompany you wherever you go. My hope is that you will regard this as an honor, rather than an inconvenience—or at worst, an insult."

"Your guarding me is an honor, Lord Snake." Flaming Arrow turned to the other man. "It's an honor to meet you, Lord Blade. To have the fastest swordsman in the Northern Empire guarding me is an honor I don't merit."

Small, black-eyed and brown-haired, the other man walked slowly and fluidly, as if economizing on each motion. "Infinite be with you, Lord Flaming Arrow. It's my honor to meet *you*. You're much too kind to this modest warrior."

"You're much too humble, Lord Blade. I'll feel more secure having both of you near, Lords."

Flashing Blade regarded him silently in the rain, as if assessing him. "You're very much like him, Lord Arrow." The man then looked at his companion. "Lord Snake, shall I lead?"

"Please, Lord Blade," the sectathon said. "If you'll follow, Lord?"

Flaming Arrow nodded, secretly relieved he wouldn't have to enter the fortress. Only once before had he been inside, when he'd assassinated the bandit general Scowling Tiger.

The memory-laden place felt forbidding.

"What's the hurry, Lord Snake, if I may ask?"

"The Lord Sword wants you to witness events, Lord Arrow."

The three men started north, their feet splashing in water running too slowly off the elevated road. "How am I to do that?"

"The psychic projector in Seat, Lord."

"I've heard about that, heard it violates all the ancient proscriptions against talismans. What *is* it, though?"

The rain intensified. Flaming Arrow pulled his hood back over his head.

"It translates the flow into visual and audio signals. The Lord Leaping Elk thought of it, to enable the Lord Emperor Sword to see and hear first-hand the important news that everyone else—except you—can find out simply by consulting the flow."

"I wish *I* had one of those!"

Slithering Snake chuckled. "Anyway, Lord, Raging River has just crossed the border under the Inviolate Insignia. He'll time his arrival at Emparia Castle with our 'capture' of you. By that time, if all goes well, the Lord Emperor Arrow will have captured Seeking Sword."

"Has he changed plans?" Flaming Arrow looked up, into the rain. The forests on either side of the road began to encroach, but ahead the road widened.

"Yes, Lord. He has more allies now, and he sees an opening in your father's armor."

"His thrust for the jugular will come without hesitation."

"That's what he plans, Lord." Slithering Snake smiled.

Flaming Arrow still didn't know what to think about his twin brother. He'd had little time to assimilate that he had one. If he is my twin brother, he thought. "The Lord Colonel Probing Gaze tells me you're slippery as a snake."

The large sectathon laughed. "How is the Lord Gaze, eh? When you see him, tell him that I miss those days when he commanded that battalion at Burrow Garrison."

"Happily, Lord Snake, but I hope that you can tell him yourself."

"I hope so as well, Lord Heir."

The three men trudged companionably north through the rain. Flaming Arrow contemplated the day when they might be friends instead of enemies. He didn't object to Slithering Snake's addressing him as the Heir. He'd held the position so long it was unthinkable that anyone else could be Heir. Even so, he admonished himself to remember that he wasn't the Heir. Since he was actively helping the Emperor Seeking Sword, he might never again wield the Eastern Heir Sword. As Guarding Bear had said two days ago in Bastion, Flaming Arrow's helping Seeking Sword was a form of treason.

Guarding Bear had left the room to avoid listening to their treason. Flaming Arrow had known that in some respects the old General had been right. Treason and loyalty were opposite edges of the same knife, loyalty to one cause being treason against another. Later that evening, after Healing Hand had spoken with him, Guarding Bear had apologized to him.

* * *

"I'm sorry, Lord Arrow," the General said, a deep sadness in his eyes. "When I stomped from the room, I told myself the only way I could stop you was to tell your father what you planned to do. I guess that you suspected I might, eh? I would have, but—" He suddenly bit his lip.

"Listen, Flaming Arrow," Guarding Bear continued, suddenly looking much older and much smaller. "I'll always support you in what you do. I may not agree, as in this instance, but I know you'll do what you think is right. *That's* what I support. I always have. Thank the Infinite we've never disagreed over anything important. I hope the Bandit's plan works and that he is, as you suspect, your brother. I want you to have a close friend when the Infinite takes me onward, a friend from whom you need conceal nothing."

"If he's my identical twin, I *couldn't* conceal anything, eh? Besides, you'll live forever, Guarding Bear. Didn't you know that?" Flaming Arrow grinned at him. "By the way, why'd you change your mind? What did Healing Hand say to you?"

"Remember the other night, when he fell on top of my bear?"

Flaming Arrow nodded, curious.

"Infinite blast! I promised I wouldn't tell. Listen, Lord, Healing Hand will tell you when the moment's appropriate, eh?"

"That's what he said, and I trust that he will," Flaming Arrow replied. "Why'd he tell *you* already?"

"My appropriate moment came before yours did." Then, a wealth of joy in his eyes and beneath it a little sadness, Guarding Bear threw his arms around him and hugged him tightly. "I love you, Flaming Arrow."

"Did you hear me, Lord?" the larger man asked, running beside him.

Flaming Arrow returned to the present, to the pouring rain on a road in the Northern Empire. "Forgive me, Lord Snake, no. I was ... elsewhere."

"The Lord Sword has sent us several messages during the last few days. Are you truly his brother, Lord Arrow?"

"Yes, Lord Snake, I think I am," Flaming Arrow said. "Tell me about Seeking Sword. What's he like?"

The sectathon smiled. "How can I describe someone I've known all his life? I remember him as an infant a few days old, as a five-year old boy with a sword as long as he was tall, as a long-limbed youth with a nearly indomitable sword arm. He's many people, Lord Arrow, and he's more than them all. What can I tell you?"

Nodding, Flaming Arrow smiled. "Ambiguous question, wasn't it? Tell me about the first day you saw him."

"His father, Icy Wind—who we all found out later was Lofty Lion—brought him to the Elk Raider cave a few days after he was born. The three of us, Leaping Elk, Fawning Elk and me, were discussing your brother's and Lurking Hawk's deaths. We were speculating that the Traitor had finally betrayed your father by killing your brother. Is it true that Flying Arrow faked his death?"

Trudging beside the large man, Flaming Arrow couldn't have said much was true. Too much had changed too quickly for him to say he knew anything for certain, anymore. Regardless, he said, "Yes, I think it's true. Go on, Lord Snake, I'd like to hear this."

"Yes, Lord. Icy Wind appeared with the crying infant boy, claiming that the mother of his child had died in the earthquake. He said that he couldn't get the boy to eat. Fawning Elk had just given birth to Rearing Elk and offered to feed the infant. The malodorous man moved in to the Elk Raider cave for about a year, until she weaned the boy. That old man had such a stench that I thought about living elsewhere!"

Flaming Arrow smiled. "How did you discover he was Lofty Lion?"

"Several factors, Lord," Slithering Snake said. "Shortly before you were born, the menagerie tiger collided with Icy Wind and knocked the staff from his hand. The tiger saw the circuits and told Leaping Elk, who guessed that Lurking Hawk had made the staff. After you were born, Leaping Elk concluded that Icy Wind was a Northerner from the expressions he used. Such as 'sharper than a lion's claws' or 'thick as a lion's mane'—expressions common during Lofty Lion's reign, eh? Lurking Hawk wouldn't make such a complex talisman for an unimportant, stench-ridden old man who looked as if he wouldn't live another year. Who else could Icy Wind be but Lofty Lion? He certainly *acted* like an Emperor! Haughty and disdainful—to everyone."

Flaming Arrow nodded, remembering his dream about the staff. "The designer constructed the staff to obey anyone with a certain signature. I'd guess Lurking Hawk used it to control Lofty Lion."

"How do you know that, Lord?"

"I dreamt about the staff on the night of Aged Oak's assassination. In my dream I emulated the signature and disabled the circuits. I woke the next morning without the bruises he gave me."

Slithering Snake glanced at him sharply. "I met the Lord Sword at the fortress the next morning. He looked as if someone had beaten the Infinite out of him. His injuries were nearly the same as those Aged Oak inflicted on you, Lord."

Flaming Arrow nodded. "That's one example in which our purported talents protected us, one reason we think we might be identical twins."

Grunting, the large sectathon lapsed into his own thoughts.

Flaming Arrow was grateful for the reprieve. His legs propelled him northward through rain-drenched forest. "If this rain continues, we'll have another flood."

"Hopefully, the roads won't wash out again," Flashing Blade said over his shoulder.

"You're having problems too? Is that why Seeking Sword ordered the Windy Mountains reforested?"

"That's the reason, Lord. The denuding of the mountains over the past thirty-five years is probably the reason that the River Placid flooded two years ago. So much alluvia chokes the river that the water has no place to go except over the levees. I'd suggest when you return south—"

"That we begin the reforestation of the southern Windy Mountains."

"Yes, Lord."

Flaming Arrow sighed. If he had an Empire to which to return. I've gained a brother, but what have I lost? he wondered, remembering his mentor's words. "I've never won a duel, battle, or war without paying for what I won." Would the price that he paid for gaining a brother be losing his Empire? If that weren't the price, what *would* he pay?

To reduce his anxiety, he began to meditate with the monotony of travel. He focused on the wet surface of road that slipped continuously past him. Within he searched for that source of strength on which he'd recently drawn so much. The love of the Infinite began to fill him. His eyesight narrowed to a distant point of light. The sounds his ears heard withered to whispers. The smell of wet woods receded. The feel of heavy raindrops became the touch of feathers.

When he returned to the present, the world had changed. They'd left the forests behind and now traveled across farmland.

Ahead, beyond an arch, was Seat, the center of the Northern Empire.

He slowed as they approached the arch, looking up at it. He felt he had seen it before, but he'd never seen it, not with these eyes.

Stopping, Flaming Arrow stood in the mud below the arch. Bowing his head, he prayed for the souls of the bandits he'd killed during his manhood ritual five years ago. Ten times the number who'd died in Guarding Bear's siege of the Tiger Fortress. "What a waste," he whispered in the rain, hating himself for what he'd done and aching inside for the more than thirty thousand dead.

Slithering Snake put his hands on Flaming Arrow's shoulders. "Forgive me, Lord. We have to hurry. Raging River has crossed the River Placid."

Nodding, Flaming Arrow collected himself. How can he be so gentle with the man who'd wrought such killing? "I wish … I hadn't thought it necessary," he said.

Seeking Sword had said the same of his own acts.

At the time Flaming Arrow hadn't believed his brother's words. He did now. In assassinating the bandit leaders, he'd sacrificed his own beliefs to his loyalty to the Eastern Empire. How easily I forgot that bandits are human beings first and very secondarily bandits, he thought.

Rising, Flaming Arrow looked at the two men. "I pray that killing on such a scale never occurs again."

His reservations on his face, Slithering Snake simply nodded.

Flashing Blade also looked doubtful.

Realizing he probably couldn't prevent it's happening again, Flaming Arrow turned and resumed the journey, Seat less than a mile distant.

At the gates of the city stood Fawning Elk. Her hair was dark brown; her features were pretty. Her robes were of quality make and thick with padding to ward off the cold. She was completely dry, standing in the pouring rain. "Infinite be with you, Lords," she said as they approached.

"And with you, Lady Elk," Flaming Arrow said, bowing to her.

Returning his obeisance as an equal, she searched his features with hazel eyes set wide on her face. "If you'll come with me,

Lord Arrow? My home is near the council amphitheater. You have time yet for a quick bath and a meal." Turning, she entered Seat, gesturing Flaming Arrow to walk beside her. The other two men fell behind.

"The Lady Matriarch Water sends her condolences on the death of your mate the Lord Elk," Flaming Arrow said. He noticed that she always walked on dry ground, and that the packed earth beneath his feet was also dry. A few feet away was the churned mud of a heavily-frequented, rain-soaked avenue.

"The Lord Emperor Sword has already sent the Lady's condolences. Thank you, Lord, Infinite bless you both." She glanced at him, a thousand questions in her eyes, her age plain only in their webbed corners.

"I've other messages for you, Lady Stream."

She smiled at him with what seemed an inner amusement. "Events in Emparia City may indispose us later, Lord. I'd like to hear them now please."

"As you wish, Lady," he replied, seeing her strength and resilience and liking her. "The Lady Matriarch formally absolves the Lady Trickling Stream and all her daughters of dishonor. Since the Lady Stream did not deviate from her loyalty in serving the Matriarchy, the Lady Matriarch Water invites, but doesn't require, her daughter to lead her life henceforth as she wishes, without restriction and without obligation to the Lady Matriarch Water."

Trickling Stream smiled, her silky brown hair flowing freely around her shoulders. "I think I'll do that, Lord. Thank the Lady Matriarch with all my gratitude—if you see her before I do, of course."

Laughing, Flaming Arrow nodded, knowing somewhere deep inside him that most of the strife between Bandit and Empire was over. "I'll do that, Lady. There's more. Shall I?" he asked.

She nodded for him to continue.

"The Lady Matriarch Water humbly asks you to consider becoming liaison between herself and the Lord Emperor Sword. She prefers that you make your decision without fear of punishment, without hope of reward."

"I had hoped she would ask, Lord. 'Happily,' you can tell her. You know that I practically reared the Lord Emperor Sword, don't you?"

"So I've heard, Lady. Was he as stubborn as I was?"

" 'Determined,' I'd call it, Lord."

They shared a laugh, knowing the distinction superfluous.

She looked at him and smiled. "I'm happy that you've found each other."

Flaming Arrow nodded, happy too.

He slowed with her as they approached a modest house. Farther down the street was a large building, a set of wide steps leading to double doors. Emblazoned above it was a single purple sword on a green background.

"That's the council amphitheater, Lord. This is my humble abode."

He followed her to the door and into a simple dwelling, the home smelling of good cooking and bountiful love. The two men followed and stayed in the central room while Fawning Elk led him to the excretory-bath. He began to strip off his sodden clothes. "Why didn't you get wet in all that rain?"

"My talent, Lord—dehydration." Smiling, she gestured at the excretory-bath. "You'll find everything you need here. Forgive me for not having a blue and white robe for you. I've brought one of Seeking Sword's, if you don't mind wearing purple and green."

"No," he said, chuckling, "I don't object at all."

"I didn't think you would, Lord. I'll return in a moment with food."

Nodding to her obeisance, Flaming Arrow dipped the sponge into a bucket of hot soapy water. Lathering himself, he blessed his brother's good fortune to have such caring friends.

Finished washing, he emptied the bucket, drew a full bucket of clear hot water from the bath and poured it over his head. Easing himself into nearly scalding water, he thanked the Infinite for hot baths, especially those that followed long journeys through rainstorms.

He relaxed, content.

"Here you are, Lord," said a beautiful, black-haired woman with penetrating gray eyes. Setting the platter beside the bath, she turned the bucket upside down. Sitting on it, she fixed her gaze on him as if to insure he ate every morsel.

"Thank you, Lady." Flaming Arrow sat up in the bath, picking up the plate. He thought for some reason he should know her name. "Where's the Lady Elk?"

"She's finding dry clothes for the Lords Snake and Blade. You traveled quickly, Lord. You must feel tired."

Shaking his head, he began to eat. "I've adjusted to extensive travel. Thank you for your concern. You're very kind." Her voice sounded familiar on some level of consciousness he couldn't name.

"It was nothing, Lord. You flatter this humble lady." She picked up his discarded clothes and weapons, hanging his sword on a wall peg.

Biting into hot chicken, he realized he felt so safe here that he hadn't kept his sword nearby. Already, he'd developed an implicit trust of his brother's friends, his nominal enemies. "May I ask your name, Lady?"

"Forgive me, Lord Arrow, I forgot to introduce myself. I'm Purring Tiger."

He nearly choked. Quickly, he swallowed and set the plate beside the bath.

"Isn't it to your liking, Lord Arrow?" she asked, mischief in her eyes.

"Uh, well, uh ... " She doesn't *look* dangerous, Flaming Arrow thought.

She looked solicitous. "I'm sorry, Lord. I'll bring you something else." She stepped toward the bath to take the plate.

"No, Lady Tiger, the food's delicious. It's just that I ... I expected you to be ... different."

She grinned. "Forgive me my mischief, Lord Arrow. I did that deliberately. I confess I wanted to see you squirm."

Still nervous, he frowned. "You *could* want my head off my shoulders. You certainly have reason enough."

"I do," she said factually, nodding. Then, wilting, she shrugged. "My mate the Lord Emperor Sword tells me that you're his brother, and that I need to forgive you. I guess I need to forgive ... quite a few people. Myself-included. Easing Comfort is treating me for ... for my symptoms. He suggested that I come here to ... to forgive you. I don't know if I can."

Watching this woman who killed faster than she blinked, he picked up the plate again. "I don't understand how you *could* forgive me. I'm sorry I killed your father. I wish I hadn't. I wish he were still alive, still a citizen, with a large family, many friends, and his self respect." Flaming Arrow looked down at his plate, then up at her. "Lady Tiger, your father was as loyal to the Empire as Guarding Bear."

Biting her lip, Purring Tiger eased herself back to the bucket and dropped her gaze to the floor. "Thank you, Lord," she said quietly.

Eating slowly, he contemplated the feud that had sprung from a simple rebellion against inequitable taxation. He found it difficult to believe that a single unfair law could, and did, engender two generations of vendetta and eventually claim almost a hundred thousand lives. The law of their society was *lex talionis*, the law of retaliation. As implemented, it had no restrictions, no limitation to its infectious spread. The law was more a pandemic than a code of behavior, leaving devastation behind.

We have to find a better way, Flaming Arrow thought fervently.

Fawning Elk strode into the excretory-bath. "Lord Arrow," she said, her manner grave, "It's time."

Rising from the bath, Flaming Arrow prayed for Seeking Sword's success.

Chapter 22

LL THE peoples of the four Empires, whether bandit or citizen, peasant or noble, poor or rich, young or old, regard the Inviolate Insignia as sacrosanct. During times of war, the Inviolate Insignia might establish truce in the midst of battle. During times of peace, the banner might lend inviolacy to the participants at negotiations. The single proscription of the Inviolate Insignia is simple and clear. This pennant protects all persons at functions over which it flies from all forms of interference by all parties inimical. The penalty for violating this proscription or for employing the standard for subterfuge is severe, the violators pursued and prosecuted more relentlessly than those who traffic in contraband talismans.—*Essays on Government*, by Guarding Bear.

* * *

"Lord Arrow," the thin, nasal voice said.

Seeking Sword rose from his obeisance and settled back on his haunches. The feel of the eastern audience hall in Emparia Castle was familiar despite his having never been here. "Infinite be with you, Lord Emperor Arrow." Seeking Sword looked closely at his reputed father—who shoots pointless arrows, he reminded himself.

With his gray-streaked brown hair, crimson laced blue eyes, five foot, six-inch height, thin arms, gaunt face, and weak chin, the Emperor needed every inch of the six foot pyramidal dais to look the least bit imposing.

Behind and above him shimmered an old silken tapestry depicting a quiver of arrows, blue and white the predominant colors. Seven arrows portrayed seven Emperors, each shaft distinct from the others. Woven into the tapestry more than thirty-five years ago was an arrow with white, glittering wings, representing the present Emperor.

"And with you, Lord," Flying Arrow said amiably. Then he frowned. "What are you doing here? I thought you'd gone north to silence that blasphemous Bandit."

Seeking Sword looked for some sign that Flying Arrow saw who he really was—and found none. "I wanted to say something to you, Lord Emperor Arrow. About that Bandit, and about the delegation on its way to the castle."

Under the Inviolate Insignia, a delegation had crossed the border at dawn and had entered Emparia City minutes before.

"What's that rogue Emperor Sword doing, anyway? I can't believe he'd have the unmitigated audacity to use the Inviolate Insignia! As though he *were* a legitimate Emperor, eh? No respect for custom or ceremony at all. They're probably assassins! When they violate the Insignia proscriptions, the East, West and South will fall on the North like wolves in a pen of sheep!" Flying Arrow laughed heartlessly.

The last time someone had abused the sanctity of the Insignia was at the negotiations between the Southern and Eastern Empires, twenty-one years before, when Guarding Bear had attacked Snarling Jaguar. Only the Southern Emperor's refusal to take offense had prevented the obliteration of the Eastern Empire.

"Yes, Father. They'll slit their own bellies, eh? I want to tell you something. Would you ask the others to leave, please? It's private."

"Eh? Private? Must be important. Begone, all of you!"

The guards lining the walls filed from the audience hall. The few castle officials who'd appeared out of curiosity also departed. As the last person left the hall, someone came through the door behind the dais. The woman was red-haired and tall, wore rich robes of pale blue, and walked with uncommon ease and dignity.

"Forgive me, Lady, I must ask you to leave," he said, not knowing her. She looked oddly, vaguely familiar, but he could not have said why.

"You can ask all you want," she said impertinently. "I stay."

"Eh?" Seeking Sword said, startled. "Who are you?"

"I'm your mother," she stated, looking puzzled. She strode to a forward corner of the dais, watching him closely.

Flying Arrow glanced between them, frowning. "Has the Infinite addled your brains so much that you don't even recognize your own mother?"

They were now alone in the audience hall—he, Flying Arrow, and Flowering Pine.

Seeking Sword had never seen her image on the psychic projector in Seat. He realized that last week first he and then she had met with the Matriarch Rippling Water successively. They had not met each other only by chance. "No, Father. I didn't recognize her because I haven't seen her in twenty years."

The man on the dais peered at him. "Twenty *years*? You're speaking nonsense, Flaming Arrow! You saw her two weeks ago!"

"No, Father, I'm not Flaming Arrow. Forgive me, I mustn't have introduced myself properly. My apologies. My name is Seeking Sword, and I'm Emperor of the Northern Empire."

Flying Arrow laughed heartily, as if appreciating a good joke. "That's hilarious, Flaming Arrow. I almost believed you for a moment. I didn't know you could be so funny. What did you want to tell me?"

Seeking Sword smiled. "I just told you, Father."

"What's he talking about, Flowering Pine?"

"I heard him say he's Seeking Sword, Lord Mate." She frowned and chewed on her lip.

"Has Guarding Bear's insanity infected you? Besides, you can't be my son *and* Seeking Sword, eh? Which are you? Decide, eh?"

"But, Father, I *am* your son and I *am* Seeking Sword."

Flying Arrow glanced at the ceiling and sighed. "Do *you* know what he's talking about?" he asked the woman.

"No, Lord Mate. Flaming Arrow, what are you talking about?"

"Lady Pine—Mother—forgive me for correcting you. I'm not Flaming Arrow. I'm your son Seeking Sword. Don't you recognize me?"

"I recognize Flaming Arrow," she replied, stepping toward him.

Seeking Sword glanced toward the ceiling. Of all the problems he'd anticipated, their refusal to believe him hadn't been among them. Well, soon now he wouldn't need to convince them. "Truly, Mother, Father, I'm the Emperor Seeking Sword."

Three paces away, Flowering Pine stopped to glance back at Flying Arrow, a frown wrinkling her brow.

"Come closer, Mother, if you don't believe me. I'm your son, Seeking Sword."

She stepped so close to him he could hear her breathe. "Incredible." She stepped back two paces and half-turned to look at Flying Arrow. "Lord Mate, he's … I don't know … All that I can truly say is that this young man is convinced of what he's saying."

"What?" Flying Arrow snorted. "What do you mean?"

"He truly believes what he's saying."

"So you believe you're the Lord Emperor Sword, eh Flaming Arrow?" Flying Arrow chuckled. "Not having the Heir Sword for a week appears to have addled your brains."

"On the contrary, Father. In fact, I've come to ask something from you. I want you to give me the Imperial Sword."

"Eh? You've come to usurp the throne?" Flying Arrow laughed out loud, this time derisively. "I always wondered when you would." He laughed again, then abruptly stopped. "You can't have it!"

"Forgive me for not being clear. I don't want *your* Imperial Sword, Father. I want the *Northern* Imperial Sword, the one you can't wield."

"The Infinite *has* addled your brains! It'll kill you, Flaming Arrow! Instantly!"

"No, it won't, Father. For fifteen years I've wielded the Northern Heir Sword, a long enough time to have prepared me to grasp the Imperial Sword, eh?"

Flying Arrow looked at him for a long, silent moment, a deep frown on his face. "That's enough, Flaming Arrow. If you don't stop this foolish charade, I'll invest Rolling Bear as the Heir and lock you in the dungeons until you decide to come to your senses."

Flowering Pine backed away another pace from him.

Seeking Sword smiled. "You'd imprison your own son, Father? Oh, yes, I forgot. You don't have any scruples anyway. If you'd fake the death of your own infant son and give him to the deposed Emperor Lofty Lion, then imprisoning that same son won't cause you a moment of insomnia."

Flying Arrow's face was blank.

Seeing the Emperor's expression, Flowering Pine turned to face Seeking Sword. "Is that servant's story true?"

"Yes, Mother, Singing Star told the truth."

"Oh, dear Lord Infinite, help us all. My son, If I'd known, I ... I'm sorry this happened. Can you ever forgive us?" She turned to face Flying Arrow. "How could you do this to me?! To *him*!"

"Eh? Are your brains addled too? Who's Singing Star? He's insane! Can't you see that?" Flying Arrow's face became flushed, and a vein pulsed at his temple.

From the door behind the dais rushed the Sorcerer Delving Thought. "Lord Emperor Arrow, forgive me for interrupting but the bandits have captured—" He saw Seeking Sword and stopped in mid-stride.

"Captured whom?" Flying Arrow asked irritably. "Spit it out, for Infinite's sake!"

"The Lord Heir Flaming Arrow, Lord," Delving Thought answered, staring still at Seeking Sword.

"Everyone's insane around here!" Flying Arrow shouted. "What's this nonsense, Lord Sorcerer? As you can see, Flaming Arrow's right here! How can the bandits have captured him, eh?"

"I don't ... I don't know, Lord. That ... doesn't make sense."

"I repeat, Father. I'm the Northern Emperor Seeking Sword and I want the Northern Imperial Sword. Please give it to me. *NOW*!" Blast them! he thought, getting angry.

"No, Flaming Arrow! I won't! I've decided!"

"Uh, Lord?" Delving Thought said meekly.

"What is it?"

"The, uh, bandits also claim that the Lord Emperor Sword has the Northern Heir Sword. They've broadcasted an image of it on the flow. It looks like it might be the Heir Sword. They demand that you give them the Imperial Sword."

"They're lying!" Flying Arrow roared. "Lofty Lion destroyed the Heir Sword thirty-five years ago!"

A servant rushed through the main double doors and bowed quickly. "Lord Emperor Arrow, the delegation from the north, they're asking … demanding entrance to the castle! What do we do?"

"Tell them to go to the Infinite."

"They … but they said they won't leave until you see them, Lord Emperor."

"I told you to tell them to go to the Infinite!"

"Yes, Lord Emperor Arrow." Bowing, the servant quailed under the wrathful gaze and left.

"You, Flaming Arrow!" the Emperor roared, pointing at Seeking Sword. "You cease this foolish … What happened to the shields?"

"They're down," Flowering Pine said. "The castle shields have fallen!"

"Sorcerer!" Flying Arrow bellowed. "Repair those blasted shields!"

"Yes, Lord Emperor." Delving Thought rushed from the audience hall, panic on his face.

Catching the open door, a man strode into the audience hall, truculent. Seeking Sword had seen his face many times on the psychic projector at Seat. "Lord Emperor," the Commanding General Scratching Wolf said, his obeisance less than obligatory. "I came as soon as I heard about the Heir's cap—" He stared at Seeking Sword. "I thought bandits captured you, Lord."

"I repeat, Father," Seeking Sword said, as if the General hadn't spoken to him. "I am the Emperor Seeking Sword and I demand that you give me the Northern Imperial Sword."

Scratching Wolf walked right up to him and peered into his face. "Your brains addled? I don't know whether to shit or vomit! Did you say you're Seeking Sword?"

"Who are *you*?" he asked rudely, staring at him haughtily.

"Don't you recognize me, boy? I'm your reputed grandfather, Scratching Wolf! What's the matter with him, Lord Emperor?"

"He's insane, Lord General. So's your daughter. She actually believes that nonsense," Flying Arrow said, sounding much calmer than he looked.

If the castle shields are down, Seeking Sword thought, then the Empire is now observing events in the castle on the flow.

Scratching Wolf frowned at Flowering Pine, then shook his head.

Guarding Bear—who Seeking Sword remembered had served as Security Commander of Emparia Castle for a single day more than twenty years before—entered the audience hall, grinning madly. "It was I who disabled the castle shields, Lord Emperor," he said.

"Why the Infinite did you do that, Lord Bear?" Flying Arrow asked.

The old General threw back his head and guffawed, face to the ceiling.

Through the double doors came the sound of a woman enraged. "Get the Infinite out of my way, blast you! Move, or I'll rip your testicles off and feed them to you!"

In strode Rippling Water, towing a frightened woman behind her. "Lord Emperor Arrow," she said, scowling. "The next time your monkeys try to keep me from seeing you, I'll decorate your walls with their brains!"

Wilting, Flying Arrow put his face in his palms. "What do *you* want?"

"I want to know what the Infinite you're going to do about my mate, Lord Emperor Arrow. Didn't you hear? Bandits have captured him! The flow is screaming with the news. You ought to listen to it on occasion. Why are the castle shields down, Lord?" She stopped beside Seeking Sword. "Infinite be with you, Lord Emperor Sword." She bowed to him, then looked at the Emperor Arrow. "Well?"

"Well, what?" Flying Arrow said. "What do you want *me* to do? Declare war or something?"

"They'll kill him if you do that!" Rippling Water said, looking frustrated. "Why don't you give them the Sword?"

"Eh? Infinite blast you, Lady Matriarch, that's treason!"

"Is it treason to preserve the life of your son?"

"I don't know! Why are you asking me? Ask him! Yes, your mate, Flaming Arrow, whom the bandits have supposedly captured!"

"Eh? Are your brains addled?" Rippling Water asked. "This isn't my mate!"

"Then who *is* it?"

"That's the Lord Emperor Sword. Can't you tell?"

"No, I can't tell!"

"Why not, Lord Emperor?" Rippling Water spat. "Is that because he's Flaming Arrow's twin brother? Is *that* why you can't tell them apart?"

"Flaming Arrow's brother died at three days old!" Flying Arrow shouted.

"You faked his death, you despicable bastard," she said, her voice calm.

"How dare you accuse me! I'll have your head for that! I'll—"

"I dare because I have proof!" she interrupted him.

Flying Arrow laughed at her. "Present your 'proof,' Lady!"

Rippling Water turned and began to speak to the woman behind her.

The entrance of the Northern Delegation interrupted her. At the head of a contingent garbed in purple and green strode the ancient Eastern expatriate Raging River, his sword loose in his hands, the blade half out of its scabbard. The Inviolate Insignia floating behind Raging River wouldn't stop him from taking heads.

Most everyone spread toward the sides of the hall to make way, only Seeking Sword and Rippling Water remaining where they were. The woman cowered behind Rippling Water.

"How'd you get in here? I thought I told you to go to the Infinite!"

"Coming here was worse, Lord Emperor Arrow," Raging River said gruffly, making no obeisance. He looked at the man beside him. "Infinite be with you, Lord Emperor Sword." The gristled General bowed deeply to him.

"Lord General River, a pleasure to see you." Grinning, Seeking Sword nodded to acknowledge the obeisance.

Raging River turned toward the dais. "Lord Emperor Arrow, I've come at the behest of the Lord Emperor Sword to negotiate a place and time for the exchange of prisoners."

"What prisoners, blast you!"

"The Northern Empire has captured the Heir Flaming Arrow. The Lord Emperor Sword has ordered me to arrange for the exchange of the Lord Heir for your prisoner, the Lord Emperor Sword."

"I haven't *taken* him prisoner." Flying Arrow looked exasperated. "I haven't taken any prisoners!"

"Then you'd better do so quickly, eh Lord?"

"How will I do that, eh? I don't even know where he is!"

"Eh? He's right here, Lord Emperor Arrow. Is your eyesight bad? Don't you recognize him?" Raging River turned to the man beside him. "Didn't you introduce yourself, Lord Emperor Sword? How disrespectful!" He turned toward Flying Arrow. "My apologies, Lord Emperor Arrow, for the uncouth behavior of this curmudgeon." Raging River gestured at Seeking Sword. "Please allow me to introduce the Lord Seeking Sword, son of Lofty Lion, wielder of the Northern Heir Sword and de-facto Emperor of the Northern Empire."

"That's not Seeking Sword," Flying Arrow protested. "That's Flaming Arrow!"

"You're wrong, Lord Emperor Arrow. Can't you tell the difference between your own son and the Lord Emperor Sword? Are your brains addled?"

250

"Of course I can. That's Flaming Arrow!"

"No, Lord Emperor Arrow, that's Seeking Sword!" Rippling Water said, stepping forward, dragging the woman with her. "This woman has proof that you faked the death of Flaming Arrow's infant twin brother!"

"You faked your own son's death?" Raging River asked, aghast.

"I didn't fake anyone's death," Flying Arrow said calmly.

"I have proof that you did, Lord Emperor!" Rippling Water said. "Tell him, Star."

"No!" Flying Arrow yelled, his face turning crimson. "Begone! All of you! This is my castle and I command you all to leave!"

"Tell him, Star!"

"Forgive me, Lord Emperor," Singing Star said meekly. "The … image of your … son … of your dead son … wasn't your—I can't, Lady, I can't say it! Please don't make me!" She put her face in her palms and sobbed with terror.

Flying Arrow laughed derisively, the sound inhumane.

The attention of those in the audience hall focused on Singing Star.

The hair on Seeking Sword's arms rose, as though from static electricity.

Puzzled, he whispered to Rippling Water, "What's happening?"

* * *

Energy began to gather. Those present and those beyond the castle observing on the psychic flow began to emanate confidence and sympathy. Singing Star looked up in awe. The energy began to build; courage infused her. Rippling Water amplified the energy, mentally encouraging the woman to speak, narrating to Seeking Sword in a whisper.

"What the Infinite's happening here?" Flying Arrow screamed.

Streaks of tears on her face, Singing Star looked at the Emperor. With the confidence and conviction of the psychic flow behind her, she said, "The boy who died wasn't your son, Lord Emperor Arrow. It was my son. Exploding Illusion took my baby and killed him. *My* son!"

"You're lying!" Flying Arrow raged, his left arm beginning to quiver. Lofty Lion had sliced into Flying Arrow's left shoulder in the final battle between Northern and Eastern Empires.

On the flow, the Empire questioned Singing Star. In a burst of repressed shame and despair, she bared her soul upon the flow, telling them all what'd happened twenty-one years ago. The citizens of Empire recoiled in righteous indignation and asked Flying Arrow if her story were true.

"I don't know what you're talking about!" Flying Arrow screamed at her. "You, Flaming Arrow, take that smile off your face! You look like the old insane General when you grin like that! Stop it, I say! Stop it!" The arm lashed out as if to strike something. "You're all insane, and you're trying to make me think I'm crazy, aren't you?! It's a conspiracy, isn't it? Isn't it!"

Twitching as if electricity coursed through it, the left arm danced spasmodically. "I know you're plotting against me! I can smell a plot when I'm drowning in a cesspool! It won't work! You can't fool me! I'll have every last one of you decapitated, your bodies obliterated, and all your sons and daughters executed! I refuse to succumb to your plot! It won't work, I tell you! It won't!" Suddenly he lay his right hand on the Sword.

Blinding electricity surged toward Seeking Sword.

A foot from the Bandit, a wall of energy stopped the electricity.

Flying Arrow gaped, his mouth a maw, his arm writhing. "Who did that?! Infinite blast you, I'll—"

"I did, Lord Emperor Arrow," Flowering Pine said. "My name is Breaking Arrow, I'm Brazen Bear's daughter, and I'm leader of the Breaking Arrows like my father before me."

Flying Arrow looked at her in disbelief. Everyone else watched his flailing left arm, the motion hypnotizing. The Emperor seemed not to notice, looking quickly from face to face as if expecting each person to attack him. "What do you want from me!" he screamed suddenly, his neck tendons straining as he leaned forward.

"I want the Northern Imperial Sword, Father," Seeking Sword said.

The flow reinforced the answer, and those in the room added their voices.

"What do you want from me!" he yelled again, staring at them through eyes just recognizably human.

"Give him the Sword!" an Empire replied.

"What do you want from me!" he yelled again, sweat pouring off him as if a storm had just drenched him.

"Give him the Sword!" an Empire yelled back at him.

"What do you want from me!" he yelled again, his left arm thrashing wildly, his back arching as if someone tortured him.

"Give him the Sword!" an Empire demanded.

"All right!" he screamed finally, gasping. "Let him have it, even if it kills him! Bring him the blasted thing," he said, his voice weakening. "He can have the Sword. Bring it to him, I say. Oh, please bring him the Sword," Flying Arrow pleaded, his voice a strangled sob. The left arm fell limp at his side.

An Empire sighed, suddenly quiescent. Those in the room waited, psychically following the progress of the four servants running to retrieve the Northern Imperial Sword.

"Medacor!" Seeking Sword called, not liking Flying Arrow's pallor.

"Here, Lord," a woman said, stepping forward. Her blond hair framed her drawn face. "Lord Emperor, may I approach?"

Flying Arrow nodded, looking defeated.

In the now unshielded treasure rooms of Emparia Castle, the Imperial Treasury was visible to all. The vast complex of rooms high in the castle looked nearly empty. In one room was a single object, a brass-colored Sword adorned with a ruby. The four servants entered and lifted the silk sheet on which the Sword lay. None of them touched it directly, as it would have killed them. The servants descended through the maze, making their way ever downward toward the eastern audience hall. Through the rear door they entered, bearing their precious load. Gently they lowered it to the floor in front of Seeking Sword.

He looked at it, then raised his gaze to Flying Arrow.

"Go on!" rasped the Emperor, slumped across the throne. "Isn't that what you wanted?!" His face was pale, his eyes hooded, his voice slurred.

Guarding Bear stepped up next to Seeking Sword, nodding to Raging River. "Infinite be with you, Lord River."

"And with you, Lord Bear," Raging River replied, bowing.

Guarding Bear turned to Seeking Sword. "We've been waiting for thirty-five years for a new Northern Emperor. Will you disappoint us?"

It seemed so superfluous.

"For the moment, Lord General. I'd like my brother to be with me. He deserves that much." Careful not to touch the Sword, Seeking Sword wrapped the silk sheet around it.

He picked up the bundle and turned toward Flying Arrow, then knelt and bowed. "Thank you, Lord Emperor Arrow. You will know the wisdom of your choice." And to honor the Emperor further, Seeking Sword held his bow.

"Walk with the Infinite, Lord Emperor Sword," Flying Arrow said, his voice faint. "Lord General River, Lord General Bear, would both of you do me the honor of escorting the Lord Emperor Seeking Sword back to the Northern Empire under the Inviolate Insignia?"

"It would be an honor far beyond my station, Lord Emperor Arrow," the gruff, grizzled General said. Both he and Guarding Bear bowed to Flying Arrow.

"Oh, and if it pleases you, my son, Lord Emperor Sword, would you mind releasing my other son, your brother, Flaming Arrow?"

Something deep inside Seeking Sword shifted at hearing his father acknowledge this simple fact. "Of course, Lord Emperor Arrow, I'll order his immediate release. Please forgive my subordinates their opprobrious behavior, holding my own brother hostage like that. Infinite be with you, Father."

The Northern Emperor straightened and looked at the two older men. "Let's go, Lords."

* * *

Flaming Arrow stepped out of the just-opened southern entrance of the Tiger Fortress.

"This way, Lord Arrow," Purring Tiger said, guiding him to a promontory where the trail began to descend.

He had traveled to the fortress after witnessing the events at Emparia Castle on the psychic projector at Seat. Was that just yesterday? he wondered.

A people were freed yesterday, and an Empire reborn. Seeking Sword had obtained the Northern Imperial Sword and was returning it to its rightful home, thirty-five years after Flying Arrow had defeated Lofty Lion.

Below Flaming Arrow on the slope leading to the fortress, a contingent approached under the Inviolate Insignia—Seeking Sword's contingent.

He sighed. Among them he saw his mate Rippling Water and his mother Flowering Pine. Then a flash of burning ember snared his eye. Under the hair of ember were the bluest eyes he'd ever seen, eyes he'd previously seen only at in a mirror, and one time before at Bastion.

The eyes caught his.

Flaming Arrow knew his mate Rippling Water had run up to him and now held him, but he didn't notice. He knew his mother Flowering Pine was weeping softly on his shoulder, but he didn't notice.

All he saw was his own blue eyes staring back at him, the black-haired Purring Tiger on the other man's arm equally unnoticed.

The two women looked at each other, he saw, then linked arms and stepped back.

He didn't look away from his brother. He wondered why his brother was crying.

"Brother, why are you crying?" Seeking Sword asked him.

"Brother, why are *you* crying?" Flaming Arrow asked him.

They stepped forward as if to hug but Flowering Pine stepped between them. "My sons, remember that you're twins, and remember your talents."

They both snorted. "Never had a trace of one, myself," Flaming Arrow said.

"Nor I," Seeking Sword added.

"I know," Flowering Pine said. "That's what worries me."

"And me, Lords," said Healing Hand, coming out of the fortress. Behind him was his father, Easing Comfort. Further back, still in the passageway, were Spying Eagle and Melding Mind, the latter leaning heavily on his son. "Lords, I've been concerned from the time I realized you were brothers. Something has repressed your talents all your lives, more than likely Lurking Hawk's implantation of you both at three days old. We don't know what will happen when ..." Healing Hand let his speech trail off, his palms beside his shoulders.

Flaming Arrow looked at Seeking Sword. "Our lack of discipline might be dangerous, brother."

"We've lain around gorging ourselves on delicacies for too many years, brother." Seeking Sword slapped his belly. "Such indolence."

"Neither of you are prepared for what might happen," Flowering Pine said. "No one knows what *will* happen."

The brothers nodded. "You're right, Mother. no one does," they said in unison. They looked at each other, then both looked up the mountain. "Up there."

"I'll lead the way," Seeking Sword said, taking Purring Tiger's hand and bidding her to walk beside him.

Flaming Arrow followed, taking Rippling Water's hand.

The two men strode into the fortress, heading for the central core.

"Lord Arrow," said a deep voice from behind them, "You'll want this. Your father asked me to give it to you." There stood Guarding Bear. Hand on the sheathed blade, he held out a sword with a diamond on the pommel.

Flaming Arrow smiled and took it. "I'm not sure that I do want it, Lord Bear," he said, but secured the Eastern Heir Sword to his side anyway.

As they entered the mountain core, Slithering Snake intercepted the group, resplendent in his purple and green robe. "Lord Emperor, you'll want this." Hand on the sheathed blade, he held out a sword with a ruby on the pommel.

Seeking Sword smiled and took it. "I'm not sure that I do want it, Lord Snake," he said, but secured the Northern Heir Sword to his side anyway.

Halfway up the core of the mountain, Healing Hand said, "It's fitting that you'd choose to reunite here, from whence the Peregrine Twins ruled their respective Empires."

They stopped at the entrance to the Lair, Scowling Tiger's erstwhile throne. "We'll need shields, Lord Snake."

Slithering Snake held up four small metal spheres.

Nodding, Seeking Sword headed for the stairs.

Atop the mountain, Flaming Arrow gawked. "I didn't realize you could see so far." He strode to the southern edge of the mountain cap.

The day was exceptionally clear. To the north, shimmering as though chimera, was the Castle at Seat. To the south, also shimmering as though fading into the mist, stood Emparia Castle.

Flaming Arrow gazed to the south, lost in thought.

Seeking Sword gazed to the north, standing at the northern rim and looking pleased.

They turned toward each other.

Seeking Sword lay the Northern Heir Sword on the parapet.

Flaming Arrow did the same with the Eastern Heir Sword, then stepped toward the center.

Seeking Sword joined him there.

"Do you think everyone else should go below?" he asked.

"They should do what feels right to them," he replied.

Flaming Arrow turned to Rippling Water. "I won't be the same after this, you know."

"But you'll be the person you were meant to be." A tear trickled down her cheek, and then she kissed him and took a step backward.

Purring Tiger caressed Seeking Sword's nose, kissed him and stepped to Rippling Water's side. "How will we tell them apart?" Purring Tiger asked.

Rippling Water giggled.

"Here, let me turn this on," Guarding Bear said, adjusting the settings on the electrical shield in his hand. He set it at their feet. "Infinite be with us all, eh?" He chuckled mightily and stepped backward to stand beside his niece, Flowering Pine. His bear, sitting near the parapet, towered over them all.

The twins looked at their mother.

"The luck of the Infinite be with you, my sons," she said.

They smiled at her and nodded, then looked at each other, standing a pace from each other on the mountain cap.

"Last time we did this, I couldn't remember the next thirty minutes," Seeking Sword said.

"Neither could I," Flaming Arrow replied. He lifted his left hand and set it on Seeking Sword's right shoulder. Seeking Sword's left hand landed on his right shoulder. Their eyes met.

Flaming Arrow smiled and threw his arms around his brother.

The shield could not contain the shock wave—nor did it need to. The observers gasped at the impact, some of them taking a step back. The twins' mind hesitated only a moment at Guarding Bear, knowing now the great joy and tragedy that he represented. Below the twins, shields fell one after another, the psychic energy finding a way through them not by overpowering them but by finding their imperfections. People's mindshields similarly fell, saturated by energy, disarmed by comfort. The wave reached the base of the mountain, passed the twin towers at the northern entrance, eased east toward Cove, hurtled south toward Burrow, radiated west along the Windy Mountains.

Their mind entered Burrow, disassembled its electrical defenses, dismantled its human defensiveness, and moved toward the River Placid, spreading its own placid river.

The northward edge entered Seat, where they quickly found Fawning Elk and the two children, Burning Sword and Stalking Tiger.

The southern edge of their mind touched Emparia Castle, where they hesitated, ambivalent. They knew what awaited; they didn't know the response. It was in the hands of the Infinite. Their plunge into Emparia Castle was brief. Flying Arrow seemed to be expecting them, his relief profound as though being Emperor had become overwhelming.

West toward Nexus, where the four empires met, their mind went. East toward the port of Cove, south toward the Craggy Mountains, and north toward the tundra. At Nexus their mind paused; they considered the consequences of crossing into the Western Empire and decided to delay. At the Craggy Mountains they considered the same but only briefly. Snarling and Stalking Jaguar had long maintained alliances with both the Eastern Empire and the nascent Northern Empire. Their mind moved swiftly to and through the castle shields and linked with Stalking Jaguar's mind, and then they were gone before his surprise had faded.

Their mind snapped back to the mountain top an instant later.

Most the observers were still in shock. Only Flowering Pine was not.

She stepped to their side and took Flaming Arrow's left hand and Seeking Sword's right in both of her hands. She looked forlorn. "I'm sorry I couldn't tell you sooner about Guarding Bear," she whispered, looking back and forth between them imploringly.

"There is nothing to forgive," the twins said with one voice and one mind, emitting comfort. They looked past her shoulder to Guarding Bear, then the other direction at their mates. Gesturing them closer, Flaming Arrow and Seeking Sword put their arms around their mates and their father. Their father Guarding Bear.

"It's both a joy and a sadness, this new knowledge," the twins said. "Healing Hand," they called, looking over their mates' shoulders.

The blond priest in the black robe nodded. "Yes, Lords?"

"Tell everyone how this happened."

He nodded. "At Flying Arrow's behest, Lurking Hawk implanted the eight-month-old Rippling Water with an illness so severe that only the Imperial Medacor Soothing Spirit could cure her. To obtain his help, Bubbling Water and Guarding Bear had to come to Emparia Castle to ask Flying Arrow …"

"And during our visit," Guarding Bear said, "Flying Arrow poisoned me. How did I let myself be duped so easily?" The old General groaned and hung his head.

"After being poisoned," Healing Hand continued, "Guarding Bear impregnated Flowering Pine."

Rippling Water began to weep softly.

Purring Tiger looked from face to face in disbelief. Her hands leaped to her sword. Healing Hand leaped to her side, his hands over her hands. Seeking Sword grasped her arms at the elbows. Her arms immobilized, her gaze locked with Seeking Sword's, Purring Tiger wilted into his arms, wailing.

The twins made a psychic request of Healing Hand. The medacor-priest touched Purring Tiger's shoulder, and she passed out under his anesthesia.

Spying Eagle and Healing Hand helped lay her on a robe, a bunched up sash her pillow.

Flaming Arrow held Rippling Water, the whispering breeze and her soft sobs the only sounds.

Chapter 23

OW DOES a person recover from a tragedy like that?

For Seeking Sword and Purring Tiger, discovering that they were siblings cemented a decision that they had been coming to on their own, even if they had not recognized it yet.

For Flaming Arrow and Rippling Water, who had grown up nearly equal in station, in families at the apex of their power, learning from the same tutors, thrown together at nearly every social or diplomatic function, and expected by their elders and indeed by every citizen of the Eastern Empire to become mates, how does a person cope with the tragedy of discovering that the person each has mated—and loves deeply and has two children with—is his or her sibling?

How does a person recover from a tragedy like that?—*The Fall of the Swords*, by Keeping Track.

* * *

"Lord Emperor Sword, Lord Emperor Arrow," Stalking Jaguar said, looking from one to the other, as if undecided. He straightened from his bow. He was easily the eldest among the four Emperors at Nexus that day.

Flaming Arrow and Seeking Sword had dressed identically. Only the jewel on the pommel distinguished them. They straightened from their bow, having held the obeisance a moment longer to honor the Emperor Jaguar.

Careening Condor, Emperor of the Western Empire, also studied the twins. At his side was the Western Imperial Sword, on the pommel an emerald. He'd arrived at Nexus a few moments before Stalking Jaguar, and had already made his obeisance. Behind each of the Emperors from the West and the South stood a large contingent of warriors, eyeing the other group suspiciously.

Five paces behind the twins stood the six-foot-six Probing Gaze and the smaller, stouter Slithering Snake, chatting amiably. They had fought each other along the Windy Mountains for twenty-five years. Now they looked like old friends.

"I was sorry to hear of your father's retirement, Lord Emperor Arrow," Stalking Jaguar said, his brown and gold robes shimmering in the morning light.

"I will convey your sentiments, Lord Emperor Jaguar," Flaming Arrow replied affably.

"And my condolences to both of you, Lords, on your respective losses."

The twins each nodded, gazes on the ground.

The twins had invited the other Emperors to Nexus, where the four Empires met. A four-posted arch adorned this crossroads of Empires. Under this arch, for the first time in a thousand years, stood all four Emperors. Under this arch, carved into the flagstones on the ground were the impressions of eight swords, four Imperial Swords with their hafts nearly touching at a nexus, and nearly touching their sword points, four Heir Swords pointed toward the nexus. The first to arrive at Nexus at dawn, Seeking Sword and Flaming Arrow had thought the design somewhat curious.

"Thank you for coming, both of you," Flaming Arrow said, looking up and sighing.

Seeking Sword looked over his shoulder and gestured to the two erstwhile enemies. Together, they dragged a sheet forward between them.

On the sheet lay two Imperial Swords and one staff.

"As you know, we haven't been formally invested as Emperors," the twins said, gesturing at the Swords on the ground between them. "We've asked you here to inform you of our intent and to request that you join us in our endeavor."

"Eh? What endeavor, Lords Emperor?" Careening Condor asked abruptly, his syllables oddly pronounced but easily understood.

"Here in the year of the Swords ninety-three twenty-four, we stand at Nexus—at *the* nexus," Flaming Arrow said.

"A nexus of change," Seeking Sword added. "We have a choice to move forward in the same direction that we've followed for over nine thousand years, or to choose another direction."

"A direction made available to us," Flaming Arrow said, "by the auspicious circumstance of our rejoining."

"A rejoining that indicates a potential beyond anyone's expectation."

During the pause, Stalking Jaguar spoke. "Your emergence into our collective consciousness has certainly raised hopes in both your Empires, Lords. And in mine. But, pardon me, what direction, Lords Emperor?"

Flaming Arrow smiled and looked at Seeking Sword. Behind them, a group approached along the road leading from Emparia Castle.

"Lords Emperor," Seeking Sword said, "a month ago as I traveled along the northern shore of the River Placid, I passed the place where Lofty Lion tried to assassinate Flying Arrow with his staff. If you'll remember, four different people tried to pick up that staff after the assassination attempt, and they all four died instantly." Seeking Sword bent down and picked up the staff from the sheet. "I recognized it there on the riverbank, given that my father Icy Wind used it to discipline me a thousand times. I picked it up without thinking. It's now harmless." Seeking Sword tossed it to Stalking Jaguar.

A strong black hand caught the staff. After a moment, the Southern Emperor nodded. "Indeed, Lord Emperor Sword, it's now harmless."

"In my dream at a crossroads hostelry," Flaming Arrow said, "I wrestled with the electrical circuits of this staff, and ultimately defeated them." He paused. "In my dream."

"What you're proposing is preposterous," Careening Condor said.

Stalking Jaguar looked puzzled. "Perhaps my disbelief obscures my understanding. Just what *are* you proposing, Lords?"

As one the twins replied, "We are going to disable the electrical circuits in both of our Imperial Swords, and we are inviting the both of you to allow us to do the same with your Imperial Swords. And end the reign of the Swords forever."

"And leave my Empire vulnerable to him—and you?" Careening Condor pointed at Stalking Jaguar.

"We will stop him," the twins said simply. "As for us, if we had any desire to govern your lands, we would simply take them over, right now."

Careening Condor threw his head back and laughed.

The twins looked at each other and smiled. "Who is your Heir, Lord Emperor Condor?"

"Eh? I don't have one yet. Everyone knows that!"

"And where's the Western Heir Sword?"

"It's safe in my castle, of course!"

Seeking Sword closed his eyes, and Flaming Arrow stated, "It was." Seeking Sword opened his eyes, and a sword appeared at the Western Emperor's feet, on the pommel an emerald.

"What?!" Careening Condor gawked at it.

Flaming Arrow gestured at it. "Would you like to verify that the Sword in front of you is indeed the Western Heir Sword?"

"I *know* that it is, Emperor!" Careening Condor spat the title. "Are you provoking me to war, you impudent puppy?!"

Seeking Sword closed his eyes. The Sword disappeared. "Not at all," Flaming Arrow said. "Would you like to verify that the Sword is now safely back where it came from?"

Careening Condor touched his Imperial Sword. The emerald glowed. "What trickery is this? How did you do that?"

The twins shrugged and spoke in unison. "Again, Lord Emperor Condor, if we wished to rule your lands and people, we would simply take them over, right now. What we're asking is that you consider the prison which currently cages you, and to give us permission to let you out of that cage."

"What cage, Emperor?!"

"Lords Emperor?" Stalking Jaguar said. "May I?"

The twins shrugged again, and gestured for him to try.

As the Southern Emperor spoke in low tones with the Western Emperor, the group coming from Emparia Castle hailed Slithering Snake and Probing Gaze. Among them was a blond man in black robes talking intently with a somewhat older man with brown hair.

"Lord Emperor Arrow, Lord Emperor Sword!" Healing Hand said, seeing that they were looking in his direction. He loped ahead of the contingent to greet the twins. He leaned close to them, giving no obeisance. "It is done, Lords," he said in a low voice. "Your father is well, as you foresaw."

The twins sighed, relieved. "No ill effects from not having that?" Seeking Sword said, and Flaming Arrow gestured at the Eastern Imperial Sword on the ground.

"None, Lords, other than a mild setback. The neurological reconstruction that Spying Eagle and I did after his brain injury was lacking plasticity, so some additional rewiring was necessary."

Flaming Arrow looked at Spying Eagle as the brown-haired Wizard approached. "Thank you, my friends, I was ... afraid."

Spying Eagle bowed deeply. "Anyone would be concerned, Lord Emperor Arrow."

Flaming Arrow nodded in return.

Seeking Sword gestured over his shoulder. "How do you think they'll respond, Lords?"

Healing Hand looked past them at the Emperors Condor and Jaguar, still deep in conversation. "There will be some risks for the Lord Emperor Jaguar, given his age, but little risk for the Lord Emperor Condor."

Wielding Imperial and Heir Swords caused changes to the brain, and taking those Swords away was likely to induce injury. Heirs had died upon disinheriting, their brains having become dependent on the Sword. In the nine thousand years of Sword-based rule, few Emperors had been deprived of their Imperial Swords. Lofty Lion was the only Emperor in recent memory to have survived the removal of an Imperial Sword from his possession, and he had been kept alive in part by the talisman staff that Lurking Hawk had built for him. Before that, Stalking Jaguar's great-grandfather had wrested the Southern Imperial Sword from the previous Emperor with the help of a specially-bred animal; that Emperor had died instantly when the Sword was taken from him.

Flaming Arrow glanced at Seeking Sword. Together, they turned toward the Emperors Condor and Jaguar.

"What wizardry are you cooking up now?" Careening Condor said, when he saw their attention on him.

"No wizardry, Lord Emperor Condor, none at all," Seeking Sword said. "Your decision is entirely your own to make, Lord. We will abide by it to the end of our rule."

Flaming Arrow nodded.

"What were you just talking about with those Wizards?"

The twins looked at Healing Hand.

The black-robed priest knelt deeply. "Lord Emperor Condor, the peace of the Infinite be with you."

"And with you, Lord Priest. Or Warrior. Or Wizard. Or Medacor. Or whatever you are."

"Yes, Lord, I am. My apologies for having such a confusing signature. I am Healing Hand. This is my friend, Spying Eagle."

Spying Eagle bowed.

Careening Condor spat. "A traitor like his father before him and his father before him."

"I pray that the Infinite finds the Lord Emperor Condor at peace," Spying Eagle said, a hint of sadness in his voice. He stepped backward, looking unperturbed.

"If I may describe for the Lord Emperor Condor what my friend and I did for the former Lord Emperor Arrow?"

Careening Condor shrugged.

Healing Hand kept the explanation simple, knowing the Eastern language not the Emperor's native one. He then offered to explain in more detail in the Western tongue.

"Not necessary," the Emperor Condor said, looking between Seeking Sword and Flaming Arrow. "I'm not convinced. You two do what you like with your Swords. With all due respect, Lords Emperor, I think you're shoving them into your own back passages."

He then looked at Stalking Jaguar. "Well met, Lord Emperor Jaguar. I'm glad there's peace between us. I hope it remains. Infinite be with you." He bowed deeply to Stalking Jaguar, then turned and strode away, issuing orders.

Straightening from his own bow, Stalking Jaguar sighed and looked at the twins.

"Not much benefit in compelling him," Flaming Arrow said.

"We may not have a choice," Spying Eagle said.

"Eh?" said four other men.

Spying Eagle gestured at the ground, at the shapes carved into the flagstones. "I'm wondering if the Swords are linked and protect each other. Lay your swords in these impressions," he said.

The three Emperors glanced at him curiously but complied. Using their feet, Seeking Sword and Flaming Arrow gingerly nudged their Imperial Swords into their respective impressions, trying to avoid touching them directly. Then they each set the Heir Swords into their slots. Each of the gems began to emit a slight glow.

Missing still were the Southern Heir Sword and the two Western Swords.

Flaming Arrow looked to the west, where the battalion of Condor Warriors was forming up, wondering what he might do to persuade the Western Emperor to join them.

Healing Hand was explaining to Stalking Jaguar what the consequences might be, and how he and Spying Eagle were prepared to help.

Seeking Sword shared his thought with Flaming Arrow that everyone but they two should be shielded. They looked down at the five Swords, both of them wondering what impact the absence of the other three would have.

Stalking Jaguar picked up the thread of their thoughts. "Why not bring the Southern Heir Sword, as well?"

Seeking Sword smiled. "With your permission, Lord?"

Stalking Jaguar nodded.

Seeking Sword blinked and the Sword appeared at his feet. "I'm getting better at this."

Stalking Jaguar placed the Southern Heir Sword in its respective slot. The glow from the gems brightened somewhat. "I'll inform them not to be alarmed," he said, and touched the hilt of his Imperial Sword. Then he and the others backed away and switched on an electrical shield, leaving Flaming Arrow and Seeking Sword standing under the four-posted arch.

Flaming Arrow shrugged. "Together, or one at a time?" Behind him, unnoticed, Healing Hand stepped away from the electrical shield, outside of its range.

"Together," Seeking Sword said. He knelt to one side of the Northern Imperial Sword and poised his left hand inches above the haft.

Flaming Arrow did the same.

They dropped their hands to the cold, pewter-colored hafts.

* * *

Seeking Sword felt accepted, welcomed, invited, drawn. The Sword enfolded his mind with comfort and warmth, and graced him with a sense of completion and attainment. He felt successful and competent, as though all his needs had been met, as though spiritual enlightenment were within his grasp. He felt as though he could conquer the world, and that it would be a better place if he were to do so.

The ground at his feet glowed as if he were seeing it for the first time. A few feet away, the lands not under his dominion held no such allure; it was just dirt. The memory of the moment he learned of his father's death came upon him, when he realized he was Lofty Lion's son, when he realized he would rule the Northern Empire.

They need my guidance and sagacity, he thought. Without me, they're lost.

He glanced over at Flaming Arrow.

He'll try to stop me, Seeking Sword thought. He covets my lands and wants to dominate my people. He thinks he's superior. He'll persecute me and try to wrest the Imperial Sword from me. He'll send spies to spy on me, and assassins to kill me. He'll stop at nothing to …

The kick to his wrist ripped his hand from the Northern Imperial Sword.

Healing Hand then kicked Flaming Arrow's hand away from the Eastern Imperial Sword.

"My apologies, Lords, I had to stop you both."

Seeking Sword felt empty inside, as though something deeply important to him had been stripped from his soul. He yearned to put his hand on the Sword again. Then he felt Flaming Arrow's presence inside him, and like Flaming Arrow, realized that he had lost his link with his twin at the moment he had touched the Imperial Sword.

"Insidious," Flaming Arrow said, standing.

Seeking Sword also stood, not wanting to be tempted. "Seductive," he said, frowning at his brother. "Thank you, Lord Hand."

"An honor to be of assistance," he replied, his ice blue eyes warm and kind. "I'll be blunt, Lords. You've never had conscious exposure to psychic manipulation. You're immature in that area—infantile, even. Lurking Hawk's manipulation of your minds at three days old arrested your psychic development."

"We can't do this, then," Seeking Sword said.

Healing Hand held his palms up to his shoulders. "That's for you to decide. I would certainly say that you don't have the skill. However, if I may speculate further on some confounding factors?"

The twins nodded.

"First, your 'lack' of psychic power throughout your lives was simply their suppression, as we now know. To what extent your minds were changed by the Heir Swords is only speculative, since no one was able to monitor it. So there are three possibilities: Your minds have been molded to an extent adequate to allow you to wield the corresponding Imperial Swords. Or your minds were inoculated by Lurking Hawk's manipulation and received no molding at all. Or some variation in between."

"If our minds weren't molded at all, the Imperial Swords would have killed us, wouldn't they?"

Healing Hand shrugged. "We've always assumed that an Heir Sword prepares the Heir's mind for the Imperial Sword. What if we have that wrong? What if the Heir Sword simply provides the Imperial Sword with enough information that it can then take over the Heir's mind? Then we're left with the question of whether the Heir Swords penetrated your minds or were able to interpret enough of your psychic patterns to provide the Imperial Swords with sufficient information."

"It felt as though they did 'take over,'" Flaming Arrow said, frowning.

"That's what it looked like," Healing Hand said.

"You said we don't have the skill," Seeking Sword added.

The Medacor-Priest nodded. "Against a staff, perhaps, you do. These Swords have proved invulnerable for nine thousand years."

"Do you have the skill?"

Again, Healing Hand shrugged. "Even if I did, there's more than skill required."

The twins looked at each other. Their psychic dialogue was brief. They did not question their need to disable or destroy these Swords.

"What would Guarding Bear do?" Seeking Sword asked.

Flaming Arrow smiled. "Something impulsive, stupid, and incredibly courageous."

Healing Hand nodded. "His protective power saved him even from his own folly. And based on your incredible luck, Flaming Arrow, I'd say you inherited that power in abundance."

He looked at his twin and pointed at the Northern Imperial Sword. "Any objections?"

Seeking Sword shook his head, bent to grasp the Sword by the blade, and extended it haft first toward Flaming Arrow.

The Eastern Emperor grasped the Northern Imperial Sword.

Time stopped.

The Sword turned to liquid fire. Its psychic arsenal assaulted Flaming Arrow with a barrage, enveloping him in a glow so bright they couldn't look at him. Later, Healing Hand recalled that the stones embedded in the pommels of each sword lit up, all six of them.

At first he felt curiously unaffected. Then the pain hit him. Pain unreal, as though every nerve were aflame with the heat of a thousand suns. His body tried to convulse in agony, but he had no access to his muscles. He tried to throw away the Sword; his hands would not obey. The psychic energy ate into his brain toward the very center of his soul.

Something stopped it.

Underneath the pain he felt the presence of his brother. Together they held fast against the onslaught, their raw power matching that of the Sword. The Northern Sword shifted its focus to its rightful wielder, pumping superiority and paranoia into Seeking Sword's mind. Flaming Arrow countered, frying the circuit. Seeking Sword engaged the Sword, pulling its protective embrace further into his mind; Flaming Arrow delved into its structure, searching for its reservoir. As the Sword raced to control Seeking Sword's mind, Flaming Arrow raced to find its source of energy.

There! Like a pool of water under a thicket of thorns, the deep reservoir of psychic power lay under a tangled array of electrical circuits. He found the conduit where energy pumped into the surrounding circuitry, and he shut it off.

Flaming Arrow snapped back into his body, his knees weak.

Seeking Sword slumped to the ground beside him, and Healing Hand knelt. His brother's pallor was travertine, his skin just as cold.

"No!" Flaming Arrow gasped, wilting inside. The Sword clattered on the stone.

Healing Hand placed one hand on Seeking Sword's chest, the other on his forehead. The Medacor closed his eyes.

A memory came to Flaming Arrow. Healing Hand once showed him one of Guarding Bear's statues, had placed his hands upon the stone squirrel, and had lowered a live wriggling squirrel to the ground.

Sweat pearled on Healing Hand's brow. His eyes rolled back in their sockets, and his skin went gray. Seeking Sword's chest heaved and his body convulsed; then he coughed and rolled to his side.

Flaming Arrow knelt to hold Seeking Sword. "I thought I lost you."

Taking deep breaths, Seeking Sword began to regain his color.

Healing Hand looked up, his gaze a daze. He shook his head. "Much worse than I thought."

"Thank you, my friend," Flaming Arrow said. Then he looked into his brother's eyes. "I would rather live under their dominion than lose you."

Seeking Sword expelled a breath. "I wouldn't." He looked over at the Sword.

Flaming Arrow probed it—and sighed.

It was just a sword. Once, it might have been important. And, now, it no longer was.

Epilogue

HERE WERE eight Swords.

They had once been important. Three feet long and slightly curved, the blades looked tarnished. The metal's dark color suggested it was simply brass. The edges were sharp and without a nick. The hafts were pewter-colored, contoured for the human hand, and unremarkable—except for the single jewel set in each pommel.

Despite their modest appearance, the Swords were skillfully constructed. The blades themselves had been made from microscopic sheets of a chromium-antimony alloy layered one atop the other. The painstaking process made the blades very flexible and the edges very sharp. Even the best Swordsmiths found the alloy difficult to work, however, making reproduction improbable.

In addition to their precise construction, the Swords were ancient. Forged more than nine thousand years before, the Swords had withstood all manner of use and misuse. The number of warriors who'd wielded the Swords was a figure lost in the past. The number of warriors who'd died on their edges was many times that. The number of warriors mortally wounded while wielding these Swords, however, was fewer than a thousand.

The Heir Swords had assured successions by preparing Heirs' minds for the Imperial Swords. No different in appearance other than their slightly larger gems, the Imperial Swords had extended the range of Emperors' psychic powers to the farthest corners of their Empires. Thus, the Imperial Swords had been the figurative and literal source of Emperors' authority. The Imperial Swords had killed any unfortunate (or treacherous) soul inadequately prepared by the Heir Swords. Thus, the Heir Swords had been the only way to obtain that authority.

Each of the four Empires had had its own pair of Swords, a different gem adorning each pair. The four Imperial Swords had all served the same function: To grant the current Emperor total dominion over his or her Empire. The four Heir Swords had all shared their own function: To assure a smooth succession.

The eight Swords now ruled nothing. The four-posted arch above the flagstones has long since rotted away, the borders of the four Empires no longer fixed by the dominion of the Swords. Their continuing importance is captured in the few sentences etched in the stone in which they are encased. "For ten thousand years, we were imprisoned by our own devices. Here lie the devices of our imprisonment. The objects in whom we placed our trust did predicate the course of their history. A Sword innately predicates victor and vanquished, master and slave, dominance and subservience. Our political systems faltered, even though the eight Swords had been forged to preserve them, because these Swords were the devices of their own destruction."

The eight Swords now preserved at Nexus remain important, if only to remind us that what preserves also imprisons.—*The Fall of the Swords*, by Keeping Track.

* * *

About the Author

Scott Michael Decker, MSW, is an author by avocation and a social worker by trade. He is the author of twenty-plus novels, mostly in the Science Fiction genre and some in the Fantasy genre. His biggest fantasy is wishing he were published. His fifteen years of experience working with high-risk populations is relieved only by his incisive humor. Formerly interested in engineering, he's now tilting at the windmills he once aspired to build. Asked about the MSW after his name, the author is adamant it stands for Masters in Social Work, and not "Municipal Solid Waste," which he spreads pretty thick as well. His favorite quote goes, "Scott is a social work novelist, who never had time for a life" (apologies to Billy Joel). He lives and dreams happily with his wife near Sacramento, California.

How to Contact/Where to Find the Author

Websites:
http://scottmichaeldecker.com/
https://twitter.com/smdmsw/
https://www.facebook.com/AuthorSmdMsw
http://www.wattpad.com/user/Smdmsw
http://www.creativia.org/scott-michael-decker.html

Lightning Source UK Ltd.
Milton Keynes UK
UKHW011234091120
373077UK00006B/1020